SEAL THE DEAL

KATE ASTER

Cover design: The Killion Group, Inc.

DEDICATION

To my husband—my inspiration and my hero.

And to Chuck, U.S. Navy Captain and editor extraordinaire.
Come home safely, my friend.

PART I

SUBURBAN CHICAGO

EIGHTEEN YEARS AGO

She really *had* thought they were fixed.

Lacey stared down at Taffy and Buster's progeny, seven adorable bundles of fur, as they explored the inside of a crate beneath her homemade "Rabbits For Sale" sign.

Clearly she had been wrong.

With a defeated sigh, she watched people bustle in and out of booths at the weekly Farmers' Market. They held in their hands a tomato here, a head of lettuce there, as though each locally grown fruit or vegetable was a treasured prize. At just twelve, Lacey couldn't quite appreciate the difference between the produce here and the massive shipments trucked into the grocery store every day. But it was a fun atmosphere, with the regulars chatting among themselves and crowds of preschoolers eagerly awaiting one-dollar pony rides.

The Farmers' Market was only a short walk from home, but her parents had never taken her or her sister here. Lacey couldn't imagine them waiting till a particular day of the week to buy fresh produce. They would certainly never spare the extra hour or two to wander aimlessly from booth to booth, squeezing peaches and tapping melons. Time was money, after all, Lacey reminded herself as she glanced at her watch.

The morning was passing without a single sale. Lacey had started the day with confidence, ambitiously writing "$10 each" in thick marker on her poster. By mid-morning, she had replaced it with a more modest "$5." Now she resorted to flipping the poster over and starting fresh:

"FREE to Good Home."

As the minutes ticked away, she began imagining the looks of reproach in her parents' eyes if she returned home unsuccessful, recalling her recent Girl Scout Cookie sales effort that hadn't met the Owens' high standard for success.

Even worse, what would become of the bunnies?

Lacey shielded her eyes from the sun to see if there were any interested prospects in her midst. A familiar shape was approaching, dark against the glare of the sun. But her sister's stride was easy to recognize. Also just twelve, Vi walked as though she should be pounding the pavement of Wall Street rather than marching through a suburban Farmers' Market carrying a bright pink piece of poster board.

Standing above her now, Vi glanced down at the crate, quickly counting heads. "No luck yet."

It was more of a statement than a question, but Lacey answered anyway. "No."

Vi looked sharply at Lacey, as though she was staring down an unruly bunch of stockholders at an annual meeting. "Okay. Here's the deal. If I sell every one of these rabbits by the end of the day, I get a 50% cut."

"50%? But I feed them out of my own money."

"You're not going to get anything if you keep doing things your way. Besides, you might be surprised what I can sell them for."

Lacey eyed the pink poster board that Vi held protectively to her chest. "Okay. Deal."

With great resolve, Vi ripped Lacey's poster off the stake and taped up her own.

Lacey's jaw dropped when she read it:

"Rabbits for Sale: $20 each. Perfect for Sunday Dinner!"

"That's horrible, Vi! I don't want people to EAT them," Lacey gasped.

"These are the suburbs, Lacey. No one's going to skin a rabbit out here." Vi then leaned over, lowering her voice. "But every little kid who reads this sign isn't going to let Mommy or Daddy let these cute animals be stewed up. Parents will have to buy them just to stop the crying."

"That's wrong, Vi. We can't do that."

"Who says? It's not a lie. People do eat rabbit, you know."

As always, Vi's logic sent Lacey's head spinning. Or maybe it was the heat. "Well…"

"Besides, Mom will make you get rid of these little guys one way or another." Vi did a slashing movement with her finger at her throat for added emphasis.

Lacey's eyes widened.

Vi knew she had won. She turned triumphantly toward the crowd. "Rabbits for sale! Rabbits for sale! The sweetest meat you'll ever eat!"

Heads whipped around.

"Rabbits for sale! The sweetest meat you'll ever eat!" Vi's chant was as effective as the best advertising jingle that ever came off Madison Avenue.

A stampede of children dragging their parents was followed by high-pitched squeals.

"You're not really going to eat them, are you?" one whined.

"But they're so cute," another chimed in.

Tears rained a downpour.

"I don't want anyone to eat this one. I would name him Charley."

Helpless parents reluctantly pulled out their wallets.

Less than an hour later, Lacey handed over the last rabbit to a freckle-cheeked boy, while Vi smoothly accepted a stack of bills from the father, swift to point out that he was one dollar short.

When the boy and his father were out of earshot, Vi yanked the sign out of the ground, saying under her breath, "Let's split up the money at home. We don't want to look too mercenary."

As Lacey watched her adopted sister load their belongings into their red wagon, she was reminded yet again of the undeniable difference between the two of them. Lacey, the only biological daughter of the successful Gerald and Hilary Owens, did not have nearly the business sense or ambition of either of her parents.

Yet with irony, her adopted sister resembled them in every way possible.

Despite the day's windfall of cash, Lacey felt strangely inadequate as she lifted the empty crate into the wagon. She was uncomfortable with this new feeling she had as she looked at Vi.

She felt envy.

CHAPTER 1

TODAY

ANNAPOLIS, MARYLAND

Not another open casket.

Stepping through an arched doorway and into a sea of gray hair and solemn faces, Lacey quietly groaned at the sight of Dr. Donald Baker at the other end of the room. Through the hushed crowd, she waded toward the casket that rested in front of a stunning wall of floor-to-ceiling windows overlooking the Chesapeake Bay. The well-appointed funeral home was easily the most expensive place to mourn on the Eastern Seaboard.

Death, Lacey had discovered recently, came with a hefty price tag.

Holding her breath apprehensively, she gazed down at

Dr. Baker as he lay in an impressive mahogany casket. He looked just like the photo that had caught her eye in the obituary section of the newspaper three days ago. Even stone cold, his face had a kindness that brought tears to her eyes. Absurd, of course, since she didn't even know the man.

After so many funerals, she should be callous to this part of her job.

With a little digging online, Lacey had learned that the late Dr. Baker owned a chunk of waterfront property crowned with a stately Colonial. For a real estate agent just starting out, selling a listing like that would upgrade her life from ramen noodles to Chinese take-out for at least a year.

She bolstered her determination, recalling the image of Vi gracing the cover of *BusinessWeek*. Lacey doubted she'd ever climb to such lofty heights of success as her adopted sister, but it would be nice to have something to boast about.

Besides, she had rent to pay. So she dabbed her tear-moistened eyes and scanned the room.

Lacey had memorized the face of Dr. Baker's widow from a photograph online. Spotting her immediately, she felt a small surge of excitement. *Too easy.* She might even get out in time for the next funeral on her schedule.

Taking no more than three brisk strides toward the widow, she slammed into something as unyielding as a six-foot-three slab of concrete. Two jarring steps backward and she slipped, suddenly seeing nothing but a blur of vertical motion.

It was an out-of-body experience, as though she could actually see her own mortified expression as her head made its rapid descent toward the floor. She vaguely heard a few foul words strung together, which was likely her own voice cursing her friend Maeve for convincing her to wear stiletto heels to a funeral.

Completely inappropriate—both the stilettos and the curse.

In a flash, she saw her life rush past her, an unimpressive sequence of failed careers and failed relationships. She could see her parents and sister standing over her casket, shaking their heads and muttering, "You just couldn't get it together, could you, Lacey?" Then her head smacked against the marble slab floor, the impact thankfully softened by the updo in her hair.

Opening her eyes, she thought she must be looking at the face of God, or maybe St. Peter ready to usher her through the pearly gates. Whoever he was, the man hovering over her was sex in a suit.

"Are you all right?" the Vision said.

Lacey just stared. His image was decadent—piercing blue eyes, classically chiseled features, and skin that begged to be touched. His short, military-style haircut seemed to accentuate his broad shoulders subtly bulging with muscles beneath his tailored suit.

Mercy.

Definitely not God, or she wouldn't feel this surge of desire burning just below her stomach. At least she hoped not.

"Wow," she said in quiet admiration.

"You fell and hit your head. Do you remember where you are?"

A flurry of other heads, mostly topped with silver hair or half bald, invaded her vision.

"Yes, I'm at the funeral of..." Donald, was it? Or was that last week's corpse?

"Donald Baker." The man kneeling beside her said and called out over his shoulder with fierce authority, "I need some ice right now. And this woman needs an ambulance. Call 911."

"No, no. I'm really fine. I just bumped my head." Despite the dull ache at her temple, Lacey struggled to get up and the room swayed in response. His firm yet gentle grip held her still. Another fluttering below her stomach, and she wondered if it was sheer lust or nausea from a mild concussion.

Or maybe both.

"It would be better if you didn't move."

"I'm really fine." She pressed her palm against his chest to nudge him aside and felt a hint of the rock-hard pecs beneath his neatly pressed shirt. Involuntarily, her hand strayed an inch or two to savor the feel of a tempting ripple. She couldn't resist; men who looked like this didn't grow on trees. If they did, women would never get any work done.

Feeling his chest rise as he took in a breath, the alluring warmth of his skin seeped through the smooth cotton to her hand. She could swear she heard her body sizzle in response, and pulled away as though she had touched the burner on Maeve's new industrial gas range. "I'll just sit down somewhere and catch my breath."

"I really don't recommend..."

Strangely feverish, she shrugged herself free from his too-titillating grip and began to stand.

"Okay, if you're going to be stubborn." With a slight shake of his head, he lifted her into his arms so easily that her breath caught. Unconsciously, she let out a whimper. Every muscle in her body savored the feel of his thick, corded arms enveloping her and she fought the urge to nestle into his broad chest. She silently prayed he would carry her out the door and to the nearest secluded area without delay, but he carried her to a nearby couch instead.

His fingers probed gently around her head as he searched for swelling. With one careless touch of his hand against the side of her face, Lacey's body melted into the sofa cushions like a pool of hot wax. She briefly fantasized about pulling his face toward her so she could feel the sweet pressure of his perfectly formed lips.

It really had been too long, she realized. Immersing herself in her work had definitely made her sex life come screeching to a halt. But hanging out in funeral parlors was generally not the best way to meet men...until today.

His hand became entangled in her updo as he continued to feel for inflammation. He must be a doctor, Lacey decided. He couldn't be an E.M.T. or every unattached woman in Annapolis would be dialing 911 more frequently than Papa John's.

"Do you mind?" he asked.

"Not at all," Lacey responded breathlessly before realizing she had no idea what she had just agreed to.

He pulled out her hair clip and let her brown locks tumble around her. The tiniest hint of arousal sparked in his eyes, but it disappeared quickly replaced by a stoic countenance.

Damn.

"Can you tell me your name?" he asked, slipping her hair clip into his pocket.

Lacey's heart soared a moment with the hope he might be interested in her. She hadn't attracted a man this hot since... well, *never*.

"Lacey Owens."

"Who is the President of the United States?"

Crash and burn. He was only concerned about whether she had a head injury. "No one I voted for," she muttered, her ego deflating. "Really, thanks for your concern, but I'm perfectly fine." She felt the sting of disappointment as he let her stand up on her own, secretly hoping he'd throw her back on the couch and ravish her. Except for the fifty or so people crowded around them, it would have been the perfect opportunity.

An elderly woman approached, extending her hand. "My dear, that was quite a fall. Are you all right?"

It was Edith Baker, the woman she had been trying to talk to when she crashed into...

Him! Lacey suddenly realized that her knight-in-wool-blend-Brooks-Brothers was the reason for her fall. No wonder he was so interested in whether she was all right. He probably thought she was planning on suing him.

Figures.

"Are you all right?" the woman repeated. "I really think you should sit down again."

"No—I mean—I really am fine." Brushing herself off, she struggled to regain some shred of dignity. "You're Mrs. Baker. I wanted to extend to you my sympathy. I'm Lacey Owens."

"Thank you. I'm so glad you're all right. How did you know Don?"

That question used to stump Lacey. But after a year of honing her funeral crashing skills, she could smoothly answer, "I only knew of him. But he's done so much incredible research for the hospital, I felt compelled to pay my respects."

"So you are a doctor, too?"

"No," Lacey laughed. "Actually, I'm a real estate agent. But I read all the hospital newsletters, so became familiar with his work." She felt a wave of skepticism coming from the muscle-bound specimen who stood protectively at Mrs. Baker's side. "What your husband achieved in his cancer research has saved so many lives." She sinuously shifted the focus off of herself like a pro.

"He was a dedicated man," Mrs. Baker agreed, "and a wonderful husband."

"He obviously loved you a great deal."

"Owens," the elderly woman suddenly repeated thoughtfully. "You sent that lovely flower arrangement with stargazer lilies, didn't you?"

"I had read once that your husband said it was your favorite flower. As a surprise for you, he filled the room with them for the hospital fundraiser you chaired last spring. I can't imagine having a husband who cherished me like that."

The once-grieving face of the widow instantly transformed with a smile from the memory. Lacey saw the man standing next to her soften, and he touched the older woman's arm tenderly as though he might be her son.

Odd, though. Lacey hadn't discovered a son in her research.

Mrs. Baker patted Lacey on the arm. "You'll have that one day, too, my dear. Thank you for reminding me of such a wonderful memory."

"It was my pleasure. I've taken more of your time than I intended, though. I'm sorry I caused such a disruption."

"I'm just glad the color has returned to your cheeks, my dear."

Lacey smiled, moving in for the kill. "And please, if you ever need a volunteer for your charity work at the hospital, I'd love to help in any way I can." She adeptly reached into her purse and passed the woman a business card.

"Thank you. I will. Are you sure you are all right?"

Lacey was taken aback, so engrossed in her smooth business transaction that she had nearly forgotten her head-on collision with the floor. "I'm fine. I think I will slip out now though, rather than staying for the service. You don't mind?" Lacey directed the question to the woman, but could not help glancing at the hulking man next to her. She wondered if he had to turn sideways to fit through doorways with shoulders like that.

"Of course not. You're all right to drive?"

"Absolutely. Thank you for your concern," Lacey said, and quickly turned to walk out the door.

A voice behind her sent a tingling up her spine. "I'll walk you to your car."

She felt a warm hand touching the lower part of her back and another gently gripping her elbow.

Her heart fluttered a moment until panic set in. She *had* detected some skepticism from him as she was talking to Mrs. Baker. Was he onto her real estate scheme? "You really don't have to follow me to my car."

"I want to make sure you're all right. I'd feel better if I could put you in a cab."

"I'm fine, really. Please don't make such a big deal of this. I'm embarrassed enough."

With a slight grin, he held up his hands. "Okay. I'll stop."

Lacey couldn't resist glancing down at his left hand. No ring. And such nice strong hands.

She gave herself a light shake to snap out of it. Strong hands or not, he was not worth the risk of losing a possible listing. With her husband now deceased, Edith Baker was the sole owner of a waterfront home too large for one woman to live in alone. There was a good chance Mrs. Baker would consider selling her home soon, and every real estate agent within a fifty-mile radius would be flooding the old woman's mailbox with slick brochures, full-color calendars, and handy refrigerator magnets—agents with bigger advertising budgets than Lacey's.

But Lacey's business card was already snug in Mrs. Baker's pocket, and the fondly-remembered scent of stargazer lilies was wafting past her nose. Lacey's foot was in the door. She had no intention of messing up now by getting too friendly with this mystery-in-a-suit, no matter how nicely he filled it out.

"So are you a family member?" she asked lightly.

"Not by blood. But I love them like my parents. I'd do anything for them." He said it with such conviction that he might as well have said, "I'd kill for them."

His tone made Lacey's eyes widen. *Definitely too defensive. He must suspect something.* Every instinct told her to escape him as quickly as possible, except for that primal instinct that wanted to tear open his shirt with her teeth.

"She seems like such a lovely woman," she said instead, trying to shake his half-naked image from her mind.

"She is. And you're a real estate agent?"

"Mmhm." Lacey's hands trembled as she fumbled through her purse looking for her keys. He was definitely onto her. She could see the potential listing slipping through her fingers, and her name being blacklisted from the best funeral home in town.

"I might need to buy property one day." His voice was so smooth it could butter toast. "Can I have your card?"

"I, uh, actually think I gave my last one to Mrs. Baker. I wasn't really expecting to do business at a funeral." She let out a little laugh.

He seemed taken aback.

Lacey babbled, "I can't believe I slipped and fell at her husband's funeral. Talk about making a scene."

"Those were slick floors for such high heels." He looked down at her shoes and pointedly let his gaze linger a little too long on her legs. "And you were definitely walking too fast."

Lacey bristled, quickening her pace. "I wouldn't have fallen if I hadn't walked into someone. You, if I remember correctly."

When he smiled, she couldn't help wondering how his teeth got so white. They looked positively…delicious.

"I'm very sorry if I had something to do with your fall, then. How can I make it up to you? Dinner?"

"No, thank you. It really wasn't your fault." She averted her eyes to avoid getting sucked into the vortex of his sexual magnetism. It was a losing battle.

"Well, I'd love to take you to dinner anyway. It would make me feel better to check up later on that bump on your head." He gently brushed his fingers along the side of her head. A jolt of electricity raced up her spine.

This man was dangerous. Given the choice between a night with him and a multimillion-dollar real estate listing, Lacey was strangely tempted by her carnal side.

He continued tracing the side of her cheek. "But if you have someone in your life who will check on that—" he paused, "—bump, I'd understand."

Her breathing quickened. Her knees weakened. Feeling lightheaded, she steadied herself against her car. "No one checks on my bumps." *Ugh. Did I really just say that?*

Smiling slightly, his hand stilled against the side of her face. Gently, he brushed her hair behind her ear, then more forcefully plunged his fingers into her long locks. First one hand, then his other. As he toyed with her hair, his head lowered so close to her own that the feel of his warm breath against her forehead fully awakened her once flat-lined libido.

Instinctively tilting her head upward, she locked her gaze on his tempting mouth, the subtle curve of his lips, his clean shave that still smelled a bit soapy, the perfect cleft in his chin that she longed to touch. She leaned into him, aching to be sandwiched in between his steel-hard body and her car.

His mouth only inches from hers, her lips opened slightly and her eyes began to close—just as she spotted her hair clip in his hand and heard him click it shut.

She pulled back from him, mortified.

He was grinning. "Your hair clip. Remember?"

"Of course," she barely whispered, raising her hand

against the makeshift ponytail that now stood out from the back of her head. She hoped he hadn't noticed how close she had come to plastering her lips against his. But from the smug look on his face, he apparently had.

"So. Dinner at eight then?"

Her lips yearned to say "yes." Yes to dinner and anything else he might suggest. But a sudden breeze blew in from the water drawing Lacey's eyes away from him and out to the Chesapeake Bay. She rallied her defenses, narrowing her gaze on the waterfront homes in her view and picturing "For Sale" signs in front of every one of them.

"No, thank you," she said, quickly hopping into her car.

As she pulled away, she glanced out her window to see his stunned face as he stood in the parking lot alone.

Air. Air. I need cold air.

Her body still smoldering, Lacey frantically pressed the buttons of her car's AC as if pushing them multiple times might get the air to cool faster.

She glanced again in the rear view mirror as the image of the man became nothing more than a speck in the distance. She could still see him though—as clear in her memory as if his face was hovering above her dashboard.

His supremely sexy face.

She felt hot. Too hot to drive. Too hot to do anything but jump into the Severn River as she crossed the Naval Academy Bridge heading into West Annapolis.

What had just happened? Had she really been that close to planting her lips on that man? On his lips...or any other body part he had readily available? No woman would kiss a man she had just met at a funeral. Especially when she's there on business.

Of course, few women went to funerals for business. But that was beside the point.

"There's no one to check on my bumps?" she repeated to herself with self-loathing. Just once, she'd love to come up with a clever reply the way her friend Maeve always did around men.

Glancing at the clock on her dashboard, she noted that she could make her next funeral. Then she replayed the last few minutes of the previous funeral in her head, wondering if she should go at all. Clearly she was off her game.

Lacey changed lanes, narrowly missing a car in her blind spot. Letting out a breath, she pulled into the parking lot of the Navy Stadium, deciding to cool down before driving further. Maybe it was the effects of that fall. Maybe she really should go to the doctor.

Maybe she should just go home and have a drink.

Resting her head on her steering wheel, she started to laugh and then surprised herself when tears started to fall. Could it be PMS? She quickly visualized a calendar in her head. No. She couldn't even use that as an excuse.

What a wreck she was. Swept off her feet—literally—by a man with a bod like the statue of David, and she completely loses it.

The stress of the real estate business here in Annapolis was obviously killing her. Or maybe she was breathing in too much formaldehyde at all these funerals.

Or it was the lack of sex. That's what Maeve would tell her. Hell, that's what every cell in her body was screaming right now.

Suddenly, she was laughing again, nearly hysterically at the memory of herself falling flat on the floor in the middle of a funeral home. She didn't know if she should feel humiliated, angry, or—remembering the final thirty seconds in the parking lot—turned on.

Yep, she was definitely turned on.

That, she decided, is exactly the type of man she had to avoid until this newest career of hers takes shape. Just a little time off from distractions, she had convinced herself. With a string of pathetic dates still fresh in her memory at the time, a temporary hiatus from men hadn't seemed like much of a sacrifice.

Of course, she hadn't been counting on meeting a guy who looked like...*that*. The man radiated sex from his pores.

No, no, no. Letting out a breath that would have made her yoga instructor proud, she attempted to mentally purge his delectably yummy image. She was not going to spend her thirties the same way she had killed time in her twenties—dabbling in dead-end jobs, distracted by whatever or whomever crossed her path.

Just once, she wanted a business card with a boast-worthy tagline:

Lacey Owens: Ranked #1 in Real Estate Sales in Annapolis.

And finally, she had come up with a foolproof plan for making it reality. It was a plan even worthy of Vi. She just had to stay focused.

With a sigh, she pulled an obituary from a file she had stashed in her back seat, and punched another funeral home address into her GPS. She might just be able to make it.

CHAPTER 2

Lieutenant Commander Mick Riley played those minutes in the parking lot with that leggy brunette over in his mind as he stood in front of his bed, pinning medals to his uniform with precision that bordered on OCD.

He gave himself a slight nod. Each one was perfectly straight, perfectly aligned with the next, in exactly the spot dictated to him by Navy Uniform Regulations.

Something about putting on his uniform made him feel more in control. It defined him. It gave him direction. If he'd had his uniform on, he never would have been distracted by some cute real estate agent in her prim little suit and too-high stilettos.

Getting rejected was not a pleasant experience, especially when the woman was hot enough to get him half-chubbed at a funeral. But with hair the color of cinnamon sticks and legs as silky as a pint of Haagen Daz vanilla as she lay prone on the floor, Mick was instantly aroused. Not the most appropriate reaction, especially with Doc's dead body lying peacefully only twenty feet away.

Women like her shouldn't be allowed around men fresh from deployment.

Narrowing his eyes at his reflection, Mick adjusted the warfare insignia pinned above the coveted Navy Cross awarded to him just before he shipped off to Annapolis. He couldn't help the scowl that passed over his face. He wasn't in the mood to remember that day in the mountains outside Kandahar, hauling his near-dead teammate three miles under heavy fire.

He cursed the quiet around him. He was a SEAL, not an instructor. He should be heavily armed with an HK416 assault rifle right now, leaping from a helicopter into enemy territory.

Instead, the Navy expected him to stand in front of a room of green midshipmen droning on about the basics of leadership and ethics.

Ethics. What an irony, considering the unethical backstab dealt by his Commanding Officer that had landed Mick here.

At least he was here for Mrs. B when Doc died so suddenly. Don and Edith Baker had been his sponsors during his plebe year at the Academy more than a decade ago. They were like parents to him over the years. When Doc died, Mick feared he'd never see Mrs. B smile again.

Then along comes that woman at the funeral and some story about stargazer lilies, and Mick saw the light return to Mrs. B's eyes.

That must be why he was so attracted to her. It was simply gratitude he felt for her.

Satisfied with his reasoning, he gave a slight nod to his reflection in the mirror. "Gratitude and a nice ass," he said to himself as he put on his cap and headed out the door.

Stepping from his historic townhome on the Academy campus, the "Yard" as midshipmen called it, he glanced warily around him out of habit, still not used to being able to walk around on a work day without his SIG Sauer pistol at his side and the weight of body armor on his back.

It was a beautiful campus, and a hell of a lot prettier than his surroundings during his constant deployments. Being a naval history buff, he might enjoy a little time here in Annapolis. But two years? He vowed to do whatever it took to get his career back on track before then. Even with his injuries from his last mission barely healed, he wanted to be back with his team. They were probably back in Afghanistan or maybe off the Horn of Africa right now.

And here he was, he thought with regret as he passed a mob of tourists being led by a guide in a colonial era costume. May as well be stationed at Disneyworld from where he was standing. He wasn't even armed.

What is the point of having a job in which he isn't armed? Why even bother qualifying as expert on every weapon from pistol to machine gun, if the most dangerous thing he can carry right now is a can of Raid?

A brisk ten-minute walk across the parade fields led Mick to the door of an unimpressive office he shared with a Lieutenant slated to teach nuclear engineering. The damn kid looked so content sitting behind his computer, Mick momentarily hated him.

The Lieutenant quickly rose from his seat at attention when he saw Mick. "Sir."

"Lieutenant, if we're going to share an office all year, let's forget the formalities."

The Lieutenant smiled. "That extra stripe on your shoulder board tells me to stand up, Sir."

"Yeah, well, this extra stripe reminds me that I shouldn't even be teaching. Don't remind me of that by jumping to attention every time I come into the room."

"Done, Sir."

"Mick," Mick corrected. "Mick Riley."

"Got it. Mick. Jack Falcone." The Lieutenant offered with a firm handshake. "So what are you doing here, then?" Jack asked, glancing at the Navy Cross Mick had pinned to his chest. "You should be writing your own ticket now. In San Diego or out in the field, I'd think."

"I pissed off my Commanding Officer after my last mission. I was up for orders. He made a phone call or two, and here I am."

Jack let out a breath. "Hope it was worth it. Pissing off your CO, I mean."

"Probably not," Mick muttered, wanting to change the subject. Truth was, he couldn't regret telling off Captain Shey that day after the Kandahar mission. If the Captain hadn't ordered the Blackhawk to change extraction points when it came under fire, Sully would still be in the SEALs rather than sent home to his wife and kids without a leg. Mick tugged at his collar. "It's hot as hell in here. Don't we have air conditioning?"

"I thought you SEALs were tough," Jack smirked.

"Yeah, I can kill a man in two seconds bare-handed. But I can't take this damn Annapolis heat in the summer."

"It's hotter in San Diego."

"It's not the heat..."

"...it's the humidity," Jack finished for him. "Yeah, I know. My ass is stuck to this chair."

Mick leaned back and stared vacantly at his computer. He didn't know the first thing about writing lesson plans or syllabi. "How about you? Big physics brain?"

Jack flashed a smile that made him look scarily like Brad Pitt in his younger years. "That's me. I'll teach here for a couple years, then back to sea as a department head. If I don't take your route and piss off my CO."

"Just don't call him a pansy-ass bastard to his face."

Jack let out a low whistle.

Mick could tell he wanted to hear the whole story, but knew better than to ask. SEAL missions were top secret, hidden behind layers of nondisclosure forms. Black ops, they called it.

Returning to typing, Jack gave a slight nod at the framed photo on his desk of him surrounded by four women, two holding infants on their laps. "I'm liking it here because my sisters are all on the East coast. I've been at sea so much, I barely get to see them and their kids." He handed the photo to Mick proudly. "I've got one more niece and my first nephew now."

Mick scowled. "You have four sisters? That would kill me."

"Are you kidding? It's great. I know everything about women. I have the inside track. I ask all the right questions, like 'what are you thinking right now?' Girls love that shit. Between that and this uniform, I can't keep women off me."

Mick laughed. One look at the young Lieutenant, and anyone would know it was true. "Well, keep that uniform on, or you'll have the same experience I did this afternoon."

Jack raised his eyebrows, a silent request for details.

Mick ordinarily wasn't the type to talk much. Some guys liked talking about life over a few beers or while shooting pool. The only male bonding Mick enjoyed was when he was headed into danger with his fellow SEALs. But, staring at a blank monitor, suddenly socializing seemed a lot less painful. "I was at the funeral of my Academy sponsor, and I met this woman. Asked her to dinner and she shot me down."

"You tried to pick up a woman at a funeral?"

"Yeah."

"You don't find that a bit...inappropriate?"

Mick paused. "I just got back from six months in a war zone. How would I know what's appropriate?"

"Poor excuse, Slick—I mean, *Sir*." Jack shook his head, his smile fading. "Seriously, man. Stay away from my sisters."

Maeve Fischer rustled the pages of the newspaper open. She took a lengthy sip from her wine glass and gazed out at the Chesapeake Bay.

Of all the rooms in her waterfront home, it was the screened-in back porch that stole her heart the most. She had big plans for rest of the house, but the porch would remain the same. Too many perfect memories of her grandparents were on this porch. She could see them right now, sipping their vodkas and holding hands as the sun set. They still had held hands after nearly sixty years of marriage.

They're holding hands today, Maeve thought, a little comforted by the idea. Her eyes got teary—must have been allergies—and she raised her wine glass just a touch to the horizon.

"Here's to love that lasts," she said quietly, and watched two seagulls rise from the water and fly into the distance.

Still holding hands definitely. Indefinitely.

A gentle breeze blew off the water causing sections of the newspaper to scatter to the floor. She sighed and let them lie on the ground. She wasn't moving a muscle for anything right now. She was just going to relax and enjoy the sun as it drifted lower in the sky.

This was the best Maeve had felt in months. She finally had both of the extra rooms of her house rented. She had a Baltimore client with a stunning property in Canton and a boatload of cash to decorate it.

She had even found a neighborhood kid to mow her lawn weekly for a song.

Life was good.

"A little early to be drinking, Maeve," noted a voice over her shoulder.

Maeve didn't even turn around. She just balled up a page of the Style section and tossed it over her shoulder at the voice.

Lacey caught the wad right before it hit her face. "Good aim. Sure you don't have eyes in the back of your head?"

"I saw your reflection in the wine glass. Grab a glass and pull up a chair. I picked up a new Cab I've been aching to try. Cabernet-of-the-year according to *Wine Connoisseur*."

Lacey went back into the kitchen and re-emerged, glass in hand. Kicking off the stilettos, she let out a sigh.

"From that sigh, I'm guessing they were pretty boring funerals."

Lacey smiled slyly. "Then I guess your instincts aren't as good as you think." She pulled a section of newspaper toward her. "Are these the obituaries?"

"I circled a couple that you might find interesting," Maeve answered and gave a careless wave to Lacey's murmur of thanks. "So what happened?"

Lacey set the newspaper down and gazed dreamily out to the Bay. "Well, the first interesting thing that happened was falling and hitting my head." She raised her eyebrows for emphasis. "Bad."

"You okay?"

"Definitely. Think it only hurt my pride. I blame these stupid shoes you made me wear."

"You just need more practice in them," Maeve said, reverently touching one of the shoes as she bent over to retrieve her scattered newspaper. "Sexy little things. And with that dark suit, it's just the perfect mix of sex kitten and real estate guru. I need them back for Saturday, you know."

"Of course."

"And the second thing that happened?" Maeve prodded.

"I met the hottest man I've ever seen in my life."

"At a funeral? You're kidding."

"Nope, not kidding."

"Were you drinking?" Maeve narrowed her eyes at her friend.

"God, no! What's the matter with you?"

"At a funeral." Maeve repeated, a statement this time, not a question. "Wait a second. It's not some old guy or something, right?"

"Oh, please. Of course not. He's probably my age. So way too old for you," she noted. It was a well-known fact Maeve preferred the younger set. "Total muffin, as you would say."

"A muffin," Maeve said appreciatively, the same way an art connoisseur might say "A Monet."

Lacey gave herself a small shake as if to break a spell. "So anyway, that's it. Bumped my head. Met a man. End of story."

"What do you mean, 'end of story'? Didn't you get his number?"

"Of course not. I was there on business."

"Oh. Family member of the dead guy?"

"No. But definitely too close for me to mess with, not that I'm looking for that right now anyway. The widow's property would be worth a ton, and she's already got my business card in hand."

"That's pathetic. You need a good date. Well, you need more than that. But let's start with a date. That woman won't be looking to sell that property for months. Maybe years."

"So, I'll be patient. It panned out for the Miron listing, didn't it? And for yours, for that matter."

"I didn't sell."

"No, but I got a cheap room to rent."

Maeve laughed. She always thought it ironic that it was Lacey who had convinced her to keep the waterfront home she inherited from her late grandmother. It would have been a nice commission for Lacey, and Maeve had been ready to sign on the dotted line. "Well, I still say you should have asked for his number. Do you know his name?"

"No."

"Where he works?"

"No."

Maeve rolled her eyes. "Did you find anything out about him at all?"

Her grin wide, Lacey leaned forward and took a leisurely sip of Cabernet. "Well, from the feel of his arms around me, he probably bench presses 425 pounds."

Maeve nearly dropped her glass, jostling it just enough that the red wine splashed over the side and onto her cream silk slacks. She didn't even give the stain a second glance as she eyed her friend. "Okay. You owe me details. Now."

As the sun completed its path toward the sparkling blue horizon, Lacey filled her in on the details, then rested her feet on the café table in front of her.

"425?" Maeve sighed. "That's Greek god material."

Lacey grinned.

"Well, you should at least have gone to dinner with him. At least. Your whole time-off-from-dating thing is just unnatural. Use it or lose it."

"It worked for Vi."

"Honey, I've seen Vi on TV, and she doesn't look nearly as sexually frustrated as you do. She's getting it somewhere."

Lacey frowned. "Then she never lets it get serious enough that it might distract her from her career. She must just use them for sex and then toss them out the door."

"Here-here!" Maeve toasted, raising her glass enthusiastically.

"I'm not very good at that," Lacey grumbled, shrinking further down in her seat.

Maeve shook her head as she refilled her friend's glass. "I

just wish you wouldn't take it all so damn seriously, Lacey. You can reinvent your career years from now. Look at me. Thirty-six years old and I've finally started getting paid for what I love."

"Dating younger men?"

"The other thing I love," Maeve clarified. "Interior design."

"Well, this is it for me. I'm sick of being the *unsuccessful* daughter."

Maeve rolled her eyes, unable to relate to the freakish dynamics of Lacey's family of habitual over-achievers. Maeve had won the lottery when it came to her own family. Of course, she'd paid her dues in other ways, she remembered sadly. Leaning back, she indulged in a therapeutic gulp of wine. "Vi is Vi. Lacey is Lacey. Stop trying to be more like her and just be who you want to be."

"And who would that be? A thirty-year-old who has no clue about what she wants to be when she grows up? Or grows old, in my case."

"No, a thirty-year-old who lives for today. Look at that view, Lacey." Maeve extended her arm to the Chesapeake. "You're sipping a Cab enjoying a view of the Bay while Vi is probably in some crowded financial district crammed in a windowless office getting yelled at by some producer."

"Or flying to Paris to cover the European Banking Symposium."

"Paris? Really? That bitch."

Lacey jumped at the sound of a door slamming inside the house. She darted a startled look at Maeve.

"Oh I forgot to tell you—I found a renter for the third room. She seems really nice. Quiet type. Perfect renter, as far as I'm concerned." Maeve emptied the last wine from her glass and finally started blotting the stain on her pants.

"Where is she from?"

"I didn't ask. She's still in college, I think. Cleans a few houses in the neighborhood. That old couple in the split foyer on the corner uses her."

"You didn't even run a credit check on her?"

"What do I need that for? I'm a good judge of character."

Lacey raised her eyebrows.

"Okay. With women. I'm a good judge of character when it comes to women. With men, my record's a little sketchy."

SLAM!

Bess cringed at the sound of the door behind her. She hadn't meant to let it slam. She didn't want anyone to think she was going to be a loud tenant.

Stepping hesitantly into the room that was now hers, she was greeted by a spindle-framed twin size bed and a dresser with worn-down varnish. The walls were painted a light shade of pink, with grey smudges from years of gentle abuse and a smattering of nail holes from pictures that had been removed. One framed photo remained with a black and white image of a couple sitting together on the steps of a back porch. It looked like it had been taken in the 1950s, though she couldn't be sure. The couple's hands were intertwined as though they would never part.

The man was gazing at the woman—his wife, Bess imagined. And the wife smiled at the camera, not in an overly happy way that would make a person think that the smile was for the sake of the photograph. Just a subtle, warm smile as though she always wore that expression. Bess indulged in a brief fantasy that the woman was her own grandmother, who was right now making cookies from scratch downstairs. For a moment, Bess could swear she smelled them baking.

The daydream dissolved with the sound of laughter

coming from somewhere in the house. It must be Maeve, talking to her other housemate. Bess wondered if she should introduce herself. She didn't want to seem rude.

Better not. The less she talked to them, the fewer questions they'd ask.

She stretched out on the bed and felt safe for the first time in days, gazing up at the watchful face of her imaginary grandmother.

CHAPTER 3

Mick juggled the casserole dish under one arm, fumbling with his keys till he found Mrs. B's. Funny how he still carried it attached to his key ring after all these years. She and Doc were like family to him, so keeping the key on hand made him feel as though he had a home to return to no matter where he was deployed.

Still, he probably should have called first.

"Mrs. B! It's Mick," he called out in the foyer. "Thought I'd surprise you with dinner and..." He stopped mid-sentence when he saw her in the living room among stacks of papers and photos, with tears in her eyes.

"Oh, Mick. You should have told me you were coming. I could have made something." The old woman blotted her eyes with a nearby tissue.

"Why are you crying?" He sat beside her, putting the Pyrex on the coffee table. Mick rubbed her back. "Sorry. Dumb question. Of course you're going to cry. I just hate to see it."

"They are happy tears. We got old and we were too busy to notice. But we had a wonderful time together." She gazed down at some photos in her hands. "It's something I hope you are blessed to have one day."

"It's a rare thing, what you and Doc had. I think I'd rather just steer clear of love entirely than be disappointed that it wasn't as real as yours was."

"You're cutting yourself off from life then," she said tenderly as she returned to sorting the photographs. "How ironic. A man who risks his life every time he is on a mission. And you enjoy every minute of it, I might add. But you won't risk your heart."

Mick didn't bother to argue. He picked up a photo of Doc and Mrs. B in front of the Eiffel Tower. "When was this?" he asked, hoping to change the subject.

"1966. Maybe '67. Is there a date written on the back?"

He flipped it over. "No."

She shook her head. "I always meant to be more organized with my photos. Even back then. But I couldn't even remember to write the date on the back. That's why I'm doing this now. I just want to put them in some kind of order as best I can. I want to remember all the places we've been and things we've seen." She reached for a photo she had set aside. "And people we met," she added with a gleam in her eye, handing Mick the photo.

Mick's jaw dropped an inch. "Is that Nixon?"

"Yes. That came as a surprise to both of us. When Don first began cancer research, he earned some kind of award for the hospital. The President was at the luncheon." She clucked her tongue. "Look at that. Don wasn't even wearing his best suit, and he's all rumpled. But he was always a bit rumpled. I loved him for it. And he knew that. He knew it every day of our life together." She touched the photo to her lips thoughtfully. "Never let the people you love wonder how you feel. It's a waste of precious time. You remember that."

Reaching for another photo, she looked down at her

much younger self. Doc's arm was around her and a cigarette was in his hand, surprising Mick. Everyone smoked back then, it seemed, even Doc.

She smiled. "I was young. You're so young right now, and you don't even know it. You'll only know it when you're my age and looking back." She took another handful of photos from a pile. "Well, my, my. Who is this lad?"

Mick laughed at the sight of himself at eighteen, standing on a picnic table pretending to be swinging from a low-hanging branch. He looked like an immature idiot. Of course, that's what he was back then. Amazing how a war or two can harden someone. "Can I burn this?"

Mrs. B snatched it from him. "Over my dead body. These are dear to me. You—all the mids we sponsored. When we learned we couldn't have children, we were devastated. But sponsoring midshipmen brought us such fulfillment." She smiled. "You were always our favorite, of course."

"You're just saying that because I brought casserole."

Mrs. B looked at the pan on the coffee table apprehensively. "Oh, is that what that is?"

"It's good. At least try it. Aren't casseroles customary when someone's lost a loved one? Thought I heard that somewhere."

The old woman laughed. "You're right, actually. I have at least three that came from neighbors over the past few days. Let's just put this in with the others." She rose from the sofa.

Mick followed her into the kitchen. He took his usual seat, a stool pulled up to the counter. Doc had replaced the old ceramic tile counter with granite as a surprise for his wife. Mick missed the old tile. He missed the mustard yellow appliances they had when he was at the Academy. Some kitchens weren't meant to be renovated.

He saw the trash was full and started to take it out to the can.

"Garbage is tomorrow morning for you, isn't it? Let me take this out," he called over the creaking of the garage door as it opened.

From the end of the driveway, he looked at the house in the glow of dusk. He felt an ache he had come to know too well in the past several days.

He missed Doc. He missed his deep, throaty laugh every time Mrs. B said anything even slightly funny. He missed seeing his weathered hand rub Mrs. B's back affectionately and the way she'd lean into him just a little, probably without even knowing it.

He couldn't imagine how much Mrs. B must be hurting.

Back in the kitchen, he heard the familiar sound of her chopping vegetables. Mrs. B could do it fast, like the chefs on TV.

"Thought I'd make some soup, Mick. Just not in the mood for more casserole. You're welcome to stay."

"How about I take my favorite lady out instead? Since my casserole's not a hit, I still owe you a good meal."

"Oh, honey, I'm not in the mood to go out just yet. I need time."

Mick kissed the side of her head with gusto. "I give you two weeks and that's it, lady, or I'll be insulted. I already got turned down once by a woman this month." *Damn.* He hadn't meant to let that slip out.

Mrs. B stopped chopping. She didn't even have to say a word. Mick knew he was required to give an explanation.

"Just that woman at the funeral. The one who fell. I asked her out to dinner. Shot me down."

"The real estate agent, right? I think she gave me her card. What was her name?"

"Lacey. Tracey. Something like that," Mick said causally, pretending not to have cared enough to remember.

"Lacey. Yes, that was it."

Mick threw a raw diced carrot into his mouth and immediately regretted it, chewing on it with disdain. He always admired people who could eat raw vegetables as a snack. He was not one of them. "Well, it's good to get turned down every once in a while. My ego gets too big otherwise."

"Is she married?"

"I didn't see a ring."

"Why would she turn you down then?"

Mick shrugged off the question. "How do you think Doc knew her anyway? He wasn't planning on selling the house or something, was he?"

"Lord, no. She probably just gave money to the hospital at some time. Or maybe she advertises in their newsletter. I didn't get the impression she knew him well. Just admired him from afar, like everyone else. A man who saved lives like my Don brings on a bit of hero worship, let me tell you." She laughed, tossing him a glance over her shoulder. "She was a pretty young woman. But not overly showy like those others you always seem to date."

Mick let out an exaggerated sigh.

She barreled on. "And such a sweet girl. Very thoughtful of her to send those lilies."

Mick's expression warmed, remembering how Lacey had made Mrs. B smile at a time when he had worried she would never smile again. "I thought so, too," he said, gazing with a hint of longing at the wedding photo of Doc and Mrs. B across the room. Their smiling faces reached across the decades and spoke of a love that is uncommon, but might be worth looking for.

His eyes drifted back to Mrs. B, noticing a curious expression on her face as she looked at him. "What?"

She quickly looked away. "Oh, nothing," she said innocently, tossing a handful of chopped carrots into a pot.

There was nothing like the smell of fresh paint, Lacey was reminded as she guided Carolyn Miron through her beautifully staged home. The open house was set for Sunday, and Lacey was brimming with pride as she showed off the transformation to the owner who had already moved into a nearby retirement village.

It was Lacey's first waterfront listing, and she had put more work into it than she had ever imagined would be necessary. Listings gained by crashing someone's funeral were a lot more difficult than the average house sale, she had learned. Now, she had contact information for everyone from grief counselors to assisted living homes to the Social Security Administration.

Emerging from the foyer, Lacey pointed to the new window treatments that framed the view of the Severn River sparkling in the morning sun. "They look like Dupioni silk, don't they? But they're really crushed voile. Much more economical."

Carolyn gave a slight nod, reaching out to touch the shimmering fabric that flowed from the new brushed nickel rod. Hung close to the ceiling, the draperies gave the illusion of height to the windows, and the creamy fabric Maeve had suggested added a hint of luxury without the sizable cost of silk.

Guiding her client into the kitchen, Lacey showed off the wood floors gleaming under their glossy finish. Steel hardware modernized the old kitchen cabinets since new ones were not in Carolyn's tight budget.

Under-cabinet lighting highlighted the granite countertops that replaced the old laminate. The counters were darker than Lacey would have preferred, but the stone manufacturer had offered her a great price on the Ubatuba stone because it had been rejected last-minute by another purchaser. "There's this tiny chip right here. It doesn't affect the stone strength, and I can barely notice it myself. But the other homeowner didn't want it, so we got lucky."

Carolyn's back was to Lacey as she traced her hand along the luminous stone. "It's beautiful."

Leading Carolyn through the crisply painted bedrooms upstairs, Lacey felt a surge of excitement at the idea of showing off her work at the open house. She had even gone so far as to imagine herself announcing to her parents when she visited them Thanksgiving that she had just sold a million-dollar-plus property, if it sold in time. It would be nice to have something to boast about for a change.

When this waterfront house sold, she'd have the money to print up some marketing materials like fliers and postcards for mailings. She might even be able to give up crashing funerals for business.

Lacey ended Carolyn's tour in the living room, so caught up in her own excitement that she barely remembered to look at her client to see her reaction. She was shocked to see sadness in the older woman's eyes.

Her heart sinking, Lacey couldn't stop the words before they slipped out. "Are you really sure you want to list the place? You don't look happy about it." She could envision her profit-monger sister smacking her on the back of the head right now.

Carolyn sighed as she gazed at the view of the Severn. "I really don't have a choice. It's too much house for me. And my son thinks I should be in an assisted living home at this stage in my life."

Lacey scowled. She had met Carolyn's son once, and it was one time too many. "I'd hate to see you sell it and then have regrets."

"But my son says—"

"It's your decision, not his." Lacey cringed at her tone. "I'm sorry. It's not my business. I just want to see you happy."

Carolyn's hand gently swept over the rented sofa that faced the view of the backyard. Lacey had found movers to take some of the furniture to Carolyn's small duplex in the assisted living community. The rest was sold at auction.

"No, I really am ready." Carolyn took an audible breath and then smiled, as though making peace with her decision. "The new furniture you rented does look a lot better than what I had here. You were right. I never realized how dated it all was. It's funny. You sometimes get used to things over time, never knowing how bad they are until they're gone."

Why did Lacey think Carolyn was talking more about her marriage than her furniture?

"And I never thought to face the sofa this way. Lou always wanted it facing the TV. This looks beautiful."

"It's the view that's going to sell the house."

"I've taken it for granted all these years."

"You were busy raising children. You didn't have the time to stop and smell the roses. You could now, you know. Just give yourself a few months to think it over."

The old woman smiled. "You're a terrible businesswoman."

Lacey knew Carolyn hadn't intended to hurt her, but the words stung. She could hear her parents saying the same thing.

"I'm ready for a change, Lacey. This house is beautiful now. But it holds memories I'll be glad to shed." Carolyn's hand toyed with the fixtures on the new French doors. "Besides, do you know how close I'm living to the mall now? What old lady could resist that?"

Lacey's cell phone rang. "I'm sorry. I thought I turned it off," she said, intending to ignore it.

"No, no. Take the call. I think I'll just sit here and enjoy the view a bit."

"If you're sure." Lacey glanced down at the number. She didn't recognize it. "Lacey Owens."

"Lacey, this is Edith Baker. I met you at my husband's funeral."

Lacey's heart rate sped up, the image of the breathtaking Baker property dancing in her mind. "Of course, Mrs. Baker. How are you?"

"As well as can be expected, I suppose. It's been a difficult week."

"I can't begin to imagine. Is there anything I can do to help?"

"Well, actually, there may be. You had mentioned you might be interested in doing some volunteer work for the hospital, and I'm chairing a fundraising event there this fall. With all that has happened, I'm too tired to do some of the planning. I could use some help."

Lacey swallowed a sigh. She needed an income. She didn't have time to volunteer. But she had offered and it would put her in a good position if Mrs. Baker ever did decide to sell her house. "I'm not certain I know much about throwing a fundraiser, but I can help if you'll guide me, Mrs. Baker."

"Perfect, Lacey. And please call me Edith. Would you be available to come by Thursday evening to talk things over?"

"Absolutely."

The house was empty when Lacey came home. She was alone, except for a shirtless young man with washboard abs mowing the lawn. She laughed quietly. When Maeve had told her that she had hired a neighborhood kid to mow the grass, Lacey had pictured some wiry fourteen-year-old. But considering who was doing the hiring, Lacey should have known better.

The "neighborhood kid" looked to be about twenty-two by Lacey's estimate, as she peered through the blinds at his perfectly cut body.

Lacey waited as her coffee slowly brewed, impatiently tapping her toe on the imported Italian kitchen tile Maeve had installed last week. Her mind drifted to the phone conversation she had just had with her father back at the office. "A volunteer opportunity?" he had chided when she mentioned working on a hospital fundraiser. "That's a contradiction in terms. If you're wasting your time without getting paid, there's no 'opportunity' there, Lacey."

Maybe he was right, but it was too late now.

She shrugged it off. Serves her right for taking a personal call during work hours, she supposed. Lesson learned.

Reaching for a mug in the cabinet, Lacey's eyes wandered again to the man mowing the lawn. She noticed the sheen of sweat that glistened over his ripped chest and bulging arms, seeming to accentuate each sharp curve. How could she *not* notice, especially in the midst of her self-imposed dating drought?

Inevitably, the image of the man she had met at Dr. Baker's funeral popped into her mind. She cracked a smile, remembering the feel of his strong arms sweeping her off the floor with such ease. Lightly tracing the rim of her coffee mug, her fingers tingled recalling the feel of his hard pecs through his shirt.

Bet he looks a bit like that with his shirt off, she thought with a sigh that sounded more like a purr.

"Enjoying the scenery?" Maeve leaned against the doorway of the kitchen, catching the longing stare of her friend out the window.

"I didn't hear you come in."

Maeve smiled knowingly. "Yeah, I know. Distracted. Bess is here, too. Went up to her room." She joined her friend in gazing out the window. "My, my. He doesn't even have a shirt on. That's a little unprofessional for his first day of work. Bad boy. I might have to spank him."

Lacey laughed. "You're too much. He's definitely not what I was picturing."

"Figured. He charges more than that pre-pubescent down the road, but I don't feel like I'm breaking child labor laws. Not bad to look at either," Maeve continued, admiration clear in her voice. "And you know how I like..."

"...surrounding yourself with nice things," Lacey finished for her as the last drops of coffee poured into the pot.

"Mmhm," Maeve answered dreamily, helping herself to the first cup. "Is this the high octane stuff?"

"Yeah. I'm exhausted, but I still have some calls to make. I've got that open house coming up this weekend."

"Great! Want me to come by and act like an interested buyer?"

"Sure, if you have the time. Oh, speaking of, there were some boxes that I wanted cleared out of her house before it goes up. Carolyn didn't feel right putting them in storage. Just papers and personal things. Photos probably, too. You know how sentimental old people get. She says her new duplex is too small for them."

Maeve winced. "How many?"

"About six. Mind if I put them in the attic for a little while? She said she just needs some time to sort through them, but she's not up to it emotionally right now."

"Sure, but it gets really hot up there. The stuff might get damaged."

Lacey hadn't thought of that. She groaned inwardly, foreseeing herself tripping over the boxes in her small bedroom for the next several months.

All the more reason to get that house sold fast.

"I could put them in the office," Maeve offered. "We've got a huge storage space in the basement we never use."

"I swear if you were a man, I'd marry you. Thanks. It sounds perfect."

"But you really do let people take advantage of you, Lacey," Maeve said in her usual big-sister-like tone.

Lacey sighed. She knew that was coming.

"She's got a son, right? Why can't he store them?"

"The guy's a prick. I wouldn't trust him with anything important. She probably feels the same."

"Great to have kids, huh?" Maeve said sarcastically. "Glad I'm not going down that road." She raised her coffee mug as though it were a toast. Or a vow. "They're helpless, loud, smelly when they pop out, and they only get worse with age. Thanks, but no thanks."

Lacey couldn't say she felt the same. But right now, career was her only priority.

She hates kids.

Bess sat on the staircase with her head between her knees. She had been halfway up the stairs when she felt dizzy and had to stop. She hadn't intended to listen in on their conversation. But it might be for the best that she did.

Better start looking for another place to stay. Instinctively, she held her hand to her belly. She wasn't showing yet, but would soon. Baggy clothes could only hide so much.

She raised her head slowly and gradually stood up.

Where could she go from here? No one would want to rent a room to a single mom of an infant. And she certainly couldn't afford to get an apartment on her own yet.

I could go back to my parents, she thought, her heart filling with dread.

But *he'd* find her there. It was still too soon for her to risk seeing him again.

Her parents were not an option then. She'd have to let them live with the blissful story that she had gone to explore Europe for a few months. When a few months turned into a year, she doubted they'd even notice.

With any luck, if Dan went to her parents to try to track her down, they'd share the story with him. And with a little more luck, he'd take it as gospel.

What a fool she had been. The bruises, the swollen jaw, the black eye, and the empty apologies she accepted afterward.

Yes, she had been a fool.

Until the day she found out she was pregnant. Her cheekbone was still swollen from a few days before. But at that moment, staring at the yellowish mark on her face in the bathroom mirror and holding a positive pregnancy test in her hand, she knew her child deserved better than a father like him.

So for now, she'd cover her tracks.

Bess rubbed her belly and looked around the room she now called home. Tracing her hand along the headboard, she gazed at the picture on the wall. It was Maeve's grandparents, Bess had been told. The grandfather's loving gaze at his wife reminded Bess that all men weren't like Dan.

But it was the image of the grandmother that really touched her. Her joyful eyes seemed to reach out from the photo with warm welcome.

"Gram." That was what Maeve had called her. What a lovely woman she must have been. Even now, as Bess closed her eyes, she could feel the grandmother's smile watching over her.

She sighed, for now simply content to have a soft bed to rest, and sent a silent request to a grandmother she never knew for a little more time in this sanctuary on the Chesapeake Bay.

And she smiled, feeling the old spirit's answer.

CHAPTER 4

Lacey pushed another open house sign into a patch of soft soil alongside the road. Her blouse was already sticking to her chest after standing in the heat for only a minute, and her hair had doubled in volume.

Cursing Annapolis's oppressive humidity, she jumped back into her car and blasted the AC. Fortunately, she had plenty of time to cool down at the house before people would start arriving.

If they arrived. Half of Annapolis was probably bobbing around on their boats on a hot day like today.

She parked her car along the street so that she would not obstruct views of the house. It looked perfect. Even the black-eyed Susans had seen fit to hold their blossoms for her open house. She hoped it was a sign of good luck ahead.

Stepping into the house, Lacey held her breath. She had stopped by yesterday evening to make sure everything was ready for today, half-expecting a pipe burst or roof leak to delay today's open house. But everything was perfect then, just as it was today.

Odd, though. She was certain she wouldn't have left the coat closet open like that.

Lacey shut the closet door firmly and opened the French doors that led to the patio so people could hear the enchanting sound of water lapping against the rocks.

Turning on the lights upstairs, she noticed another closet door open. An uncomfortable chill raced down her spine. She never would have been careless enough to leave two closets open last night.

For that matter, she didn't even remember having opened them.

Her eyes darted around. Nothing was missing, and it certainly didn't look as though anyone had broken in.

She whipped out her cell and started dialing.

"Hey," Maeve answered.

"Do you believe in ghosts?"

"Uh, no. Don't think so anyway."

"Then explain this. When I came into the house, two of the closets were open. I know for a fact they weren't open when I left last night."

"Why are you still in the house? If you think someone's broken in, get the hell out of there!"

"But that's just it. Nothing's missing."

"Are you sure you didn't leave those doors open?"

"Positive."

"How about the old lady? Would she have stopped by last night?"

"Not unless someone drove her. She has bad eyes and can't drive at night."

"Well, somebody else must have the key. Didn't you say she had kids?"

"Yeah, and the son lives in town. I guess that must be it," Lacey decided with some relief. "But why would he stop by here? She doesn't live here, and there's nothing left here of hers."

"Maybe he got sentimental about the place and wanted to see it again."

"Believe me, this guy is not the sentimental type."

"Are you sure you're safe there? Keep me on the line while you check the place out, okay?"

Grateful for Maeve's caution, Lacey checked all the closets, under the beds, and even climbed up the rickety ladder to the blistering hot attic.

She was definitely alone.

"Well, it had to be the son," Maeve said with confidence. "Who knows? Maybe he just remembered a stash of *Playboy*s he had hidden away when he was a kid."

"I guess you're right."

"I'll stop by later to check on you. Anything you need at the store?"

Lacey rattled off a few items and hung up the phone in time to catch her breath before one o'clock. At that precise moment, she hoped she'd be welcoming hordes of eager potential buyers into the house, their checkbooks open.

It was a great dream, anyway.

Maeve clicked her phone shut.

"Is everything okay?" Bess asked.

"I think Lacey is crumbling under the pressure," Maeve answered with a laugh, turning the corner into a parking lot. "I have to stop in and pick up some wine. Do you mind?"

"No, go ahead. I'll just wait in the car."

"It's too hot. Come on in. You can pick out something you like. I've noticed you're not into my choice of reds."

"Actually, I, uh, I just don't drink."

"Oh," Maeve said, at a surprising loss of words. "Okay. Well, if you really want to wait here, I'll leave the car running so you can at least keep the AC on."

"Thanks."

Maeve slammed the door behind her and charged into the store on a mission. The selection of wine was a sacred act. One didn't just grab the first thing they saw on the shelf, or God forbid, purchase a bottle simply because it had a pretty label.

Instead, Maeve religiously read about wine, sought out recommendations, attended tastings. As a rule, she didn't drink much. But she made every glorious sip count.

Maeve shook her head as she explored the import aisles. *What is this about Bess not drinking?* she wondered uneasily as she lightly traced the wines lined up on the shelf with her discerning finger, the same way another person might scan books in a library.

Maeve had a hard time trusting people who didn't drink. Her ex-husband had given up alcohol about halfway through her short-lived marriage. At first, she thought it was admirable. Unlike Maeve, he had trouble stopping after just one glass—or six or seven, for that matter. But Maeve had later learned that he only gave up drinking around *her* because he couldn't afford a careless slip of the tongue while under the influence. It would be in poor taste to accidentally call your wife the name of your co-worker in the middle of a moment of passion.

Not that there had been much passion in the end.

People who didn't drink might be hiding something, Maeve's experience had taught her. Not always. Maybe even rarely. But sometimes. So what was Bess hiding?

Not her business, Maeve reminded herself. Bess seemed like a good person, and she was the perfect renter. Always quiet, almost painfully so. Meticulously clean, too, which made Maeve think her housecleaning clients must be in seventh heaven.

There was definitely something going on with her. But everyone was entitled to her own secrets.

Lord knows Maeve had her share.

Lacey's face was starting to ache from smiling. "Thank you so much for coming. I'm glad you liked the house. Please give me a call if you have any questions," she said, handing two business cards to a young couple on their way out the door.

Her smile faded as she saw the man approaching the house. It was Carolyn's son.

"Hello, Mr. Miron." Something about him made Lacey wish there were other people in the house. She glanced in both directions down the street, silently willing cars to stop and see the house. But no one stopped.

"Call me Jeff, please. Nice to see there are people checking out the house," he said as he watched the couple get into their car. "Has it been busy?"

"Yes, very."

"Well, I won't stay long. I was just in the neighborhood and thought I'd stop by and see if there was traffic. I know my mother's anxious to sell," he said, slowly giving Lacey a head to toe appraisal. "Care to show me around?"

Lacey didn't budge from the foyer. "I'm sure you know your way around."

His face fell with displeasure.

Lacey remembered the open closets. "But if you come here again like you did last night, I'd appreciate it if you would shut the closets next time. Now that the house is on the market, I'd like it looking pristine when buyers come."

He was unmistakably flustered. "What are you talking about?"

"You were here last night."

Annoyance flashed in his eyes. "Yes, I stopped by hoping to see you. I figured you might be checking on the house. I lost your card."

"What did you want?"

"I thought you might like to catch dinner with me. You know, to celebrate the open house."

Lacey didn't disguise her disgust. He was old enough to be her father, and worse, he was married. "No, thank you," she said firmly, suddenly feeling the need to open the front door.

He blocked her hand as she reached for the knob. "Just business, Lacey. I might have some useful input on selling this place. I did live here for a number of years. I'd hate to see you lose this listing," he finished, the threat evident in his tone.

"At the end of the six month contract, your mother is free to look elsewhere. But having dinner with you is nowhere in the fine print. Now if you'll excuse me." Lacey opened the door.

"You're rude for a real estate agent."

"I'm not talking to you as a real estate agent. I'm talking to you as a woman who doesn't appreciate threats of any kind." Lacey felt a rush of relief as she saw Maeve's convertible pull into the driveway. She sent her a meaningful look.

"Excuse me!" Maeve quickly called from her car the moment she opened the door. "We're not too late for the open house, are we?" She darted up the driveway with Bess following close behind.

"Not at all," Lacey called back. "Please come in."

"I'll talk with you later," the man said to Lacey in a low tone.

"No," Lacey said with conviction. "I don't think you will." She reached out to Maeve to shake her hand. "Thank you for coming. I'm Lacey Owens. Do you mind signing the book on the kitchen table?"

Maeve and Bess walked into the house, with Maeve shutting the door behind her. "Who the hell was that?"

"That was Carolyn's son. Creep. He actually asked me out, and basically threatened to take away the listing from me when I said no. He's married, by the way."

"And old, ugly, with poor taste in clothing," Maeve finished for her. "And that was just my first impression."

"I've never been so happy to see you two. Your timing couldn't have been more perfect." Lacey let out a long breath, eager to change the subject. "So, how does everything look?" she asked as she guided her friends into the living room.

Bess gasped at first sight of the view. "Oh, it's just beautiful. Maeve was telling me you completely redid the place."

"Just some fresh paint and new fixtures. Rented furniture, too."

Maeve glanced upward. "Is that crown molding new?"

"No. It's just more noticeable now with the new colors, isn't it? Check out the chair rail I had installed in the dining room, though. Really adds some character."

Maeve peered through the doorway and nodded her approval.

Bess smiled up at the sparkling chandelier and the tiny reflections that it sent dancing on the walls. "Look at how that captures the light at this time of day."

"Don't be too impressed. It's not real crystal. But you wouldn't believe the fixture she used to have here. Way too 1980s for this price bracket."

Tracing her finger along the chair rail, Bess's eyes wandered dreamily out the window to the water view glistening in the late afternoon sun. "I'm ready to move in. How many houses do I have to clean before I can afford this?"

Lacey handed her the flier in answer.

Bess groaned. "Yikes."

"Actually, it's priced higher than I recommended. But that son has Carolyn convinced this is what it's worth." Lacey shrugged. "It's close enough that it will be a starting point for negotiation, I hope."

"That will be a sweet commission when it sells," Maeve said, glancing at the flier. "I may raise your rent."

"*If* it sells. And if that freak son of hers doesn't convince her to get a different agent when the contract is over."

"Did you ask him if he was in the house last night?" Maeve raised her eyebrows.

"Oh, I didn't ask him. I pretty much cornered him so that he couldn't deny it. And you'll love this. He said he came to the house last night looking for me."

Bess's face paled. "What?"

Maeve scowled. "Creep. Looking for you where? In a closet? And for that matter, why wouldn't he just call you?"

"He said he lost my card."

"Right. Like it's hard to track down a real estate agent's number. Hasn't he heard of the internet? I still say he was looking for his hidden stash of *Playboys*."

Bess spoke up. "Maybe we should stay here till the open house is over. You know, in case he comes back. There's something weird about him."

Lacey took Bess by the hand and couldn't help noticing it was trembling. "That's sweet, but I'll really be fine."

"Okay," Bess said uneasily, then surprised Lacey by pulling out pepper spray from her purse. "Just keep this handy till you get home, okay?"

CHAPTER 5

Clenching her Spode china teacup in a death grip, Lacey sipped her tea. She could tell just from the feel of it that this single cup was worth more than her entire dining collection purchased in an economy box at Target.

Carefully, she eased back into Edith Baker's down-filled sofa and gazed at the impeccable surroundings. When Lacey had first driven up to the house, she had been beyond intimidated. The property jutted into the Bay on three sides like its own small peninsula, offering sprawling views from nearly every room. Her mouth had gone dry at the sight.

It was gorgeous, from the manicured gardens that led to the water's edge to the cathedral ceiling crowned with a genuine Waterford chandelier.

Definitely a far cry from the Miron property that had so desperately needed a sharp eye for detail and hard work before going on the market. Nothing needed her here. Anyone could sell a property like this. It didn't take anything but a simple listing online and the right price. No challenge at all.

Easy money. How refreshing would that be?

Lacey flexed the muscles in her fingers after safely settling the tea cup back on its saucer.

"Is your hand bothering you?" Edith walked back into the room carrying a fresh pot of tea. "I've been having you take down too many notes."

"No, it's not that at all," Lacey confessed. "I've been gripping that tea cup too hard because I'm scared I'll drop it. Your china set is beautiful. At my house, the finest china is a set of coffee mugs that read 'I love firemen.' Maeve got them on Ebay."

"Your housemate sounds like quite a character," Edith laughed as she refreshed their cups, her gentle tone making Lacey feel surprisingly comfortable. "I like her already. It's good to have friends who keep your heart light." She sat next to Lacey and picked up one of the crust-less finger sandwiches she had placed on the coffee table.

A voice called in from the foyer. "I'm here. Where's the most beautiful woman in Annapolis?"

Something about the voice sent Lacey's heart racing.

Edith put a hand to her mouth to conceal a laugh. "Such a tease. Time must have gotten by me," she said apologetically to Lacey, glancing at her watch. "We're in the living room, dear."

"Just grabbing one of these cookies off the counter. You sure know how to keep a man happy, Mrs. B. I came straight from work, so didn't have time to—" He stopped short in the doorway when his eyes met Lacey's.

Shocked by the jolt of recognition that shot between them, Lacey's tea cup splashed onto her linen capris at the sight of the man she had met at Dr. Baker's funeral.

"Let me grab a towel for you," he said, darting back into the kitchen.

"I'm such a klutz," Lacey said to Edith, as the man returned with a dishtowel.

"Well, you weren't expecting to be startled like that." Her eyes filled with humor, Edith looked at the man. "Oh, but that's right! You had offered to take my old bag of bones out for a night on the town. Time flew by me this afternoon. I've enlisted Lacey's help for the fall fundraiser this year. You remember Lacey from Don's funeral?"

"Of course. Mick Riley." He extended his hand.

She took it, and the feel of his skin touching hers in the simple gesture nearly knocked her breathless. "Lacey Owens."

Edith cocked her head to one side with a coy grin. "Lacey and I have been talking and laughing for hours. Just the breath of fresh air I needed. I really am exhausted now, though. Do me a favor and take Lacey out in my place. If I had any energy, I'd be making her dinner right now to thank her for all this help she's giving me."

Lacey tried to wrench her eyes away from Mick, looking intimidating in his Navy uniform, his chest covered in a mysterious array of ribbons and emblems. Her heart fluttered at the sight. "No, really, Edith. I feel privileged to be a part of this benefit."

"Lacey, I insist. It will lift a weight of guilt off me. I know how much time this is going to take you over the next few months. You'd be smart to at least get a nice meal out of it," Edith finished with a wink.

"I couldn't—"

Mick took Lacey lightly by the arm. "You'd better not argue with her, Lacey. I've known this woman since I was eighteen and I've never won an argument with her."

Helplessly, Lacey was escorted out the front door by Mick, the feel of his gentle touch on her arm sending tiny shivers down her spine. "But we took separate cars," she protested feebly.

"Details, details." Edith waved her hands lightly.

Mick shook his head as Edith closed the door behind them. "I have to apologize for her. She and Doc were my sponsors my plebe year at the Academy, and she's been trying to set me up with women ever since."

"Plebe year. That's your freshman year, right?"

"You're obviously not from Annapolis. Don't have the terminology down yet, do you?"

"I'm working on it."

"During your first year at the Academy, you get assigned a sponsor. Sort of a second family for while you are here. For some, the family title sticks."

"She seems like a wonderful woman."

Mick nodded. "I'll take full responsibility for explaining why we didn't go out later. She shouldn't have put you in that awkward position."

Lacey felt an odd disappointment when she realized he wasn't taking her to dinner. She knew she should refuse anyway. But if she had been *forced* to go out with him, well, then she'd just have to suffer through the dinner.

Though looking at him now, impressive in his khaki-colored uniform that fit snugly across his broad shoulders, maybe "suffer" wasn't quite the right word.

They began walking back to their cars.

"I'm actually glad to have run into you again. I wanted to apologize," he said, surprising her.

"For what?"

Mick laughed quietly. "Hitting on women at funerals is conduct unbecoming an officer. I think you could get me court-martialed for that."

Lacey grinned. "If it makes you feel better, I nearly said 'yes.'"

"Yeah, that's the vibe I was getting."

Lacey flushed, remembering how close she had come to lip-locking him in a parking lot. "Um, yeah. To be honest, I was very attracted to you. I'm flattered that it seems to be mutual."

"Seems to be."

His eyes met hers. As sparkling blue as she had remembered, they were homing beacons for undersexed women. Soft lashes. Tender lids she longed to kiss. She was losing herself in them again, enraptured, when she suddenly blurted, "It's just that I'm really not in a place where I want to date anyone right now."

He held back a laugh at the desperation in her voice. "I've been there myself. So I'll respect that."

She held his gaze, instinctively trusting him. Once a woman drew a line in the sand, she could tell he would not cross it. Unless she begged, she considered hopefully. Because looking at him right now, she realized it might come down to that.

Mick moved to open her car door for her. "Well, with all that settled, will you let me at least buy you dinner as friends? I don't want to have to explain to Mrs. B why I let her down."

Lacey smiled, tempted. He *did* say that he was buying, she considered, her thoughts drifting to her bleak checking account and the dry pouch of Easy Mac awaiting her in Maeve's kitchen cabinet. She relented too easily. "Okay."

"Great. We'll drop off your car at your place, and go from there."

She couldn't help noticing his take-charge attitude. "You have a knack for talking people into things. You'd be a good lawyer."

"Who says I'm not a lawyer? The Navy's got enough on staff."

"I say. My mom's a corporate finance lawyer. I know a lawyer when I see one. Besides, lawyers don't have those." She gave a slight nod at his arms.

"Those what?"

Lacey felt a surge of boldness, a sudden need to touch him, and reached out to lightly trace her hands along his upper arms. The damn things were like tree trunks, as hard and thick as she had remembered. Her body temperature rose by ten degrees. "These. You can't get arms like this pushing papers or sitting in court all day. I don't know what you do for the Navy, but you're no lawyer."

Feeling his biceps constrict under her fingertips, her eyes widened. Hunger flashed momentarily in his eyes, but then just as quickly, the spark disappeared and he patted her on the shoulder.

"Well, you'll just have to control yourself. We're just friends, remember?" He winked. "I'll follow you back to your place. Hurry up. I'm hungry."

"Me, too," Lacey answered quietly. He had no idea what she was hungry for.

Or maybe he did.

They found themselves lingering, taking too long to order, to eat, to sip the last of the bottle of wine Mick had ordered. Lacey took a long look at the label before the waiter took it away so that she could recommend it to Maeve when she got home.

Under the blurring effects of a French Pinot, Lacey had to keep reminding herself to steer clear of funerals or the late Dr. Baker as a topic of conversation. Surprisingly, it wasn't that difficult. He was fascinating, she thought as she comfortably rested her head on her hand and gazed at him.

Of course, everything was more fascinating after sharing a bottle of wine.

"So do you like teaching?" she asked as her coffee arrived.

Mick passed her the cream. "I'm hoping it will grow on me. I'm a SEAL. I like work that's a bit more physical."

Lacey couldn't resist sending a discerning gaze across his impressive shoulders. Yeah, I'll bet, she thought.

He continued, obviously energized by talking about his preferred job. "SCUBA, parachuting, hand-to-hand combat. SEALs have the best training out there, and I'm not exactly putting it to use here." He gave an almost imperceptible stretch that broadened his chest even more.

Lacey's mouth watered.

"And I know it sounds crazy, but I miss the risk." He paused, sending a nod of thanks to the waiter as he took away his dish. "So how about you? Why real estate?"

"Oh, I just love the risk, too," she joked, tossing his own words back at him. "I never know when a seller might have a Doberman that they failed to tell me about. And there's the physical challenge. When I show a townhouse, there's a lot of stair climbing involved."

"Climbing stairs." Mick glanced downward. "So that's how you keep those great legs in shape."

Lacey fought the blush that was creeping up her neck. "Seriously, though, I don't know why I ended up in real estate. I've barely been at it a year now. I think it's the only career I hadn't tried." She sighed, suddenly feeling pathetic sitting next to a man who had done so much in his career. Sort of like how she felt sitting next to her sister, come to think of it.

"Are you liking it?"

"Real estate? I like some parts of it. People sell or buy homes when there's something major going on. I like being there to help them through it. Job changes, marriage, babies, d—" Lacey cut herself short from saying death, remembering where she and Mick had met. "d—divorce," she finished quickly.

"So you're a people person."

"Yeah, that's me. Unfortunately, I'm discovering that I'm not the best salesperson, and that's what it really takes to succeed. I attract the 'lookie-loos'—the people who just like looking, but never buy. I probably rack up a thousand miles a week just driving people from house to house. What I need are more sellers. That's where the money is." She reached for a packet of sugar just as he did, the touch between them only lasting an instant. Yet still, her breath caught. Her eyes locked on his, and she memorized them, the delicate pattern of his irises, a striking steel blue with indigo flecks that looked like turbulent waves on the sea.

A smile curved his lips as he took the sweetener from her and poured it into her cup. Stirring for her, he paused thoughtfully. "There has to be some way to find people who seriously want to sell. Maybe advertising or networking?"

Lacey's eyes widened, realizing they were treading into dangerous territory. "What I need—" she began, quick to change the subject, "—is to be more like my sister."

"Your sister?"

Lacey nodded. "She's a huge success. Started out in financial planning like our dad, and now she's on all these finance shows on TV."

"Really?"

"She'd never put up with clients walking all over her like I do. The minute she figured out someone wasn't serious, she'd literally dump them on the curb and move on. She was on the cover of *BusinessWeek* last month, you know." She couldn't help being a bit boastful about her sister. Lacey was proof that sisterly pride could blend seamlessly with envy.

Mick studied Lacey for a moment. "Huh. What's her name?"

"Vi Owens."

The recognition in his eyes was obvious. Lacey had seen

it so many times before. Right now, he was picturing Vi with her perfect hair, doe-like eyes, and full lips. It was an injustice that someone so successful could be drop-dead gorgeous, too.

Mick quickly glanced down at his water glass and took a sip.

Lacey grinned. "You know her. I can tell."

Their eyes met and Mick tried to sound casual. "Yeah, I might recognize the name. I watch CNBC sometimes."

Lacey warmed inside, realizing that Mick was trying to look unimpressed by Vi to protect her feelings. It was adorable. "It's really fine. I'm proud of her."

"I can't believe she's your sister. You look nothing alike."

"Hey, that's not a nice thing to say since she's Wall Street's equivalent to Angelina Jolie."

"You're *both* beautiful, just in different ways." With a fleeting look downward, he added, "And you have better legs."

"Thanks." Lacey blushed. "Vi was adopted. That's why we look so different. But what's ironic is that she's so much more like my parents than I am. They're so driven. Very successful. Just like Vi."

"And you're not driven?"

"Not like Vi always has been. She was a Wall Street profit monger before she even knew there *was* a Wall Street. I mean —" she paused, seeing an example was necessary, "—she used to sell her Halloween candy piece-by-piece for profit to kids in school."

Mick choked back a laugh. "She *sold* her Halloween candy? Lacey, that's not driven. That's insane."

"She did it every year till we were too old to trick-or-treat. And a million things like it. The topic of her sixth grade term paper was compounding interest. In high school she started an investing club." She looked into the distance thoughtfully. "Even back then, Mom and Dad would boast about her to everyone. One time I actually overheard one of their friends say, 'Are you sure *Vi's* the adopted one?'"

Mick winced. "How old were you?"

"Oh, I don't know. Eight. Maybe nine."

"Hell of a thing to hear at that age."

Lacey's lips pursed together, strangely tempted to confess how much it really had hurt her. That comment. All the comments she heard as she was growing up.

She shook her head. "So anyway, that's why I'm focusing on my career until I have a few good listings go to settlement. I've actually got my first closing next week. It's not much, but I also have a waterfront that I just put on the market."

Taking a sip of her coffee, her eyes met his again. She didn't *want* to like him. Didn't want to think of him as any more than a perfect face topping a just-as-perfect body. But she found herself opening up, easing into the conversation as naturally as she had leaned in toward him that day in the funeral home parking lot. As though some inexplicable magnetic force would draw her toward him even if she couldn't see his mouthwatering presence. Even if the lights were out.

The lights out. Now, there was a thought.

Clearing her voice awkwardly, she hoped he couldn't see the steam she felt rising from her body. She glanced out the window. "I have this crazy fantasy about sitting down at the dinner table at Thanksgiving at my parents' house and announcing my first waterfront sale. I'm sure they've always wondered if they brought the wrong baby home from the hospital." She laughed, reaching for more cream. "I guess that sounds lame—to be thirty and still trying to impress my parents."

Mick shrugged. "I've seen guys go to war to try to impress their parents. It doesn't sound too unusual to me."

"Is that why you joined the military? To impress your parents?"

"Hell, no. I did it to get laid." His eyes sparked with amusement.

"Are you serious?"

"Dead serious. I was this really skinny kid in high school. The guy no one would date, you know? But I was smart, and I got into the Academy. Got the Navy uniform and suddenly women are slipping me their numbers." He gave a wink, and then his face grew serious. "No, I'll admit there was a little more to it than that. I needed direction. The Navy gave me that. Then the war broke out and that's when I knew I wanted to be a SEAL. And that wasn't to get laid, believe me. I knew I'd be good in the action."

"Your parents must be proud."

"My mom died of lung cancer when I was nine."

"I'm sorry."

"My dad's proud, but we're not very close. I have one brother, but he's ten years older than me. I guess that difference in age stopped us from developing much of a relationship."

"That's a shame." Lacy reflected on her own relationship with her sister. It may have had its struggles, but she couldn't imagine not having her in her life.

"He lives in New Mexico now with his second wife. I saw them once before I was deployed to Afghanistan the first time. They drove up to San Diego to see me off. But, you know, life just goes on. I haven't seen him since. We email once in a while."

He reached for his water glass and swirled around the ice cubes. "I really should go out there and visit. I've been away so much, but that's just an excuse. Now that I'm stuck in

Annapolis, I'll have nothing but time on my hands, compared to my time in the SEALs."

"You don't seem too happy about being here."

A fierceness washed over his face, disappearing so quickly Lacey questioned whether she had even noticed it. "I was slated for another SEAL job in San Diego, but things changed and I ended up here." He gave a slight nod out the window to the Naval Academy across the water, with the distinctive profile of its Chapel dome illuminated against the evening sky. "Don't get me wrong. I love the Academy. But teaching isn't what guys like me are meant to do."

"How long will you be here?"

"Two years at most. Hopefully I'll be headed to San Diego, and after that, deployed. I need to get back in the action."

Lacey felt a sadness that she couldn't understand. She reminded herself that he was only—could only be—a friend. How long he stayed here shouldn't matter so much to her.

But it did.

"Well, I hope that's what happens, then," she forced herself to say.

If Lacey had looked tempting to Mick in the candlelight, then the drive home was pushing him over the edge. He had never thought the blue lights of his dashboard could make a woman look so appealing. He wished he was a teenager again, and could park the car in some deserted lot for a while before returning her home before curfew.

There was a warmth, a pure honesty about Lacey that he found so refreshing. He glanced in her direction as her tongue caught a renegade drip of chocolate ice cream dribbling down her waffle cone. Smiling, her eyes sparkled.

God, she was sexy in that sweet, girl-next-door kind of

way. He was sitting in the car with the kind of woman most men dared to wish was waiting home for them after a deployment.

No wonder he avoided this kind of woman like the plague.

As they reached a stoplight, Mick stole a long look at her, just as a drip of ice cream fell onto her shirt. Right on the peak of her breast, Mick noted, biting his tongue to stop himself from offering to lick it off.

"Nuts," she said quietly, her hand brushing lightly against her breast. Pulling his eyes away from the profile of her tight nipples against the thin fabric, the blood in his head rushed south.

Any other woman, and he'd offer her a drink at his place right now. Any other woman and he'd be using his best lines —the ones that always got him laid. He'd be talking about the war, the loss, his duty to his country, and all the other patriotic bullshit that generally sent women to their knees…literally.

But something about Lacey made Mick want to coldcock any man who used a line on her. Including himself.

Lacey was right. It was smarter to just stay friends. A woman like her might convince him to kick his Navy career to the curb, especially since he was already pissed off at his chain of command.

He had a career to focus on, just like she did.

He just hoped she didn't give him the proverbial friend-hug at the end of the evening. Holding her that close without ripping her clothes off might kill him.

"I had a wonderful time," she said with an uneasy sigh. "Look, I understand enough about men to know that they really don't want to be just friends. I had a great time tonight, though. I want you to know that."

"I had a great time, too," he admitted. And now that she

had given him the perfect out—served it up to him on a silver platter—he shocked himself adding, "And you're wrong. Friends is fine with me. If for no other reason, I just want to be around when you are voted the most successful real estate agent in the Mid-Atlantic."

She beamed.

Then the devil in him returned as he leaned in closely to her. "But when that happens, I warn you that I will seduce you to my fullest capacity."

Hearing a car door slam, Maeve raced to the window barely remembering to turn the light out so that they wouldn't see her watching. A man was approaching the passenger side door. Maeve's jaw gaped at the sight of his broad silhouette, and she nodded her tacit approval. He was a heartbreaker.

A protective feeling rose in her. Lacey was so trusting. Maeve better keep a close watch on this one.

When the man opened Lacey's car door, the car's interior lights revealed Lacey's image in her conservative capris and blouse. Maeve strained to see her shoes. *Flats?* Maeve shook her head.

She raced down the stairs when she heard Lacey come in through the door, and stopped, arms crossed and eyebrows raised, on the bottom step. "How are you supposed to seduce a man in flats, Lacey? Have I taught you nothing?"

"We're just friends, Maeve."

"Whatever. When Bess told me that you had driven off with some hot guy, I thought there might be hope for you. But I can see I was wrong. Your hair's not even disheveled." She sighed and flopped onto the sofa opening her latest issue of *Wine Connoisseur*. "What a waste. He looked delicious. Was that the guy from the funeral?"

"How'd you guess?"

"Bess said something about your meeting with that widow, so I put two and two together. From the look of him, maybe I should start hanging out at funerals." She let out a low whistle from behind the magazine.

"Where is she, anyway?"

"Bess? I think she's asleep by now. Kid sleeps like the dead. I've never known anyone to go to bed so early."

"It's the work, probably. Very tiring pushing vacuums and scrubbing floors all day. I don't know how she does it."

"It pays," Maeve said, dog-earing a page. She set it down on her lap thoughtfully. "I think she's just doing that to pay the rent while she figures out her next move."

"I can relate to that." Lacey's tone was dismal. "That's how I spent my entire twenties."

They heard the creak of the staircase behind them.

Maeve peeked over the arm of the sofa. "Hey, Bess. I thought you were asleep."

Bess's startled eyes were puffy. "I was. I heard someone at the door."

"Oh, that was just me. Sorry I woke you." Lacey kicked off her shoes.

"How was your date?"

"Well, it wasn't really a date," Lacey said, and explained to them both Edith's unexpected set-up between her and Mick.

Maeve laughed as the story unfolded. "I like this old lady's style."

"She's really sweet. But it was so awkward. And honestly, I don't think I could handle just being friends with him. The whole night, I just wanted to—"

"Pounce him?" Maeve offered.

"Yes!"

Bess grinned at Lacey's candor. "Could you maybe just keep him around a little, just in case you change your mind?"

"Or could one of us have him by default?" Maeve sent Bess a wink.

Lacey fired them both a glare and all but growled, "No!"

Maeve and Bess exchanged knowing looks.

"Just friends, my ass," Maeve said with a smirk.

CHAPTER 6

Handing a set of house keys over to Brian and Marybeth Sandoval, there were few occasions when Lacey had felt this proud. "Congratulations. There's nothing more exciting than buying your first home together."

Marybeth was beaming. "Oh, Lacey, I just can't thank you enough for all your patience. I never thought we'd need to look at so many homes before we found the perfect one."

"I'm just glad you found the right one."

Brian placed his arm easily around his wife's shoulders and gave a little squeeze. "You went above and beyond. And haggled a good price for us. Remind me to never try to sell a car to you. I'd come out in the red."

"I promise to stay away from your car dealership only if you send me a referral or two," Lacey said, handing him a few extra business cards.

"Will do."

Lacey stepped from the settlement attorney's office and into the crisp air. It was cooler than usual for early September, hinting of fall weather around the corner. The refreshing breeze only added to Lacey's good mood. She pulled out her cell phone and dialed Maeve's number as she walked down an alley toward Main Street. It went straight to voice mail.

"Maeve? Where are you? I made it through my first closing. Wish you were around. I need a drink to celebrate, and I can finally afford one. Call me."

Lacey snapped her phone shut. It wasn't a huge sale, but the small commission would at least keep her from worrying about her rent for a few months. Besides that, it was her first.

Feeling the weight of the cell phone in her pocket, she willed it to ring. She had to talk to someone. On a whim, she pulled it out again and dialed her parents.

"Hi, Mom. It's Lacey. How are you?"

"Lacey. I was just going to call you."

"Really?" Lacey asked, suddenly hopeful her mother had remembered that the closing of the Sandoval house was today.

"Yes. Your sister is going to be on CNBC this evening again. Between five and six your time. She asked me to tell you."

"I'll try to check it out," Lacey said, knowing full well she'd skip it.

"So what did you call about?"

"Nothing much." In the shadow of her sister's TV appearance, Lacey felt the need to rein in her enthusiasm. "I just finished the closing on the Sandoval home."

"Is that the waterfront property you just listed? That was quick."

Lacey's face drooped. "No. That's still up for sale. This is just a starter home for a newly married couple."

"Oh, yes. Sandoval. Now I remember them. You spent a lot of time with them. Didn't they make an offer a few months ago?"

"It's been about six weeks. There were a few things that needed to be fixed after the inspection."

"You must be thrilled to unload them. They sounded very high-maintenance for people willing to spend so little on a home."

Lacey felt the odd need to defend her clients. "They're actually a nice couple. Not everyone can spend seven figures on a house."

"Mm," her mother responded, obviously distracted by something.

She was probably turning on CNBC at this very moment, Lacey concluded. "Well, I'm at my car now. I better go."

"Of course. Have a good night."

Lacey leaned against the side of her car and suppressed the urge to throw the phone across the street. She certainly couldn't afford to replace it.

In retrospect, Mick had been pretty pleased with himself for not calling Lacey in over a week. It proved that he was still in control of his emotions. Control was important.

Of course, that was not counting when he had called Lacey the day after their dinner to tell her she had lost an earring in his car. Mick had thought it was a ploy to get him to call her, his healthy ego getting the better of him. Women were trained to "accidentally" leave things behind if they wanted a man to call them. He may be a guy, but he had some passing knowledge of that whole Cinderella-glass-slipper thing.

The fact that the earring turned out not to be Lacey's—well, he hadn't expected that. But the time they had spent laughing about it on the phone was almost worth his being wrong. He hated being wrong.

Fortunately it rarely happened.

He flicked his cell open and started dialing.

"Hello?" Lacey's voice sounded hollow on the other end.

"Lacey? It's Mick. Are you all right?"

"Oh." Her voice brightened a bit. "Hi, Mick. No, I'm fine. I just got off the phone with my mother."

"Everything okay? You don't sound too happy."

"Everything's fine. Thanks, Mick. My mom's just so—I don't know." She sighed. "How are you?"

"Fine. I just called to see how your first closing went. But I can tell from your tone that it must not have gone well."

"No, actually it went great. That was nice of you to remember."

"I'm just that kind of guy," he said with a grin. "Congratulations, then. So why do you sound so down?"

"It's just—it's complex really. I told my mom about the closing and she was her usual less-than-enthusiastic self. She managed to tell me that my sister is going to be on CNBC in about an hour, though."

Mick was glad to hear the bite in her tone. It made her sound less defeated. "And I'm sure you're racing home right now to see her."

Lacey laughed. "No way. In fact, I think I'll stay out and avoid anyplace I might run into a TV for the next hour or so."

"Well, why don't you come out sailing with me? I was just headed down to the boat basin. I need to brush up on my skills. We don't do a ton of sailing in the SEALs and I don't want to be shown up by one of these mids." Mick winced, suddenly realizing what he was offering. Offering to take a woman out on a boat at sunset. A woman he promised to keep his hands off.

Was he insane?

"You have a boat?" Lacey said with surprise.

"God, no. I couldn't afford one of these beauties at my

rank. But I'm an officer and have my C license. I can take them out anytime if they're not being used for training."

"Really?" Her voice was hesitant. "You really can take me sailing? You won't get into some sort of trouble, will you?"

Mick laughed, touched by the enthusiasm in her voice when she had only moments ago sounded so downhearted. "I really can do that."

"It's a date, then. I mean, a deal. It's a deal."

"Great. I'll meet you at Gate One to the Academy in about ten minutes. It's the one at the end of King George Street."

"I know right where it is. See you there."

It had been more than a week since Lacey had seen Mick in uniform, and she still hadn't fully recovered from the sight. Yet this evening he had unknowingly topped himself when she discovered how completely arousing it was to be with a man who warranted a salute.

"How do they know to salute you since you're not in uniform?" she whispered as a group of midshipmen passed, their hands raised quickly in the precise greeting.

"A lot recognize me. And the others are too damn scared to *not* salute and then see me standing at the front of their lecture hall."

Mick hopped onto the boat and glanced down at Lacey's feet. "I don't want to seem like I'm already trying to get your clothes off of you, but you can't come on board in those heels. Much as I love what they do for your legs."

"Oh, of course," she laughed as she leaned over and unstrapped her sensible Mary Jane-style heels, thanking God she had painted her toenails.

Reaching out his hand to help her aboard, Mick smiled.

"Welcome aboard, Ma'am." He gave her a mock salute, then busied himself with the lines.

"Is there anything I can do to help?" she asked, enjoying the sight of him managing the lines and controls as though it were second nature.

"Not a thing. Just sit back and relax," he said, tossing her a look over his shoulder. "And try not to look so damn sexy, will you?"

Lacey rolled her eyes with a grin, imagining herself shoeless in a suit Maeve would have called borderline-frumpy. She knew she was the furthest thing from sexy. Average was a word that best described women like Lacey. Mousy brown hair. Fewer curves than a highway across a Plains state. A halfway decent face, though lacking the ability or interest to play up her better features. That was more Maeve's department.

Yet something about the way Mick looked at her made her feel anything but average.

Motoring out of the boat basin as they headed to deeper water, Lacey thrilled to see this new perspective of Annapolis, with the Naval Academy's impressive buildings dotting the shoreline. She grinned as they passed the small inlet that Annapolitans called "Ego Alley" because boaters would parade in and out of the narrow strip of water to show off their boats to ogling tourists at the end of Main Street.

But it was when Mick cut the motor and the wind filled the sails that Lacey realized the true appeal of sailing. They whipped along the waves, the boat heeling only slightly with Mick at the helm. At Mick's suggestion, Lacey hung her feet over the side, enjoying the feel of the water splashing onto her feet and the slight saltiness of the brackish spray on her face.

They sailed into a quiet cove in the Severn River where the water was calm.

"This is beautiful here," Lacey said, watching a heron flying low across the river. Her breath caught from the casual touch of Mick's hand on her arm as he moved her to the opposite side of the boat so that he could pull a line tight. The muscles in his broad expanse of a back contracted as he pulled the sails down and dropped the anchor, and Lacey appreciated for the first time how a simple white t-shirt can showcase a perfect male physique.

"And now, my surprise." He grinned as he headed down below to the galley, and re-emerged with a bag filled with food and a champagne split. "The food is for us. The champagne is for you and you alone. Drinking and boating don't mix when you're the captain, especially when you're sailing government property. But I didn't want your celebration tonight to be without a bit of the bubbly."

"How did you manage this? I met you at the gate only ten minutes after we talked on the phone."

"It's something you learn in the Navy. On a ship, always make friends with the cook and you'll eat well. Same goes at the Academy. The cook at the Officer's Club and I are like this." He crossed his fingers.

"Smart man." She took the offered box of carry-out and practically purred at the aroma. Opening it, her mouth watered. "It's filet mignon. I love filet."

Mick popped the cork. "I'll admit that was just luck. I begged him for whatever he had prepared. Right now there's an Admiral and his wife waiting longer than expected for their dinners."

Lacey laughed.

Mick gave her shoulder a gentle squeeze. "That's good. You're sounding a lot better than when I first talked to you today."

"I shouldn't let my mother get to me like that. I was just

so excited about the closing. I called Maeve first, but when she wasn't home, I called my parents. Big mistake."

"You should have called me instead. We *are* friends, Lacey, as you keep reminding me."

Lacey found herself reaching over and touching his hand. His warmth seeped into her, from her fingertips, up the length of her arms, casting a fire across her breasts. A sigh escaped her. "Thanks. It was nice of you to remember. And believe me, spending the evening sailing with you is a lot more exhilarating than going for a drink with Maeve." In more ways than one, she thought, quickly pulling her hand from his as she felt her resolve slipping away.

What *was* her reason for not getting involved with him? Taking another sip of her champagne, her brain scrambled to remember.

"I'm glad you came. It's been a while since I went sailing. Now that I'm in Annapolis again, I'm even tempted to buy a boat."

"Really?"

Mick nodded, refreshing her glass. "Mrs. B was thinking of selling their boat. I figure if I bought it, at least I'd make sure she got a good price for it."

"Are you sure that's a good idea? It's so soon after her husband's death. I'd hate for her to make a decision like that without taking the time to heal."

Mick draped his arm lightly around her shoulders, then removed it, giving her knee a quick pat instead. "Don't worry. I wouldn't let her part with anything she valued. The boat was all Doc's. She hated sailing. Used to get seasick just looking at it." He reached for another steak fry. "She has to dry dock it this winter anyway, so it might be a good time for her to put it up for sale."

"Oh," Lacey responded, wishing his arm was still on her shoulders. With the cool breeze, the idea of snuggling up to him seemed so appealing. On pure instinct, she found herself leaning subtly toward him.

Their eyes locked for a moment, and Lacey could hear nothing but the gentle lapping of the waves against the hull of the boat. It seemed to echo her heartbeat pulsing inside of her. Mick shifted in his seat. Clearing his throat, he continued, "It's not like she was looking to sell the house or something. *That* I'd worry about."

Lacey's head snapped back from his several inches, remembering why he was off-limits. "Why do you say that?"

"That house—it's just not meant to belong to anyone else." He shrugged. "Maybe it's my own memories there that are clouding my judgment, though."

"You spent a lot of time there?"

Mick looked thoughtful, then laughed briefly. "I did and I didn't. It's hard to explain. Yes, I spent a lot of time there while I was at the Academy. And I visited a few times since. But it feels like I spent a lifetime there." He paused, as though trying to find the right words. "In the SEALs, I saw a lot of action. It wasn't pretty. You never really know life until you've seen it taken from others. Until you wonder if you'll live to see the next minute. I did things... saw things..." His voice trailed a moment. "I don't think I would have survived if I didn't have memories of that house."

Lacey sat quietly, trying to conceal the guilt that she felt for secretly hoping Edith would give her the lucrative waterfront listing.

Mick must have taken her silence as a request for more explanation. "There are times when you have to hold onto images just to survive, Lacey. The pain. The fear. A lot of guys would remember the home they grew up in, think of images of their wife and kids. It gets you through. It gives you strength. For me, I'd think about Doc and Mrs. B and the memories I had in that house. The way it always smelled like something was cooking. The laughter. The way you just sank into the sofa and knew you were home. It kept me alive. I know it sounds crazy because I can't say anything else."

"I understand. Too painful."

"No. Too classified." Mick gave himself a little shake. "So anyway, that house means so much to me, probably more than it should. I'd hate to see her give it up for herself, of course. But I'll admit, a lot of it is selfish."

Not as selfish as crashing her husband's funeral hoping she might sell her house, Lacey thought, realizing that even a friendship with Mick was tenuous. If he ever learned the true circumstances of their meeting, he'd never want to see her again.

Lacey couldn't shake the hurt of that thought for the rest of the evening.

CHAPTER 7

As companies of midshipmen marched by the bleachers to the triumphant rhythm of *Anchors Aweigh,* Mick's right hand snapped up in perfect unison with the other officers as the American flag passed.

Lowering his arm, he muttered through barely moving lips, "There's no way I'm seeing her again."

"Coward," came the tight-lipped reply from Jack standing at his right. "You should have joined us at O'Toole's that night instead. There were a couple redheads guaranteed to make you forget any real estate agent—I don't care how great her legs are."

"Next time, count me in." Mick was sweating bullets under his whites. The heat today was unseasonably oppressive. Hell of a day for a bunch of Four Star Admirals to visit, with all the required pomp and circumstance.

Watching the rows of midshipmen in their starched white uniforms, his mind drifted inevitably to his own Academy years and the stress of marching the parade fields under the scrutiny of senior officers.

Had it really been ten years since he was that young and fresh-faced?

Jack must have read his thoughts. "Makes you feel old, doesn't it?" he commented as the crowd finally began breaking up.

Mick nodded gravely. So much had happened since he graduated. The Navy had taken him to places he never thought he'd get a chance to see, and war had shown him things he wished to God he could forget.

Jack continued as they headed toward their office. "Makes you feel so old that you might want to settle down with a nice, hot-looking real estate agent and spawn some young."

"Shut up, Jack. I'm not asking her out again."

"Why not? I've never seen you so hung up on a woman before."

"You haven't known me that long."

"Okay, so I've never seen *anyone* so hung up on a woman before." Jack shrugged carelessly. "You brought up her name five times since zero-nine-hundred hours."

"She's not looking for anything serious." Mick picked up his pace as they headed along the pathway toward Dahlgren Hall.

"Who needs serious?"

"She's not looking for anything, period. Just friendship."

Jack mouthed the word friendship simultaneously with Mick. The dreaded "F" word. "That sucks, man."

"Yeah," Mick agreed. "She hot, and I'd do her in a New York minute—"

"I'd hope you'd last longer than that," Jack interrupted with a snort.

Mick's glare was deadly. "—but she drew a line that I won't cross."

Jack rolled his eyes, as they cut through the Officers' Club parking lot. "Yeah, whatever. But you better not back off."

"Why not?"

"Because she's like all women. They *think* they don't want a relationship, but that wears off. And the guy who wins is always the one who's lurking around waiting to move in at a vulnerable moment."

"More stuff you learned from your sisters?"

"Oh, yeah. My youngest sister got married to a guy she met two days after she had supposedly sworn off men. He just kept hanging around, and then moved in for the kill when the timing was right. Nice guy, though," he continued. "Or I would have turned him into fish food for the bottom feeders of the Atlantic."

"Of course," Mick agreed, thankful he never had sisters to protect. He'd probably be in jail by now. "Lacey's nice, don't get me wrong, but I couldn't handle an evening with her again. I'm just not into torture."

"Group date then," Jack offered up as the solution, punching Mick's arm with his fist. "That's what you need. You said she has housemates. So, we meet them for a drink. Real casual. Just friends. You get to keep her on your radar screen, and I get to meet her friends who hopefully won't have the hang-up with dating men that she does."

The idea had some appeal.

Jack's eyes brightened. "Even better, we wear our uniforms. Go to some overcrowded bar downtown. Bump into some mids. They have to be all deferential and salute us. We boss them around and make them do push-ups. Women love that. You'll get laid."

"I don't think that would be enough for Lacey."

"Who said it has to be Lacey?" Jack laughed at the withering look he received from Mick. "Dude, you've really got to lighten up."

"Okay. Maybe a group date. But no uniform. Too obvious. Next week sometime?"

"Tonight. Seems more casual to call last minute."

Lacey eyed the ripe pimple on her forehead and ached to squeeze the life out of it, wondering if the urge to pop zits was somehow coded into her DNA.

Sometimes it was good to spend a Saturday night dateless. Of course, she hadn't given herself many options lately.

Her cell phone rang. "Hello?"

"Hey, Lacey. It's Mick. How are you?"

Just like that, her body reacted to the sound of his voice. It was almost embarrassing. "Oh, hey, Mick. I'm fine. How are you?"

"We've got some visiting Admirals. It's been pretty hectic. Jack and I were headed down to O'Toole's to detox with a beer. Wasn't sure if you and your housemates might want to join us."

Lacey swallowed. Hard. She really didn't think she could handle another evening in his presence without her resolve crumbling. "Oh, thanks, but I'm not really sure what Maeve and Bess are up to tonight." That's good, Lacey thought proudly. Blame your friends.

As if on cue, Maeve peeked in through her bedroom door. "Did I hear my name?"

"It's Mick. He's wondering if we wanted to join him and a friend at O'Toole's tonight." Lacey shook her head furiously, making it obvious she did not want to go.

Maeve grinned and replied loudly enough to be heard on the other end of the phone. "Count us in, Mick! We'll be there in an hour."

Lacey sent Maeve a skewering glare. "Did you hear her?"

"Yeah. Is that Bess?"

"No, that's Maeve."

"Tell her an hour's great with us."

"Okay. See you there." Lacey hung up, looking again at the zit on her forehead. At least he wouldn't have a hard time being just friends with her looking like this. "Why did you do that, Maeve? Couldn't you see me shaking my head no?"

"Was *that* what that was?" Maeve asked with feigned innocence. "I just thought you were shaking your head at the idea of being alone…again…on a Saturday night."

Lacey pouted.

"Oh, come on, Lacey. You need to get out. Besides, I really want to get a better look at this guy." Without waiting for a reply, Maeve marched down the hall to Bess's room.

When Maeve stepped into O'Toole's, heads turned. There was simply something about her that drew the eye. Her hair was perfect. Her nails were perfect. Her outfit made her look like she had just stepped off the pages of *Vogue*. In a perpetually casual city like Annapolis, it defied the rules to wear anything dressier than jeans. But Maeve always dressed a step above the rest, this evening in her favorite Michael Kors ensemble with subtle, yet glimmering accessories.

Lacey personified dull standing beside her in her capri jeans and T-shirt. She looked down at her flip-flops and cursed herself for not at least borrowing some heels from Maeve. But that would give the wrong impression, she consoled herself. If Mick was okay with just being her friend, he better get used to the sight of her in flip-flops.

Bess trailed them reluctantly. Sullen after being awakened from a nap, she seemed to go out of her way to fade into the woodwork. Her baseball cap covered her gorgeous mop of red hair and she hadn't even bothered putting on one swipe of lipstick.

Given the choice, Lacey thought it wiser to sit on Bess's side of the table rather than next to Maeve.

Lacey smiled encouragingly at Bess. "You look great. You really put yourself together fast. I envy that."

Bess looked at her in disbelief. "What are you, blind?"

Lacey turned her attention to Maeve. "And you look fantastic, but that goes without saying." She paused, hoping someone might send a hint of a compliment her way. Her ego was sadly depleted tonight, especially with Mount St. Helens poised to erupt on her forehead at any moment.

Maeve just looked down at Lacey's feet and shook her head. "Here," she said in disapproval as she reached down to her heels. "Trade."

"No, I couldn't."

"Yes, you could. Aren't they sassy? I got them on a little shoe shopping detour when I was on a buying trip in New York."

Slipping Maeve's shoes on, Lacey immediately felt better.

Satisfied, Maeve smiled. "Now I can say it. You look great, too, and fabulous choice in shoes, Lacey. And you," she paused, eyeing Bess, "are a sport for coming. Sorry I dragged you out of bed. First round's on me. What do you want?"

"Chardonnay," Lacey said, feeling far more feminine now that she had heels.

"Ginger ale," Bess whimpered.

Maeve gave a slight nod and sauntered off to the bar.

Lacey eyed Bess. "You're really looking pale. Are you sure you're okay?"

"Fine. I'm just really tired. It was a hard week."

"I don't know how you do it. I can hardly clean my room

let alone a string of other people's houses. Are you looking for any other kind of work? Maybe something in retail or—"

"No," Bess interrupted. "I just don't have the energy to start looking for something new right now."

"Are you going to finish college? Maeve mentioned you were only short a semester or two."

"Eventually."

"You know, I have a laptop you can use. There are a lot of courses that you can take online. Maybe you could—" She stiffened suddenly, her senses stirring with awareness. Even with her back to the door, she knew Mick had walked in.

His hand brushed gently across her shoulders. "Hi, Lacey."

"Mick, hi. This is my friend, Bess."

Mick offered his hand to Bess and gestured to his friend. "And this is Jack. He works with me at the Academy. Teaches physics or some other useless science like that."

Jack flashed his pearly whites.

Looking at them as they sat down, Lacey couldn't help comparing the two men. Their short hair, perfect posture, and chiseled muscles made it obvious they were in the military, despite their lack of uniforms that night. But Mick's shoulders and chest were broader and his face more rugged. Jack favored a slightly leaner, boyish look, with a body Lacey imagined was sculpted in a health club rather than by hauling gear through the mountainous terrain of Afghanistan.

Jack was handsome, but she preferred her Mick.

Her Mick? Did she really just think that? She nearly winced. Better not let that slip, or Maeve would never let her live it down.

"What can we get you from the bar?" Mick offered, starting to stand.

"Actually Maeve is—"

"Oh...my...God." Maeve reappeared from the bar, a look of complete shock on her face. Both Bess and Lacey's heads whipped around to see what she was looking at.

"Maeve." Jack said her name in a hushed, almost reverent tone. His face slowly transformed from shock to pure joy, as though he were a kid who had just been handed his first ice cream sundae, dripping with hot fudge. "Maeve."

"Jack."

No one dared to say a word. There was an electric charge in the air, the kind Lacey had heard happened right before lightning struck.

Jack rose from his chair, shaking his head slowly. "My God, Maeve." Standing only inches away, he wrapped his arms around her, lifted her from the ground, and whirled her in a full circle causing heads to turn.

Maeve put both of her hands alongside his face and pulled him into a kiss. It was brief, but whole-hearted, the kind she could either give the love of her life after being separated for years, or a friend who had just handed her the winning lottery ticket.

"So I, uh, take it you know each other?" Mick said with a grin.

They both inhaled as if trying to find the right words.

"Maeve is...she and I...we..."

Maeve interrupted with her usual candor. "Jack was the best sex I ever had."

All eyebrows raised including Jack's, as well as about four or five other people who were within earshot.

"The best?" Jack repeated.

"Absolutely."

Jack shot a cocky grin to Mick. "I was the best."

Lacey butted in. "And this was...when?"

"Six years ago, maybe?" Jack looked at Maeve.

"Seven, I think." Maeve was glowing. "I was house-sitting for my grandma. It was the weekend after the Academy graduation, right?"

"Yep. The last weekend I was here before I went to Surface Warfare Officers School in Rhode Island. I met Maeve at a party for a friend."

"Who was that?"

"Brian something."

"Oh yeah, a friend of a neighbor."

"We walked out of the party together and weren't seen again…"

"…for the whole weekend," Maeve finished for him.

They delved into the sordid details, perhaps a bit too much, each one finishing the other's sentences as though they had been together for years.

"But you didn't see each other again?" Bess asked when there was a break in the conversation.

"Oh, no. Of course not. He had just graduated. I was maybe six or seven years older than him and looking to settle down. We didn't stand a chance," Maeve said bluntly. "In fact, I met my husband just a couple months after that."

The look of disappointment on Jack's face was obvious. "You got married?"

"Unfortunately," Maeve responded and then quickly raised her ring-less finger. "And divorced…"

"…fortunately," Lacey and Bess finished for her in unison, both having heard their fill about Maeve's ex.

Jack frowned. "You broke my heart, Maeve. I gave you my number. You never called."

"I told you I wouldn't."

"Oh, please," Mick chimed in defending Maeve. "You were a new officer and busy as hell. I remember my first job after commissioning. You never gave her a second thought."

"Well, maybe not a ton of thought. But I always remembered her."

"Ditto, sweetie," Maeve brushed his cheek in a maternal way, and Jack looked visibly slighted.

"So this all happened at your Grandma's? The same house we're in now?" Lacey asked.

Maeve just smiled in response.

Lacey and Bess exchanged a glance.

"In whose room?"

Maeve burst out laughing. "In every room. Don't you get it?"

"So you live at your Grandma's now?" Jack asked.

"Well, it's mine now. She passed away last year."

"Oh, Maeve. I'm so sorry." Jack reached for her hand.

Maeve pulled both of her hands back and gave a careless wave, seeming to reject both the sympathy and affection. "It's all right. I'm fine with it now. I was living in Baltimore at the time, and Lacey talked me into keeping the house."

"Still have that kitchen table?" he asked with a cocked eyebrow.

"Whoa, whoa. Stop right there," Lacey butted in. "Too much information. I have to eat at that table."

By the time their food arrived, Maeve noticed that even Bess looked like she was enjoying the evening, sipping her ginger ale contentedly. She had even pulled off that disaster of a baseball cap. Maeve made a mental note to hide that thing when they got home.

"Who ordered the crabs?" the waitress asked.

"Me." Maeve raised her hand. "Oh, and the oysters. No one has oysters quite like here."

"You know what they say about raw oysters." Jack sent Maeve a wink.

"Dream on. Consider me a once in a lifetime opportunity," Maeve retorted back. "Now your friend here...oh, I think he's already got his eyes on our Lacey."

"Just friends, she's telling me, Maeve," Mick grinned at her.

"Of course. Just friends. This is a very friendly table we have here. Oyster anyone?" she asked as she struggled to pull the slippery meat from the shell.

Bess recoiled at the sight.

"Squirmy little devil." Maeve dipped the oyster in cocktail sauce and hand-fed it to Jack, deciding not to offer one to Bess who was turning three shades of green. Another chunk of meat snapped from the shell like elastic and Maeve swirled it in cocktail sauce. Cocking her head, she watched Bess shrinking in her chair. "You okay, Bess?"

As a glob of sauce slid off the oyster's slick body, Bess covered her mouth. "Excuse me!" she murmured, bolting from the table in the direction of the restroom.

Lacey slapped her napkin on the table. "I better check on her."

Maeve watched Lacey race after Bess, and weighed whether she should follow. She had never done well at the sight of someone throwing up. Not even in college. And from the look on Bess's face, Maeve guessed she was praising the porcelain god right now. "I shouldn't have dragged her out."

Jack gave a sage nod. "Yeah, I think the oysters just tipped her over the edge. When is she due?"

"What?" Maeve asked blankly.

"When is your friend due?"

"Due for what?"

Mick sliced a finger against his throat to signal Jack to shut up.

Jack looked confused. "To deliver, I guess."

"You think she is pregnant?"

"Um, yeah."

Maeve bristled. Thank God Bess wasn't here to hear this. "She's not pregnant. She's not even fat. Jack, you shouldn't assume a woman is pregnant just because she's a little thick in the middle."

"I didn't say she was fat or thick in the middle. But she's definitely pregnant."

"How would you know and I not know?" Maeve said, clearly offended.

Jack began, "I have…"

"Four sisters," Mick completed. "Yeah, you've mentioned that."

Jack looked nonplussed. "Nausea, bulky clothes, not drinking, and with that kind of reaction to the sight of raw oysters? It's a no-brainer. First trimester, I guarantee it."

Maeve fell silent, staring blankly at random reflections dancing in her glass of Pinot Grigio as she distilled the information.

In a daze, she politely dabbed the sides of her mouth with her napkin. "You'll excuse me. I have to check my lipstick."

Pregnant. The word hovered in the air, thick and smothering, nearly causing Maeve to gasp for breath as she made her way across the bar.

Bess is pregnant? It made perfect sense. She should have figured it out a long time ago.

Bess. Pregnant.

How was Maeve going to stand that? Living under the same roof with the one thing she desperately wanted and could not have. She had the world convinced she disliked children—that she'd never lose precious sleep for late-night feedings or tolerate a minefield of Fisher-Price toys on her antique Aubusson rug.

But it was a lie—one that was easier to live with than the truth.

The restroom door creaked open and the stench of sickness struck her. Lacey was holding back Bess's hair as she emptied her stomach, apologizing profusely in between each heave.

Maeve covered her mouth, flashbacks to her party years in college making her feel even worse. She glanced away. "Is there anything I can do?"

Bess collapsed on the bathroom floor. She shook her head weakly.

Maeve forced herself to touch Bess's shoulder. "This is all my fault. You said you didn't want to come and I forced you. I'm so sorry. God, you were napping." Maeve suddenly saw another clue she had so easily dismissed just hours earlier. "I should have left you alone."

"It's not your fault. There was just something about those oysters."

Maeve tried to ignore the dirt on the floor as she sat on the floor next to them. "Bess, are you—maybe—pregnant?"

Lacey jerked her head to look at Maeve, realization dawning in her eyes.

Bess, already pale, turned at least three shades lighter. "Eleven weeks," came her mumbled response.

"Wow." Lacey let out a slow breath.

Bess shook her head, in obvious despair. "I'm sorry. I really should have told you before I moved in. I won't have to stay much longer, and I promise I'll be out before the baby comes."

Lacey shot Maeve a look of panic, and received an almost imperceptible shake of the head in return.

Maeve tried to sound annoyed. "Out? Out where?

Unless you have someplace better to go, you're sure as hell are not sticking me with an empty room. It's hard finding renters."

Lacey smiled. "Maeve's right. We're not letting you go anywhere."

Tears came pouring down Bess's face.

"And when the baby comes," Maeve dared herself to continue, "we'll figure something out. Hell, I was thinking about getting a dog anyway. It can't be too much more trouble than a dog, right?"

A brisk breeze hinted of autumn as Mick and Lacey walked along Ego Alley to the water taxi port with bags in hand. Lacey glanced down at the shopping list that Jack had written for them. "The only thing they didn't have was graham crackers," Lacey noted, wondering if they should have gone straight to a grocery store, rather than dropping into the small apothecary just off Main Street.

"It's not that late. We'll drop these off first and if he really thinks she needs graham crackers, we'll go out again," he offered easily, his head tilting as he looked at Lacey. "Are you okay?"

Lacey smiled self-consciously. "I'm fine. It's just a lot to take in, I guess." Downtown Annapolis was alive this cool Saturday night, crowded with an eclectic mix of overdressed tourists, midshipmen, and locals hopping in and out of shops and restaurants. Noticing couples walking hand in hand, she felt a tug of longing. She fidgeted with the list in her hands. "You know, I have to hand it to Jack. I somehow admire any man who can suggest stool softeners for a woman without even blinking."

Mick laughed. "I'll keep that in mind."

"How do you think he knows so much about pregnancies?"

"Well, four sisters. I guess he'd hear plenty."

Lacey picked up her pace to keep up with Mick's long, causal strides. "He seemed to really want to go back to Maeve's and to make sure Bess was all right."

"Uh, I think that had more to do with Maeve than Bess. Unmistakable chemistry there."

"You noticed, too?"

"Hell. Everyone in the bar noticed. He just didn't want to leave her company."

"Well, thanks for offering to pick this stuff up with me and take me home."

"Maybe I just didn't want to leave *your* company." His eyes sparked with mischief.

Lacey grinned, helpless against his charm. As they squeezed onto a park bench at the water taxi port, she savored the feel of his body where it pressed against hers. She desperately wanted to lean closer, to be closer, to feel the warmth of his lips and his chest pressed against her.

A furnace igniting inside of her, she remembered the feel his solid arms around her, lifting her, that first day they met. The sensation of his fingers in her hair. His light touch on her cheek. She ached for that moment again, only this time, she wanted it naked, skin-to-skin, his mouth on hers.

Squeezing her eyes shut, she tried to calm her senses, but to no avail. Every part of her seemed somehow more alive just being close to him.

A small, brightly lit boat docked in front of them.

Mick extended his hand to help Lacey down the narrow stairs that led onto the boat. Her heel caught, and she stumbled into Mick. His grip was firm on her arms, and they froze, their mouths only inches apart. The feel of his warm breath caressing her lips sent shivers down her spine. Paralyzed in his gentle hold, she couldn't tear her eyes from his.

"*Excuse* me!" An impatient tourist anxious to board the water taxi behind them broke the spell that seemed to have been cast on Lacey.

Mick shot Lacey an amused look and whispered in her ear, "Damn tourists."

They eased into their seats, side by side, and watched the image of downtown Annapolis fade into the distance. The taxi motored along, dodging in and out of moorings that bobbed on the water. His arm pressing against hers again, she could feel the tension in his muscles. Such power in this man, she pondered, wondering what it would feel like to have that power inside of her. She felt herself grow wet at the idea, and the heat between her thighs ached for his touch.

"So, how do you feel about having a baby in the house?" Mick's attempt at small talk was just the cold shower Lacey needed.

Feeling her temperature drop to normal, Lacey pursed her lips together thoughtfully. "I haven't even had time to digest the idea. It's just something we'll deal with together, I guess."

"Do you want to have kids of your own?"

"Me?" Lacey shifted in her seat, enjoying the way her thigh pressed against his in the act. "Well, I'd like to get my career on track first. But maybe. How about you?"

"It's a possibility," he answered noncommittally.

A sudden cold gust of wind had Lacey impulsively snuggling closer, stealing his heat. She glanced up, almost in apology, and a lock of hair blew across her eyes. As Mick lifted his hand to put the lock in its rightful place, his hand caressed her cheek.

His light touch was all the encouragement she needed. Without thinking—*finally,* without thinking—she leaned in, raising her mouth to his in silent plea. Go ahead, her heart whispered as the warmth of his lips met hers, gently at first, then with a searing passion.

Tilting her head, she savored him, breathing in his musky scent. Her hands splayed across his chest, stroking the rippling muscles. Half-growling in response, he pulled her onto his lap, and she felt the sweet pressure of his erection against the seat of her capris.

The heat between them radioactive, his grip tightened, his hands immersed in her hair. Her pulse raced at the feel of his chest and arms enveloping her, consuming all her senses. She opened her lips, full of wanting, her mouth fierce upon his.

Tasting him, she was desperate now, silently requesting—no, demanding—that they take the next step. She needed to feel him on her, inside of her. She needed it more than any damn real estate listing.

Her mouth devoured him, sending every signal she knew to tell him: *Now. Take me now. Anywhere. Anyhow you please.*

His breathing ragged, he traced the line of tender skin at the base of her neck downward to her back, and then grasped her arms like he would never let go.

Their port coming into view, the water taxi's horn blew. Mick inhaled sharply at the intrusion and he drew back suddenly from Lacey.

"What?" Lacey asked in a frantic hush, shattering inside from the parting of their flesh.

"I'm sorry." He let out a muffled string of curses. "You laid out the rules, and I slipped. *Damn*, you just look so gorgeous tonight."

"But I—"

"No. I really am sorry." His voice adamant, he forced a laugh, glancing down at the strappy sandals that Maeve had traded with Lacey earlier that evening. "Happens every time you wear heels."

"Maybe I should wear heels more often, then."

Her comment made Mick gnash his teeth. "Great friend I am. Give a girl a couple glasses of wine, ask her if she wants to have kids, then move in for the kill. Talk about sending the wrong signals."

"That's not what happened, Mick."

"Look, Lacey, I am obviously attracted to you. But if you're going to break your rule about men right now, you should probably do it with someone who can offer you some kind of a future."

"What do you mean?"

"I won't be staying here. I fully intend to go back to the SEALs when I'm done with this tour. That means I'll be headed to San Diego and then overseas. Correct me if I'm wrong, but I don't think you're looking for a relationship that has an expire date."

Lacey bit her lip uneasily, desperately wanting to lie. If she could just enjoy the passion, with no thoughts of tomorrow. But she could lose her heart to a man like Mick. And then she'd lose him, too.

The silence between them was almost painful. "You're right," she finally admitted.

They stared out at the water blankly as the boat approached the dock.

Lacey let out a slow breath. "So you'll never settle down? You know, down the road?"

Mick shook his head. "Not while the SEALs are still a part of my plans, anyway. Some guys do fine in the field, in combat, knowing they have a wife and child waiting for them at home. But I'm not one of them. As a single man, I can focus on the mission. I can put myself in harm's way without thinking twice. I don't know if I could do that if I was remembering the family I left behind."

Lacey saw the irony. "Distractions. Yeah, that's just what I was talking about avoiding in my career right now, too. We're in the same boat." She raised her eyebrows at their surroundings. "No pun intended."

Mick nodded in accord as they arrived with a gentle thud against the dock. He sent her a feisty smile as he offered her his hand to disembark. "If you are ever looking for just mindless sex with no strings attached, you'll call me first, though, right?"

She laughed. "You'll be the first call I make."

CHAPTER 8

Since becoming a real estate agent, Lacey could not help feeling as though some houses had souls. Not all, of course. The houses she and her sister shared as they grew up each held good memories, but had an emptiness, as though they were still shells waiting for the right owner to fill them with warmth.

But there was a different quality about some—like the simple waterfront Cape Cod once owned by Maeve's grandparents. The house seemed to glow when it was filled with laughter.

Sitting on the back porch with her housemates, along with Mick and Jack adding to the atmosphere, Lacey felt as though the little house was sighing with contentment down to its very foundation.

The sun had long set beneath the blue horizon and its warm rays were replaced the by hypnotic chirping of crickets. Maeve's little piece of waterfront was heaven on fall nights like this, and Lacey felt remarkably lucky to call this place home, even for a short while in her life.

Lucky, despite the pathetic assortment of letters that were staring at her, which included one sorry Q with a U nowhere to be found. Why had she voted for Scrabble tonight rather than Monopoly?

Mick was looking intense as he eyed the game board. Apparently, he approached board games with the ferocity of going to battle. There was no such thing as friendly competition for a hardened SEAL.

Sometimes when their eyes met, Lacey could still feel the warmth of his lips on hers when the memory of their kiss on the water taxi came washing over her like a gentle fall breeze. Each of them had accepted the boundaries of their friendship, but flirtation was unavoidable and sometimes unbearable. An electric current sparked between them every time they touched, even in the most casual way.

Lacey glowered as Mick placed an S at the end of Maeve's last word. "'Unsafes' is not a word."

Mick and Jack looked at each other and said in unison, "Yes, it is."

Bess raised her eyebrows. "Use it in a sentence," she dared.

Mick looked nonplussed. "The officer safes his weapon. He then unsafes his weapon, preparing to fire." The two men exchanged mutual nods, satisfied.

"What?"

"He unsafes his weapon," Mick repeated condescendingly, as though he were using a word they had all learned in the first grade. "Unsafes—as in make not safe. Makes it easy to fire."

"I repeat, *what?*"

"It is a word." Mick glanced over at Jack.

"It's a word," Jack agreed.

Maeve's eyes narrowed. "I challenge your word."

Bess, the keeper of the dictionary, searched its pages. "Maeve wins the challenge. It's not in the dictionary."

"But it *is* a word."

"Well, we agreed upon this dictionary," she said, waggling the pocket dictionary from her college days in Mick's face. "Not some Dictionary of Weird Military Terms. Here's your S," Bess said with authority pulling his tile off the board. "You lose your turn."

Mick stood. "This is so unfair, you're driving me to drink. Can I get you anything, Jack? Beer? More chips?" he asked, pointedly ignoring Bess's empty soda can and Lacey's depleted wine glass.

"Fine. I'll get ours," Lacey muttered. "Another ginger ale, Bess?"

Bess nodded her thanks.

Lacey let the screen door slam behind her as she entered the kitchen. "You are a poor loser, Mick."

"Military guys don't like it when we're not winning. Works to our advantage in war. Besides, I haven't lost yet."

"Yeah, but to resort to making up words."

"Unsafes *is* a word." Mick moved quickly to corner her in front of the open refrigerator. He gazed down at her, his lips not more than an inch from hers. "'The lady suddenly felt unsafes in the aroused officer's presence.' Unsafes: the plural of unsafe when you feel very, very unsafe." There was a playful, daring flash in his eyes. For exactly ten seconds, they both said nothing, knowing exactly what should happen next, and knowing it wouldn't.

Jack called in from the back porch. "Hey, Maeve is claiming a zovare is a kind of window treatment. Z-O-V-A-R-E. Do I challenge her?"

Lacey's eyes never wavered from Mick's. "It's a word. Zovare. My mom used to have those in our family room," she called into Jack.

"Do I trust her, Mick?"

His eyes still locked on Lacey's, Mick studied her. "Trust her. She's beyond reproach."

Sucker, Lacey thought. Zovare? That made-up word probably pushed Maeve well into the lead with that Z and V. Stepping back onto the porch, she shared a conspiratorial look with Maeve and glanced down at the score sheet. 54-point word with the triple word score space falling behind Maeve's A tile. Not bad for a bluff.

"Girls are in the lead," Maeve gloated.

Mick grunted, and seemed resigned to change the subject. "So what's the next step on the house renovation, Maeve?"

"Solarium. The guys are coming to blast a hole in my family room wall soon. There was a bit of a delay because of the permits. Damn bureaucracy."

"What the hell is a solarium?"

"A room with lots of glass—you know—like a sunroom. For plants."

"I didn't know you had a green thumb," Jack said, placing three letter tiles on the game board.

"I don't. But I had a client in DC who has a solarium. It was gorgeous, all sunny and bright and filled with orchids and exotic plants. I just knew I had to have one."

Jack cocked his head. "So you know nothing about plants, but you're building an entire addition for them?"

"I'll learn." Maeve cast Jack a sharp look. "And it's a small addition. They'll be breaking ground on it later this month."

"Handpicked the crew yourself, right, Maeve?" Lacey smiled.

Maeve batted her eyes innocently. "Now what on earth are you insinuating?"

"Oh, I don't know. It's just that any time you hire anyone, they're very, well—"

"Built," Bess offered. "I don't think I've ever seen so many hot men before in my life. And that lawnmower guy?"

All three women let out discerning sighs.

"Did you ever catch a look at him when he first revs up the motor? The way his muscles all bunch up? Oh, God." Lacey fanned herself.

Looking annoyed and more than a little jealous, Jack and Mick slouched in their chairs.

"Don't remind me," Maeve said sadly. "He told me last week that he's leaving Annapolis. I don't know who I'll get to mow the lawn."

"Is that the guy I saw over here on Thursday evening?" Mick asked.

"Mmhm."

"Well, that explains it."

"Explains what?" Jack asked with sudden interest.

Mick let out a low laugh. "I pulled up to the house, and I see Maeve handing some sweaty guy with no shirt a stack of bills."

Lacey laughed. "Why didn't you just ask who he was?"

Mick threw his hands up. "Hey, if Maeve is paying cash to some guy who looks like an underwear model, I'm not asking questions. Not my business."

Jack shifted uncomfortably. "So he's not coming back?"

"Nope. I'll just have to rely on the kindness of strangers." Maeve pulled out a little of the Southern drawl from her youth.

"Don't look at me," Jack said. "I'm not mowing your lawn without some sort of payment in return."

Maeve rolled her eyes, and then set her sights on Mick.

"Look elsewhere. Between my family's house growing up, and four years of mowing Doc and Mrs. B's lawn, I'm done with landscaping till I get a house of my own."

"You mowed Mrs. B's lawn?"

"Sure. All of us did things like that for them. We hung out at their house enough that we were glad to do it."

Maeve pulled her attention fully away from the letters in front of her for the first time all night. "You're saying that plebes will sometimes mow the lawns of their sponsors?"

Lacey groaned, realizing where this was headed.

Maeve slapped her hand on the table. "I want one," she said decisively.

"Maeve, you don't sponsor a plebe to get your lawn mowed. You sponsor someone because you want to give them a home away from home."

"That's fine with me. I can provide a home away from home. I do it for you all, don't I? My God, maybe we could find one who could babysit," she concluded triumphantly, raising her eyebrows and giving a slight nod to Bess's belly. "Do I get to pick one out? I'd want to make sure he could handle a bit of hard labor."

"No, Maeve. It's not like picking out a puppy at the pound," Jack commented.

After a brief silence, Maeve scowled at the looks of reproach from her friends. "Why are you all looking at me like that? I was just kidding."

The others narrowed their eyes on her.

Maeve relented. "Okay. I was half kidding. Give me some credit, will you?"

It really had been a grand idea. Maeve laughed to herself, picking up two empty soda cans from the table on the back porch, and envisioning a young, virile midshipman mowing her lawn for free. If only she didn't have that troublesome streak of decency. She must have inherited that from Gram.

The smell of onions and mushrooms wafted out the

kitchen window and onto the porch. Maeve usually enjoyed spending mornings on her back deck sipping her coffee. But the smell of an omelet—a real omelet, not the kind you pour from a carton—cooking up in her kitchen was something of a rarity. She headed back inside.

Lacey sat at the kitchen table watching Bess efficiently chop vegetables with the precision of a master chef. "I had no idea you could cook like this."

Bess tossed a smile over her shoulder. "It's easy, really. You just follow the directions."

Maeve chimed in. "No. Heating up a can of spaghetti is following directions. What you're doing is an art form."

"I used to love making brunch for Dan on Sunday mornings," she began, and then immediately clammed up.

Maeve shot her a questioning look. "Dan?"

Bess quickly busied herself looking for the cheddar in the fridge. "Yeah. Umm. He's my ex-boyfriend. You know, the dad."

"You mean, sperm donor. It takes a lot more than a night in the sack to make a dad," Lacey corrected, earning a nod of approval from Maeve.

"He's… umm…" Bess struggled, and the expression on her face wasn't that of frustration or resentment as Maeve would have expected. It was fear.

"He's not here," Maeve finished for her. "So that pretty much says enough to me. Is that mine?" she asked, quickly changing the subject.

"Mmhm." Bess handed her a steaming plate.

"Glad you didn't offer up these cooking skills last night or those guys would be on our doorstep every day." Maeve smacked her lips enthusiastically as she took her first bite.

Bess grinned. "Oh, I don't think it takes good food to keep them coming back. Just takes you two."

"I've made it pretty clear to Jack that I'm not interested. I don't backtrack."

"Try convincing him that."

"He'll get frustrated and move on." She went to the fridge. "Now Mick is another story. I don't know why you aren't doing a little horizontal tango with that man, Lacey. Orange juice, anyone?"

Lacey and Bess shook their heads.

"He's not interested in me." Lacey received two sets of rolling eyes in response. "Seriously. He even told me that. He's just not looking for someone to settle down with right now."

"Who said anything about settling down? You just need a regular aerobic workout. It's cheaper than joining a gym," Maeve teased as the phone rang. She picked it up. "Hello?" she snapped with her mouth half stuffed with food. "Hello-oo?" She shook her head at the silence and hung up, glancing at the caller ID display. "No one. That's the third unknown name-unknown number that's hung up on me recently."

Bess's ears perked up. "Really?"

"It's starting to piss me off." Maeve shrugged carelessly. "Anyway, I know you want to focus on career now, but you can't avoid distractions forever. And men are such lovely distractions."

"It's not just that. It's the way we met—at a funeral where I was trying to get real estate business. Some people might find that… distasteful."

Maeve snorted. "That's one word for it." Noticing Lacey's wounded expression, she followed up, "Creative is another word. Or savvy. That's what your sister would say, right?"

"Well, I'm not my sister, as I prove time and again. Besides, that house means so much to him. He'd hate thinking that I was trying to sell it behind his back."

Maeve batted a hand hastily through the air. "But you

aren't. She hasn't shown any interest in selling it, right? So, just come clean and tell him."

"Yeah, but then he might let it slip to Edith that I crashed her husband's funeral. She'd never list her house with me if she ever did decide to sell. She might even call the funeral home and complain. Or complain to my broker at the office."

"That's a lot of what-ifs, Lacey."

Lacey sighed. "You're probably right. Maybe I will fess up."

Maeve took the last bite of her omelet and fought the urge to ask Bess for another. "Speaking of funerals, are you going to that one I found for you in last Sunday's obits? It is today, right?"

"Yeah. It's got some promise, actually. I'm covering phones in the office this morning and then I'm taking a newlywed couple around town to see some homes at noon. Then I'll drive straight there. It starts at two. I think I'll make it in time."

Maeve raised her eyebrows to Bess. "She works hard for the money."

"Except that the money's not coming in yet," Lacey grumbled. "I better go get ready. There's a black suit upstairs with my name on it." She loaded her plate into the dishwasher. "Thanks for breakfast, Bess. It was incredible. For every omelet you make, I promise to change one diaper."

"Then I better see you for breakfast every morning."

At the ring of her cell, Lacey snapped her phone open. "Hello? Oh, hello Edith. How are you? ... Yes, I did make those calls about auction donations and got lucky with four of them. ... What? ... No, I wouldn't mind at all, though I really think you might want to wait before you make any decisions like that. ... Well, okay. I can draw up some comps and stop by. ... Thursday's fine. ... No, don't you dare feed me brunch. … All right then. Thanks, Edith. See you then." She slid her phone into her purse.

The silence in the kitchen was deafening.

Visibly flustered, Lacey let out a slow breath. "That was Edith—you know, Mick's old sponsor. She wants to talk to me about listing her property."

Maeve glanced over at Bess. "The plot thickens…"

CHAPTER 9

When Lacey walked up to Edith Baker's house this time, she could no longer envision the "For Sale" sign in front of it. Even carrying a heavy folder filled with marketing information and comparable real estate listings under her arm, she knew that this house was simply not meant to be sold.

But she was not a mind reader. She didn't know what might be driving Edith to consider selling the sweeping lot crowned with a too-perfect-to-be-true home. So she squared her shoulders and knocked on the door.

Edith greeted her with a gentle hug that made Lacey feel like part of the family. "Lacey, it's so good of you to come."

"Thanks for having me, Edith. I brought those papers you were interested in seeing."

"Wonderful. Come in and have some breakfast, dear."

The scent of frying bacon consumed Lacey's senses the moment she stepped in the door. She nearly visibly salivated. "That smells delicious. I didn't get a chance to eat anything because the workmen arrived so early this morning. I wanted to get out before the noise started."

"Maeve's solarium, right? What a lovely idea. I've always

wanted a place to grow more plants indoors. At my age, it's not as easy to get outside to do the weeding."

"You know, I know some great landscaping companies who might be able to help. I could get their information for you." Lacey sat on a kitchen stool, and could picture a younger version of Mick sitting on the very same stool catching up on his studies or talking with the Bakers, with the scents of home-cooked meals wafting through the air. No wonder he didn't want to see this place sell.

"That's a wonderful idea, Lacey. Thank you."

Their conversation weaved around light topics as they ate, until Edith set her eyes on the packet of information brought by Lacey. "Ahh, so this is what I'm interested in," she said, giving it a light tap with her finger.

"Yes, these are the comps. Let me walk you through the package." Lacey opened the folder.

Edith nodded at the estimated value of the property, a figure so enormous Lacey had grown lightheaded just typing it in.

Lacey sailed through her usual sales pitch, outlining her marketing plan, and doing her best to keep smears of syrup off the packet. As she shut the folder upon completion, she couldn't help shaking her head. "So professionally, that's what I'll tell you, Edith. But personally, I would hate to see you let go of this home so soon after your husband's death. I know it's not my business, but—"

Edith interrupted. "Of course it's your business. I think of you as a friend. I would appreciate your input as a friend, most of all."

"Then I'll say that unless there are financial reasons why you'd need to sell this house, I'd wait and see how you felt in a year." Lacey began taking the dishes to the sink.

"Why do you say that?"

Lacey, her hands still full, gave a slight nod to the wall

behind her. "It's all these pictures, Edith. All the photos you have on your walls. You have such a history here. Such memories. You can't put a price on that. Unless you have to, that is." She smiled, remembering. "It was the same way with Maeve's house. She wanted me to list it after her grandmother died. But one walk-through and I could tell memories were still so alive there. Even now, there are certain photos in the house that she refuses to move, let alone take down. The ones that are really special to her." Lacey sighed.

"From that sigh, I'm guessing that's what you'd like one day."

"A home like that? With those kinds of memories? Yes, I really do. One day." She caught herself gazing longingly out the kitchen window and gave herself a shake. "I'd hate to see you rush into a decision like this."

"I appreciate your honesty. Those are qualities that make you an excellent real estate agent."

Lacey couldn't resist a laugh. "Not the most prosperous one, though."

"Success is not always measured in dollar signs." She gave the packet of information a little pat as she sat back down. "If I ever do sell, you can be sure I will only go to you, Lacey. In the meantime, if you'd be good enough to give me a healthy stack of your business cards, I have a feeling I can get your information out to some possible clients in the future."

Lacey beamed. "I'll give you as many as you can handle. Thank you, Edith."

Ordinarily, the sound of a power saw slicing a hole in her family room wall would have been unnerving in the morning. But today, Maeve sat serenely sipping her morning latte, content to ignore the noise as she paged through several books she had purchased on exotic flowers and plants. No boring geraniums for her, she thought happily as she dog-eared pages showcasing the most extraordinary blooms.

Now that construction had begun on her solarium, she could throw herself head-first into her new hobby. One book was already covered in highlighter and yellow sticky notes. A second was filled with scribbles in the margins. This, of course, was why Maeve preferred to buy books rather than check them out at the library.

About halfway through her second cup, a word jumped out from the text.

Toxic.

Toxic? She hadn't really considered the threat of little fingers reaching up to grab a blossom before. It was definitely something to think about with Bess's baby on the way. She un-dog-eared the page, and flipped backwards to check the toxicity of her prior selections.

Toxic. Toxic. Toxic. Who knew there were so many toxic plants? Her heart sank. Life was going to be different sharing a house with a child.

Her gaze wandered across the room noting things like exposed outlets and unsecured garbage pails. Cup still in hand, she stood to take a look at the family room and winced at the sight of several pieces of breakable art.

Her entire life was about to change, and it wasn't even her child. Taking another sip, she made a slight grumbling noise. She had always wanted a child. It took years for her to deal with the reality that that would not happen.

With no family on her horizon, she had been free to invest in frivolous things like hand-blown glass, and imported textiles. Cringing, she remembered the new sofa she had on back-order. It would be a criminal offense to stain it with baby formula—or worse. She bit her lip, wondering if it was too late to cancel the order.

And what about her solarium? She raced back to the kitchen table and thumbed quickly through her book. My God, even geraniums were toxic!

"Glad it's not raining while they're doing that," Bess said as she walked into the kitchen, glancing at the hole which gave a clear view of the side yard.

Maeve turned. "Tell me about it. They are noisy, though. Lacey was smart to get out of here early today. Are you feeling okay? You're normally working by now."

"I have an OB/GYN appointment."

"The usual check up?"

"Actually I'm getting an ultrasound. Hopefully, I'll find out whether I'm having a girl or a boy. I've been in for one before, but the baby was turned the wrong way."

"So you don't want it to be a surprise?"

"No." Bess barely suppressed a grin. "Enough about this baby is a surprise already."

Maeve laughed. "Do you want a boy or a girl?"

"I know I'm supposed to say I just want the baby to be healthy, and that's true. But I have to admit, I'm hoping for a girl. I figure if the baby is going to grow up without a father, maybe it would be easier for a girl." There was a hint of sadness in her eyes. "I don't know. It's my theory."

"Well, then I won't mind telling you I'm praying for a girl. If we're going to turn the design scheme of this house upside down, then by God, I hope it's done with a feminine flair." She then added kindly, "But don't worry, I can make blue work, too."

"Maeve, you really don't have to do anything special. I've been saving up for a security deposit and Lacey has been letting me look online for apartments on her laptop."

"You're not going anywhere unless it's a smart move for the both of you," she said giving a nod to Bess's belly. "Juice?"

"Yes, please. And thanks, Maeve."

Maeve poured a large glass of orange juice and gave Bess a plate of scones without even asking.

Some days, like today, Maeve could swear she felt her grandmother's presence in this house. Even over the roar of a power saw in her living room, she could almost hear Gram shuffling into the kitchen in her slippers and morning robe. "In for a penny, in for a pound," Gram's voice seemed to whisper in her ear. Maeve nodded to herself. "So, you want company?"

"Company for what?" Bess asked cautiously.

"For the ultrasound."

"Really? You'd really go?"

"If my life is going to be infiltrated by the male sex, then I want to be the first to know." Maeve forced a laugh. "I'm kidding, you know. Of course, I'd like to go. I'm not expected in the office till noon today, anyway."

"I'd really love the company. I get so scared about these things. I'm always terrified they're going to find something wrong."

"All the more reason for me to come. Nothing goes wrong around me."

"I'd love that then. Thanks."

With that, Maeve felt the warm presence of her grandmother disappear, content with her granddaughter. Content and proud.

Several hundred calories later, Lacey stepped out of Edith's house, stuffed with French toast and brimming with pleasure at the thought of her business cards being passed around among Edith's decidedly wealthy friends. She had stayed longer than she had planned, but there was something so comforting in sharing that extra cup of coffee with Edith and talking about nothing in particular.

Her cell phone rang and she glanced at the number. "Hey, Maeve."

"It's a girl!"

"What?"

"It's a girl! Bess's baby is a girl!"

"That's fabulous! Did she call you from the doctor's?"

"No, I *went* to the doctor's. Honest to God, Lacey, it was the coolest thing I've ever seen in my life. I've seen the pictures from sonograms, but this was different. They had this 3-D imaging thing and I could actually see her move. I swear I think she smiled at me. And her feet. Oh, Lacey they are so tiny and precious. I can hardly wait to take her shoe shopping."

Lacey laughed. "Is Bess there?"

"Well, of course she's here. I wasn't going to leave her there, was I?"

"Put her on."

"Hey, Lacey." Bess sounded exhausted.

"I bet you're happy."

"Happy, but even more relieved. I get so stressed out over these things. But she's developing right on target. And a girl, too. I'm feeling pretty lucky. I think Maeve is even more excited than I am, though."

"Of course she is. She gets to experience all this without the vomiting and aching knees and labor pain."

"Of course. I hadn't thought of that."

"I wish I had been there."

"It's okay. We have pictures. They even gave us a DVD of it, would you believe?"

"Oh, that's great. I've got an appointment at one and then I'll be home to see them. I'm so happy for you."

"Thanks, Lacey," Bess said and handed the phone back to Maeve.

"How did the appointment go, anyway?" Maeve asked.

"Fantastic."

"You sealed the deal? She's listing it with you?"

"Well, no. But she is handing out my info to a bunch of her friends."

"That's a step in the right direction," Maeve offered optimistically.

"I know. Fingers crossed. I'll see you this afternoon."

Maeve hung up her cell as she and Bess walked up the path to her house. Opening the door, she glanced at Bess. "Do you think you can put your feet up for a bit before you go to work?"

"Yeah, I think I'll take about fifteen minutes."

Maeve's concerned gaze followed Bess up the staircase. She really did work too hard, Maeve thought, wishing she could think of a way to help that wouldn't damage Bess's pride.

Letting out a sigh, Maeve turned to look at the hole in the wall and the men working just outside of it. Her expression warmed, envisioning it. Her solarium. The bright sunlight would glimmer in through skylights, with upturned blooms soaking in the rays.

She imagined herself, feet up on the sofa in the living room, sipping a glass of Chianti in the afternoon and reading a bestseller as the exotic scents of rare flowers wafted through the French doors.

Her solarium.

Her solarium filled with toxic plants.

The timing couldn't be worse.

Feeling deflated, she walked over to the ominous hole in the wall and leaned against the side of it, ignored by the workmen as they hauled away pieces of drywall and old insulation.

What if? A little voice prodded in her brain, sounding scarily like her grandmother. What if she were to put up solid walls around her solarium? Solid walls instead of glass. And maybe skip the skylights—the darn things just leaked all the time, anyway. Perhaps a set of paned windows across the far wall.

It wouldn't be a solarium, that's for certain. But a nice extra room. Small, but large enough for a crib, a changing table, and a dresser. She could install one of those cute chandeliers with tiny crystals and porcelain butterflies that she saw in that exclusive store in upper Northwest DC.

She'd paint the room pink, of course. Perhaps put a chair molding along the walls and do the lower side in a brighter hue.

Later, she could convert it into an office. It would be nice to have a separate home office one day rather than always using the kitchen table. She'd bet that would add more resale value to her house than a solarium, and made a mental note to confirm that with Lacey.

A baby's room. Could she make room for that in her house? In her life? For a child who wasn't even her own?

She eyed the foreman as he passed the gaping hole. "Hey, Rob? Can I talk to you a minute?"

CHAPTER 10

Mick had slept on piles of rubble. He had marched across deserts in scorching heat carrying an eighty-pound rucksack on his back, not knowing if the day might be his last. He had felt the burn of shrapnel ripping into his flesh, and carried a near-dead body three miles over his shoulder, even while his fatigues were drenched in blood.

But at this moment, wedged underneath a bathroom sink with the base of the cabinet ramming mercilessly into his back and a drip soaking his head, Mick couldn't imagine anything less comfortable.

The plumber's wrench slipped again against the slick wet pipe, jamming his finger. He let out a salty curse more appropriate on a ship, then remembered his manners. "Sorry, Mrs. B."

"That's quite all right, dear. But do please give it up. I told you I was going to call a plumber."

"No," Mick said sharply. He had taken on this task—this battle—and he was not about to let the leaky pipe win.

"If you insist," she sighed, sitting alongside him on the

toilet, top-down. "I certainly didn't intend for you to fix my leaky faucet when I invited you over for lunch."

"I know," he said through his clenched teeth. "It should be a simple fix, though. Besides, that turkey club was worth it."

"I worry about you not eating well, Mick. You, by yourself all the time. You should be settled down by now, eating a nice meal with a family."

The wrench slipped again, followed by the necessary curses. This time, he felt less apologetic. "Sure, and probably deciding how to drop the news that I'll be gone to sea another six months, or how to tell my wife that we have to pull the kids out of school and move to the other side of the country. Yeah, not for me."

"Other people do it."

"Not me."

"I see that," Edith agreed, dropping the subtlety. "And what about Lacey?"

"What about her?"

"You've been spending a lot of time with her."

"We're just friends, Mrs. B. Neither of us has interest in anything else. Well, not really, anyway."

Edith lifted her eyebrows. "Not really?"

Mick remained silent, knowing it would be in poor taste to tell a woman who was old enough to be his grandmother that he was just looking for meaningless sex. Well, maybe not meaningless, but certainly sex without complications. His friendship with Lacey had come to mean too much to sacrifice it for a roll in the sack.

"Friends is fine, too, I suppose," Edith conceded. "Lacey's such a dear. She's been so helpful putting this fundraiser together. I don't know how I got along last year without her. I couldn't help hoping that there might have been a spark between you two."

A spark? Mick thought, frustrated. It was a lot more than a spark. More like the Fourth of July fireworks display on the Mall in DC. But with the wrong person at the wrong time for both of them.

"She's the helpful sort," he said with a grunt, thinking how helpful it would be to have Lacey's long legs wrapped around him on a regular basis. Yep, he could use that kind of help. "Can you hand me the towel there?"

"So long as you get along, Mick, because I've come to treasure her friendship. In fact, since you do, would you mind going to a tasting I set up for her?"

"A tasting?"

"At Eagle's Point on the Bay where the fundraiser will be. I have to decide which entrées I want served and the chef agreed to fix up some samples for Lacey and me. But I'd much rather you went with Lacey so that I could get a man's perspective on the meal."

"A man's perspective on the meal?" he repeated back to her, skeptical.

"Well, yes. I'd like the men attending to enjoy what they are eating. And if it was just Lacey and me selecting, then it would probably end up being far too... feminine. Little quiches and finger sandwiches. That sort of thing."

"Then just serve up steak and potatoes. That's what the guys want."

"Oh, Mick, don't be so difficult. They don't serve simple steak and potatoes at a place like Eagle's Point. If you saw all the options that the chef is having us sample, you'd see why I need your input. I haven't asked you to do anything at all for me."

"No, I'm just fixing your leaky sink," Mick grumbled, glaring at the old woman through the maze of pipes.

"I meant for the fundraiser. And I'll remind you I never asked you to do this," she finished, gently waving her hand at the sink.

"Sounds like a set-up to me." Mick enjoyed Lacey's company, but was happier in a group. The idea of sitting at a candlelit table with her for an entire evening without Jack, Maeve, and Bess there to play chaperone sounded like torture.

"Everything sounds like a set-up to you, young man." She slapped her hands down on her thighs. "Fine. I'll ask some other man to go with her."

Mick relaxed, picturing some ancient, harmless hospital benefactor eating dinner with Lacey. That worked fine for him.

Edith continued, "Come to think of it, there's a handsome young doctor who specifically mentioned how Lacey caught his eye when she visited the hospital with me last week. Of course! I'm sure he'd love the opportunity to go with Lacey."

Mick's blood simmered at the thought of some slick doctor moving in on Lacey. He peered out from under the sink to see if she was bluffing.

Edith wore the perfect poker face. "Or you could indulge an old woman who simply wants to see you eat a nice meal in exchange for your less-than-expert epicurean advice."

Drying the pipe, Mick let out a slow breath. "Can you turn the water on, please?"

"Of course."

He held his breath as he waited to see if the drip returned. It was uncomfortable enough laying beneath a leaky sink, but being a captive audience for this conversation made it even worse.

After a minute, he breathed a sigh of relief. "I think it's fixed." Just then, a drip landed in his eye. "Damn it!"

"Not fixed?"

"No."

"Mick, please stop and let me call a plumber. I have to run some errands now, anyway."

"No," Mick barked. "Not. Giving. Up. On. This." Each word was punctuated with a grunt as he tugged on the wrench.

"All right. But lock up behind you, dear."

Mick grumbled again.

"And can I count on you for the tasting? Or shall I call Richard?"

"Who's Richard?"

"Dr. Richard Hunt. That doctor I was telling you about. Heart surgeon at the hospital. Such a remarkable young man," she said, gently stressing the word "young."

Richard Hunt, Mick thought, noting the name and fully intending to do an internet search tonight to see if this was a bluff. "Okay. I'll go with Lacey. But I'm not eating anything that isn't cooked or has a name I don't recognize."

It was at least another hour before the drain was fixed. But he won the battle. His back was sore and he had lost feeling in one finger, but he won.

He mopped up the water under the sink for the last time and headed into the garage to return the wrench to Doc's old toolbox.

Glancing at the clock, he opted to give himself some recovery time and helped himself to one of the Sam Adams that Mrs. B always had on hand for him. Throwing back a few refreshing gulps, he sat appeased at the kitchen table, glad it was Saturday.

He had to admit, he was beginning to enjoy the concept of weekends. Who would have thought? When he was deployed, there was no time off. War doesn't take a two-day break after five days. One day just runs into another.

He had never minded because he loved his work. But

after being stationed here for a few months, he was starting to look forward to time when he wasn't accountable to anyone. He could sip a beer in the middle of the afternoon and not worry about letting his guard down. He could look forward to seeing Lacey tonight for pizza and Scrabble.

Whoever thought a guy like him would be excited about playing board games?

If he had any sense, he'd be at O'Toole's looking for any halfway-hot single woman who was content in a short-term-leading-nowhere relationship with an officer like himself. God knew this was the longest he had ever gone without sex. Well, except when he was living in a war zone.

Besides, it was just a matter of time before she sold that waterfront house she listed. And if she intended to celebrate her success in a carnal way, Mick was going to make sure he was the one she celebrated with.

Certainly not some damn doctor, he thought. Lacey was too trusting to be in the company of someone like that. He envisioned a perfectly preened guy in his Armani suit spewing smooth lines that he had perfected from years of picking up women. The guy probably waxed his eyebrows.

Mick felt his grip on the bottle tighten. He suddenly wanted to strangle the man for even looking at Lacey.

She was so unsuspecting. So honest, he thought as he took another sip. Nothing hidden. With her straightforward clothes and her light coat of makeup, Mick already could guess exactly what she looked like in the morning.

Oh, how he wanted to be there in the morning one day to see for himself.

His eyes wandered to the wedding photo across the room. Doc and Mrs. B looked so content, so complete in each other's company. That had always been the way they seemed, complete. Mick had to admit, it was a little like how he felt when Lacy walked into a room. It wasn't just a surge of testosterone that urged him to take her on any nearby solid surface. There was a feeling of satisfaction, of wholeness, just knowing she was there.

Mick let out a groan, painfully aware of where his mind was wandering…not too far from picket fences and babies and establishing roots.

Feeling oddly unsettled, he tossed back the last of his beer and put it in the recycling bin. A folder with a real estate agency's logo caught his eye. It was the same agency where Lacey worked, Mick was pretty sure. Too comfortable in his surroundings to even consider it wasn't his business, he opened the folder.

He scanned it carelessly at first. Then, his blood pressure rising with each page, he went over the contents with greater care.

It was a proposal to sell Mrs. B's house. Prepared by Lacey.

He stared at it in utter disbelief.

Lacey knew what this house meant to him. She knew how vulnerable Mrs. B was right now. Yet apparently she had no problem moving in for the kill, probably eyeing the huge commission that Mick noticed listed on page six.

His eyes darted around the room, slightly panicked, imagining potential buyers marching through this house—a house he cherished.

The heat of betrayal burned a hole in his stomach. What a fool he was, thinking Lacy was such a straight-shooter while meanwhile, she's plotting to take advantage of a vulnerable old woman and sell the only place Mick had ever thought of as "home."

He stormed out the door, nearly forgetting to lock it behind him.

Lacey sat at the front desk of the downtown real estate office and willed the phone to ring. She shouldn't mind the responsibility of covering phones. As the newest agent, she was the low man on the totem pole. But no one would call today. People were too busy picking out pumpkins with their children or taking long drives in the nearby countryside to witness the changing of the leaves.

Outside, a spectrum of fiery fall colors danced across her window as a breeze scattered leaves from the nearby maple and oak. A postcard-perfect autumn day, the kind that made Lacey long to sip hot apple cider from a mug and linger on a park bench. To complete the picture, she imagined herself nestled into the crook of the shoulder of an adorable man.

The image of Mick came to mind. She couldn't help it, even though she knew she was better off keeping him just as a friend.

Mick was already enough of a distraction in his current capacity.

So here she was. No cider. No park bench. No Mick.

Hearing her phone vibrate, she reached for her purse. "Hi, Vi," she answered, recognizing her sister's number.

"Hi, Lacey. How are you?"

"Oh, fine. What's up?"

"Not much. I just thought I'd see how you were doing."

Something must be wrong. Vi was not the type of person to call to just shoot the breeze. "I'm fine, I guess."

"How's that waterfront listing? Any nibbles?"

"A few nibbles, but no offer. They priced it too high. I keep hoping she'll let me reduce the asking price."

"Any more listings?"

"I actually just did a presentation for one woman who was recently widowed. But it's too soon for her to sell. I couldn't even recommend it."

Lacey swore she could hear Vi swallowing her disapproval. To her relief, Vi simply said, "Well, keep trying. It's a great idea you had—that funeral crashing thing. It's bound to pay off. So, are you still going to Mom and Dad's for Thanksgiving?"

"Of course. You're coming, too, right?"

"Of course."

"I'm always there, Vi. Every year. That can't be why you called. Is everything really okay?"

Vi laughed. "There's nothing wrong. Do I need more of reason to call my sister?"

"Well, no."

"I just haven't seen you in a while and thought I'd make sure you'd be there."

There had to be something more, Lacey thought several minutes later as she clicked her phone shut.

She remembered Vi had been eyeing a regular position on CNN as a financial expert. That must be it, Lacey decided, picturing Vi revealing her news at the Thanksgiving dinner table.

Well, at least the Miron listing didn't sell. Even the sale of a waterfront property would pale in comparison to Vi's news, anyway.

Before the eerie silence of the office could envelop her again, Mick burst through the door.

"You're trying to get Mrs. B to sell her house," he accused, without even offering the customary hello.

Lacey's jaw dropped. "Excuse me?"

"You're trying to get Mrs. B to sell her house."

Lacey would have felt guilty if she weren't so annoyed. "Would you mind lowering your voice? This is my place of business," she said, hoping he wouldn't notice she was the only one there. It was the principle. "I don't burst into your classroom and make scenes, do I?"

"How could you do that to her?"

"I haven't done anything. Edith asked me to write up a proposal for her house. She was interested in finding out more about the possibility of selling it. She called me. That's what I do, Mick. I'm a real estate agent."

"She's not ready to sell her house. You know that."

"Yes, I agree. Which I mentioned to her, I might add. But it's not my decision to make, is it?"

"You know how I feel about that house. You should have told me."

Her temper flared. "Absolutely not. It's not your business. Real estate may not be the top secret SEALs, but there is some aspect of confidentiality. If Edith wants to tell you that she is thinking about selling her house, that is *her* news to share. Certainly not mine."

"She didn't tell me. I saw your proposal on her kitchen counter."

"Did you ask her about it?"

"No. She wasn't there."

"So you just helped yourself to it?"

Mick shifted his weight, obviously uncomfortable.

Lacey's eyes locked on his. "And rather than going to her and asking, you came charging into my workplace—and accusing me of—what? Forcing her to sell her house or something? Pressuring her somehow? Do you really think I'd do that?"

He stood there in defeated silence.

"Is that what you think of me, Mick? For all the time we've spent together, you think it's even possible for me to pressure anyone into selling their home? Damn, I wish I could. Then maybe I'd be at a closing right now rather than answering the phones. Maybe I'd be living in my own house rather than renting a room like I'm fresh out of college or something. And now, to top things off, I have to sit here and listen to you accuse me of being just what I really, really *should* be if I'm ever going to be able to survive in this business."

"I—"

"Just leave, Mick. If you want to talk to me about this, you can talk to me when I'm not at work." Lacey cursed the moisture building up in her eyes. "And you can sure as hell use a more pleasant tone," she added.

Looking baffled and more than a little guilty, Mick opened his mouth as if to say something, but then shook his head and stalked out.

Seeing the door shut quietly behind him, Lacey wiped a traitorous tear from her cheek, her blood boiling.

How dare he?

Is this what she gets for taking the high road? She had never pressured anyone to sell anything. If she had, she'd probably be writing up the listing for Edith's house right now, and flush with money from the commission she would have earned from Maeve's grandmother's home.

Burying her face in her hands, she was grateful for the silence of the deserted office.

Damn Mick.

Damn him for this useless excuse for a friendship. Damn him for his lack of trust. At least she showed some sense to not get romantically involved with him.

The phone rang and her heart raced, hoping it was Mick calling to apologize. Instead, Maeve's rattled voice greeted her. "Hey, Lacey. Are you headed home soon?"

"Not for a while yet. Are you okay?" Lacey couldn't remember a time when Maeve had sounded distressed.

"I'm fine. But the house is a different matter. Someone broke in. I wasn't here when it happened."

"Oh my God. Is Bess all right?"

"She was gone, too. She doesn't even know yet. She went

to look at baby furniture and I don't want to upset her on the phone, you know? Not when she's alone like that."

Lacey heard voices in the background, and the sound of police radios sent a chill down her spine. "I'll lock up and head right home. It's dead here, anyway. No one will care."

"Don't worry, and don't rush. The police are here now doing their thing—reports and fingerprints or whatever. I just knew you were going to be headed home in a bit and didn't want you driving into a hornet's nest of cop cars without warning."

Maeve gave Lacey a few more words of reassurance, as well as a muffled, yet heady description of one particularly attractive police officer who apparently was not wearing a wedding ring.

Lacey put her cell phone back in her purse and stared into the empty office, her mind still trying to filter through the last ten minutes.

This day just kept getting better.

Mick muttered various obscenities as he stormed down Maryland Avenue to his car, hoping the ground would open up and swallow him whole.

No such luck.

What the hell was wrong with him?

Damn if she didn't make sense. He hadn't expected that. Of course she had obliged Mrs. B with a proposal. That was what she did for a living.

Of course she couldn't come straight to him with the news. It wasn't his business.

What made him think that the whole world owed him an explanation for—well—everything? He wasn't in command here. There was no war going on here in Annapolis. No one was shooting at him.

That, of course, was the problem, he realized as he returned a salute from a Marine corporal stationed at the gate as he drove onto Academy grounds. His world was here, on this side of the Academy wall, in a world that was regimented, structured. He belonged in a military world where decisions truly were life and death, where there was a strict chain of command.

Mick glanced in his rear view mirror at the downtown scene he had just left as it faded into the distance. Out there, on the other side of the Academy gate, was a world for civilians.

He didn't know how to live with civilians.

He watched a group of tourists pouring out of the Chapel wearing their sensible walking shoes and cameras wrapped around their necks. Not one of those people would have barged into Lacey's office, demanding an explanation for something that wasn't even their business.

Lacey didn't deserve to be treated like that.

Pulling his car into his parking spot in front of his townhouse, his shoulders slumped. He wouldn't blame her if she never spoke to him again.

Panic gripped his chest at that prospect. Dropping his keys on the table inside his front door, they seemed to echo in his surroundings as if to remind him how empty his life was. Without her in it.

Suddenly, it didn't matter if he went back to the SEALs. It didn't matter if the Navy forced a desk job on him for the rest of his career.

A realization formed in his mind. If he lost her friendship, his life was incomplete.

He couldn't let it happen.

The scene was exactly as Maeve had described it—a swarm of police cars on an otherwise quiet street, some with lights still blazing. Through the doors was a bustle of activity, the tinny, abrasive sounds of police radios filling the air. Drawers were pulled out from cabinets. Chests were opened and tossed on their sides. An entire file cabinet was emptied with its contents scattered onto the floor.

"Are you sure you're not missing anything?" one of the police officers was asking Maeve as Lacey walked toward her.

"I'll have to have Lacey and Bess check their stuff, but it doesn't look it. My laptop, TV, even my jewelry is still here. I can't believe they wouldn't take any jewelry. They obviously have no sense of style."

It was clear from the officer's face that he wasn't certain whether Maeve was being serious.

Lacey interrupted, hugging her friend. "Thank God, you are all right."

"Oh, I'm fine. Just a little shook up and wondering how the hell I'm going to clean up this mess."

"Don't worry about that. We'll take care of it together. How did they get in?"

"They broke the window on the French door and turned the knob. God, I never really thought about how easy it is to break into this place." She shook her head. "You should go up to your room and make sure they didn't take anything. It didn't look like it, though."

Dazed, Lacey stepped into her room, feeling the horror of seeing everything she owned tossed onto the floor. She tried to keep herself from wondering what would have happened had she been home at the time.

"Lacey!" A panicked shout downstairs interrupted her thoughts. Was that Mick's voice?

"Lacey!"

She darted downstairs and saw a police officer standing at the door holding up his hand as if that would prevent Mick from entering the home. "Do you live here?" the officer was asking him.

"No. I'm a friend. What's going on here?" Mick's eyes frantically searched the room.

"He's okay, Officer." Lacey stood frozen in the middle of the stairs. "What are you doing here, Mick?"

Mick pushed forward at the sight of her, and wrapped her in his arms. "My God, when I saw all the police cars, I thought the worst." He took her face in his hands and pressed kisses to her cheeks and forehead, as if to assure himself that she was real. "Are you all right?"

"I'm fine." Flustered by the feel of his lips innocently touching her skin, she had to remind herself that she was still mad at him.

Maeve's voice came from the kitchen doorway. "Uh, I'm fine, too, Mick. Do I get a greeting like that?"

Mick laughed and greeted her with a firm kiss on the cheek. "How's that?"

"You could do better. It's been a rough day," Maeve answered with a smirk.

"Someone broke into the house," Lacey explained. "The place is a mess. But nothing's missing."

"Was anyone here?"

"No one. Bess is shopping. She doesn't even know. Maeve was getting her hair colored."

Maeve sent Lacey a glare.

Lacey corrected. "I mean, highlighted. Just some summer-like highlights. I was at the office," she finished, narrowing her gaze on him. "But I guess you know that, don't you?"

"About that." Mick took a deep breath. "Can we talk?" Mick shot a look over to Maeve and the nearby officer.

Maeve touched the ring-free officer lightly on the arm and guided him into the next room. "I can't tell you how much I appreciate your thoroughness, Officer…" she began in her slightly Southern drawl as she sent a wink to Lacey over her shoulder.

Lacey looked at Mick, the remnants of anger in her eyes. "So why did you come here? Or are you just early for Scrabble night?"

"I went to your office first. It was closed, so I took a chance and came here. I couldn't say this right over the phone." He took her hand. "I'm sorry, Lacey. You'd never take advantage of someone you care so much about. And I was completely disrespectful coming to your office and blowing up like that."

At Lacey's silence, Mick looked down at their clasped hands, visibly struggling for the right words. "Your friendship—it means more to me than I ever thought it would. Or could. I don't know how to explain it. I look forward to every moment I have with you."

Suddenly, the stress of the day was pouring down Lacey's cheeks unchecked.

Mick swallowed a curse. "Oh, God, Lacey, please don't cry. I feel bad enough," he said, putting his arm around her. "Look, I've got real issues. I'm an asshole, actually."

"We've all got issues."

"Yeah, but I don't have those great legs to even things out," he said, hoping to make her smile. "I think I've got—you know—trust issues. God, I sound like Dr. Phil or Oprah or something. But I've had a hard time trusting people lately. I'm always waiting for them to put a knife in my back."

"I don't get it. Why?"

Mick let out an audible breath. "This last mission I led

with the SEALs. I can't say much about it, but it was bloody. We were under fire, made it to the extract point, but our transport left prematurely because they were under fire. My CO was in the helo and ordered a shift to a secondary extraction point even though he knew my team was on the way."

Lacey listened, bewildered by this glimpse into his other life. Half of it she didn't even understand—a litany of acronyms and military jargon. But she felt the gravity of what he was describing.

"He just left us," he continued, "smack in a valley stuck between two mountains with fire coming from both sides. Put my guys in extreme danger. We had to fight our way to the other extraction point. We made it out alive, but four of us were wounded. I took shrapnel in my shoulder and one guy lost his leg to a mortar round. I had to carry him three miles under heavy fire before we made it out."

Stunned, Lacey sat in silence, imagining a Mick she never knew existed. It was a world apart from sitting on Maeve's back porch playing Scrabble and drinking beer.

"I was pissed as hell. There was no reason for him to have ordered the shift. When I demanded an explanation, he couldn't give me one. I told him what I thought of him to his face with the use of some rather questionable language. Before I knew what hit me, he made a phone call and my orders for San Diego were changed to the Naval Academy. Completely stabbed me in the back."

Cautiously, Lacey's eyes met his. "Is it really so bad to be sent here, Mick?"

"Career-wise, yeah, it's a huge setback. I am out of my community. It's a dead end if I can't work some miracle to turn it around. And he knew it when he made the call. Since then, I've had a hard time trusting anyone. Maybe I'm not such a great friend to have, Lacey. Guys like me are good in a firefight. I'd never let you down. But in this world, I'm still learning how to live with civilians."

Lacey sighed, exhaustion draining from her body. "Mick, about Edith's house. I want you to know I didn't recommend that she sell it. In fact, I said the exact opposite."

He held his hands up. "You don't have to tell me that. It's not my business. You were right."

"No, but there is something I need to tell you." The time to tell him the truth had come, and a knot formed in her stomach at the thought.

"If it's about your work, I don't want to hear it. You were right. You're a real estate agent. You do what you have to do to make a living. I have to trust your judgment. If Mrs. B decides to sell her house, I hope you're the person to list it, because I know that you'd make sure she was treated right."

"But there is something you should know. When I started out in this business, I really didn't know too many local people," she began uneasily.

"Lacey, stop. Really. I of all people should give you privacy where your business is concerned. Half of the things I did in the SEALs I'll never even be able to tell my children if I ever have any."

"But—"

"I have no right to expect that someone else's life is supposed to be an open book for me. Much less a friend. I hope that's what you still are, right? Friends?" He extended his hand.

Lacey smiled and shook it. "Friends."

Grinning, he pulled her toward him and lightly brushed a kiss to her cheek. He touched his forehead to hers. "Thank God, because I'm still fully intending to get you naked one of these days."

Lacey burst out laughing.

With the help of Mick and Jack, the three women managed to get the house straightened up. Mick secured a piece of plywood to the broken door and tried futilely to convince them to let him spend the night on the couch near the door.

Taking an elongated sip of Merlot as she stretched out on the couch, Lacey let the oakiness fill her senses. Now, with Mick and Jack gone, Lacey couldn't help the uneasiness welling up inside of her. She savored the wine's soothing effects, even if it only offered her a false sense of calm. "I just don't get it. Why would someone break into your house just to mess it up? Is there someone who is mad at you?"

Kicking off her shoes, Maeve rested her feet on the ottoman. A small fire in the fireplace crackled in front of her. "Phil and I had to fire the receptionist a few months ago. But I can't imagine it's her."

"What about your ex-husband?"

Maeve's eyes grew visibly cold. "Believe me, if there was any reason to send the cops after him, I'd grab it. But he's very happy with his new life."

Lacey regretted bringing it up. "Well, it could be someone from any of our lives. Maybe the Sandovals aren't happy with the fixer-upper I found for them," she said, hoping to lighten the tone.

Behind them, Bess's voice was small and hesitant. "I think I might have an idea who it was."

Lacey sat up. "Bess, we thought you were asleep."

"I was for a while. But then I got something in my head and I can't go back to sleep. It's about what you said—who did this?"

"You think you know?" Maeve set her wine glass down.

"I thought of one possibility." Rubbing her belly protectively, Bess sat next to Lacey. "You both have been great, you know, about not prying about the father. But I need to tell you something."

"Only if you want to, Bess." Lacey took her hand.

Bess took a deep breath, resolved. "In college I dated a guy. He seemed great. Really too good for me, I thought. He was smart and athletic. And I was, well, really pathetic then."

"You're not pathetic," Maeve quickly interrupted.

"No, I was. I look back on all this now, and think 'God, how did I let this happen?'" She shook her head. "One night he had been drinking and he got mad at me about something. I don't even remember what, exactly. He hit me. Twice actually. That was the first time."

Maeve drew a breath in sharply, her eyes turning to daggers.

Lacey squeezed Bess's hand. "Go on."

"He was so apologetic the next day. He swore it was the beer. And I really thought I loved him. I wanted to forgive him. And he was great for about a month. But then it happened again. Much worse. He hit me a couple times and kicked me in the stomach." Bess shifted her weight in the soft couch. "I look back now, and can't believe I let there be another time. But it wasn't just when he hit me. It was his words. He always made me question myself, manipulated me —I don't know—into thinking it was my own fault. He hated all my friends, so I distanced myself from them. By the end, I really believed him about everything. I believed that I wasn't good enough for him. I believed that I had to answer to him for everything—even things I hadn't done. I was always so scared of doing the wrong thing."

The birch logs popped in the fireplace and Bess paused. "When I found out I was pregnant, something snapped in me. I realized that even if I was the worthless person he had convinced me I was, I would not live my life worrying about the day when his temper would turn on this child. No one will ever strike this child."

"You're goddamn right about that," Maeve said through her teeth.

"So that's why you told your parents you were in Europe?" Lacey asked, the pieces finally falling into place. "You knew he'd go to them first if he went looking for you."

Bess nodded. "For the first time in my life, I'm actually glad my parents cared so little that they believed me."

"And the baby?" Maeve's voice was so soft that it didn't even sound like her. "Have you given any thought to what you'll do with the baby when she's born?"

"I thought about adoption for a while. But I really want to keep her. And I think that if I can just stay in hiding for a while, until the baby is born, maybe a bit after, then I can go on with my life. I'll let my parents think I got knocked up by some hot French guy I met at a café in Paris or something." She managed a half-hearted laugh.

Maeve shared a look with Lacey, who gave her a slight nod back.

"We'll get through this together, the three of us," Lacey said, now reaching her other hand over to Maeve so that they were all three joined.

Maeve then leaned over and took Bess' other hand so they formed a circle. "The four of us," she corrected.

CHAPTER 11

"So this is the guy?" Standing behind Mick's desk, Jack studied the photo Bess had provided.

"Yeah. They thought it would be good for us to know the full story since we're around the house so much. In case we see the guy," Mick explained, his voice hardening, "so we can kill the son-of-a-bitch." He stared at the photo, memorizing every line, every curve, and the smile he vowed to wipe from the guy's smug face.

"It doesn't make sense, though." Jack settled behind his computer. "I don't think he's the one who broke in. Abusive boyfriends don't hunt down their ex-girlfriends just to throw around their clothes and files and dump some boxes. If it was him, he'd be lurking in the bushes till she got home, and then beat the crap out of her."

The thought sent a chill down Mick's spine. He had become just as protective of Bess and the baby as Lacey and Maeve were. "It's one possibility and we shouldn't overlook it."

"Did they tell the police?"

"No. Bess is too afraid that if she involved her ex's name, he'd be notified. And there's too good of a chance it wasn't him."

"So she's never going to tell him about the baby?"

"Not if she can help it."

Jack exhaled slowly.

As if reading his thoughts, Mick quickly added, "He gave up the right to know he's a dad the moment he beat his girlfriend."

"Agreed." Jack nodded automatically.

Mick leaned forward in his chair. "He gave up the right to live, as far as I'm concerned. I swear if anyone ever struck Lacey, he'd never draw breath again."

Jack raised his eyebrows. "You mean, any of them—Maeve or Bess, too—I'm sure."

Mick shrugged, firing up his computer. "Of course. Any of them."

Jack leaned back in his chair looking smug. "Man, you've got it bad."

"What?"

"You're in love with Lacey."

Mick glanced up from his monitor. "In love with her? I'm not even dating her. How could I be in love with her?"

"Are you kidding? Hell, it's easier that way."

"You've been spending too much time with your sisters, Jack. Those female hormones are rubbing off on you."

"I'll agree I have too much estrogen exposure. But anyone can see it. You've got it bad."

"Okay. You caught me. I want to fuck her senseless, okay?" Mick tried to sound as vulgar as possible to restore the balance of testosterone in the room.

"You want to do a lot more than that," Jack said grinning. "You're in looooove." He drew the last word out the way a third grader might.

Mick glared, not amused. He was not in love. "You watch too many chick flicks." He snatched the photo of Bess's ex and taped it to the wall writing in all caps in a Sharpie: THE BAD GUY.

Pulling into Maeve's driveway after a long work day, Lacey ached to take off her heels and watch the sun set from the back porch. She didn't even notice the sound of the lawn mower as she stepped into the house. Yet there were Maeve and Bess, all but drooling, perched at the kitchen window gazing appreciatively into the backyard.

Lacey smiled. "So the lawn guy is back? He didn't move, after all?"

Maeve didn't even glance away from the window. "Oh, no. He's gone and forgotten. But apparently, we've been upgraded to a better model."

Curious, Lacey made her way to the window. Her jaw dropped.

There was Mick, shirtless, mowing the backyard.

"Oh my God," was all she could say.

"Mmhm. That's about the reaction we had," Bess murmured.

Lacey had imagined Mick's body would be muscular, and make no mistake—she had imagined it plenty.

But even her wildest fantasies couldn't quite match the reality of him. His shoulders were wide and thick with corded muscles that extended down into his broad back. A scar just below one shoulder seemed to lend an air of mystery to his otherwise flawless body. As the mower made its pass, the girls exhaled in unison at the sight of six pack abs so divine, they could only have been crafted by the hand of God.

Lacey felt the urge to trace her fingers along those ripped muscles. And get naked. Very, very naked.

"I knew he'd be ripped," Maeve said with some authority, "but I had no idea he'd be that ripped."

Bess was flushed. "As a pregnant woman, I didn't think it was possible to be this turned on."

"Are you kidding? All those extra hormones you have now are just aching for some relief. Lacey, couldn't you just loan Mick to Bess for an hour or two?"

Lacey wanted to say that he wasn't hers to loan, but the words got lodged in her throat. She couldn't tear her eyes off of him. Beads of salty sweat trickled down his six-pack and disappeared beneath his shorts. She licked her lips unconsciously and struggled to find her voice. "Why is he mowing the grass?"

Maeve snickered. "Well, he comes pounding on the door about a half hour ago and says he owes you big time, and to deduct whatever I used to pay the other guy from your rent."

Lacey blushed noticeably.

Maeve finally managed to pull her gaze from the window. She crossed her arms. "So what, may I ask, does he owe you for? Must have been a hell of a blow job."

Bess snorted.

Lacey gave Maeve a light slap on the shoulder. "Nothing like that. We had an argument. But we worked it out, so I never told you guys. There was so much else going on with the break-in. I never expected him to do this." She looked outside again in sheer admiration of the male form. "Oh, Maeve. You didn't tell him he had to take his shirt off, did you?"

"Even *I* wouldn't have thought of that. It was his idea. He said he wanted to make sure I got my money's worth."

Bess whistled a little. "I think you did and then some."

Just then, Mick glanced up and saw all three women

gazing at him. He flashed a smile and flexed his muscles with flourish. "Just wait till you see me do the edging," he called out over the roar of the motor.

"Sweet Mary. We could sell tickets to this, you know." Maeve sighed and then said sharply to Lacey, "Now don't you dare tell him that the other guy never did the edging."

"So what happened, Lacey?" Bess asked. "Must have been a bad argument for a payback like this."

Lacey turned away from the window. "Well, Mick found out that I had written up a proposal for Edith's house."

"So?" Maeve shrugged.

"He went ballistic. Stormed into my office, telling me I should have told him, and all that."

Bess lost the color in her cheeks. "Was he violent?"

"Mick? Oh, no. Just loud. So I told him to leave and he did. That's why he came early Saturday night. To apologize. And that was that. I had no idea he was going to do this." She gestured to the backyard.

"He said he'll keep doing it till winter, too," Maeve said with a grin. "So you'll have a bit more spending money in your pocket for the holidays."

"He really didn't have to do this. It wasn't such a big deal."

Crossing her arms, Maeve leaned against the counter. "So when are you going to take that hard body out for a spin, Lacey?"

"I'll probably never have the honors."

"For God's sake, Lacey, how settled in your career do you have to be to have sex again? This is getting absurd."

"It's not just that, Maeve. He still doesn't know that I crashed Doc's funeral to try to get the listing," Lacey explained. "After seeing how he reacted last week, now I *know* he'd hate me for that. How can I get involved with him now?"

"Honey, I've got news for you. You're already involved with him."

Bess gazed out the window again thoughtfully. "Why don't you just tell him the truth?"

"I tried to last week, but he cut me off. Said that he was wrong to stick his nose into my real estate business, and he didn't want to know anything more about work."

Maeve brightened. "There you go, then. You're free and clear. Jump the poor bastard before he explodes from sexual frustration. Or before you do."

"I'm not like you, Maeve, I can't just jump in the sack with someone when I feel like I'm hiding something from him."

Bess winced. "Ouch. Lacey."

"I'm sorry—I didn't mean it that way."

Maeve waved her hand carelessly, "I know you didn't. No worries. So then just tell him and force him to listen."

"I know that's what I should do. But the more feelings I get for him, the harder it is. Besides, a relationship with Mick isn't good for me right now. He's already clouding my thinking. Last Thursday when I went to that Parker funeral all I kept thinking was, is this ethical? I couldn't even bring myself to introduce myself to the widower. I just slipped out after the eulogy. Even now, look at me. I walked in the door in a great mood. Then I took one look at him and I'm confused, unfocused, and pretty much just want to cry."

"Holy Hell. You're in love," Maeve concluded.

"No!" Lacey insisted firmly, despite the tears building up from the realization… and the guilt. Why was she reacting this way? "Absolutely not. He's just my friend. I feel the same way you two feel about him."

Maeve and Bess exchanged a look.

"Uh, but we're not crying right now," Bess observed.

The mower outside stopped. Lacey glanced out the

window as Mick powered up the edger. Licking her bottom lip involuntarily, she let out a slow breath when she saw his muscles bunch as he revved the motor.

Maeve raised an eyebrow to Bess. "If this keeps up any longer, we'll be buying her a vibrator for Christmas."

CHAPTER 12

Lacey stood in front of her closet wishing some new outfit would magically appear. Her wardrobe was dismal. Browns, grays, black. Lots of black. But since attending funerals was part of her job, the drab palette was a necessity.

She slipped on a gray skirt with a black sweater. Glancing at herself for no more than ten seconds, she ripped the sweater off and replaced it with another black one. Shaking her head ferociously, she tore off the skirt and tried some jeans. At least they were blue, and this was Annapolis, after all. No one ever wore much more than jeans in this town.

Feeling defeated, she flopped down on the bed.

What was wrong with her? This wasn't a date. It was just two friends going to sample some foods together. It didn't matter what she wore.

The hell it didn't.

She stormed into Maeve's bedroom on a mission.

"Looking a little flustered," Maeve observed, eyeing the light sheen of sweat on her friend's brow. She lay sprawled out on the bed in a silk robe reading *Architectural Digest.*

Desperate, Lacey's eyes were wide. "I have no clothes. I have no shoes."

"As I've been telling you for months now."

"Can I borrow something?"

"Duh. Of course. What do you need? What are you dressing for?" She lifted herself out from a pile of fluffy pillows.

"Mick and I are going to sample those entrées at Eagle's Point tonight."

"Hot date clothes, then."

"It's not a date."

With a smirk, Maeve snuggled back into the poof of her bed linens. "Well, then what you're wearing should do just fine."

Lacey sighed. "Okay, okay. Sort of hot date clothes. Everything I have is either super casual or bland work clothes."

"Ah, yes, the Lacey Owens Funeral Collection," Maeve nodded solemnly, rising from her bed with greater enthusiasm. "I can do better than that."

Lacey bit her tongue and let her friend take over, watching her pull out stacks of shoe boxes and armloads of hangers from her closet.

Maeve barreled through an assortment of colorful attire, sorting and paring down until she settled on a combination that resembled something ripped from a magazine. She dressed Lacey like a life-sized doll, topping her effort with a light squirt of perfume.

"There. You are now ready," Maeve said triumphantly, turning Lacey around to see herself in the mirror.

"I am indebted to you forever." Lacey gazed at herself in Maeve's selection of a silk blouse with a cashmere sweater, and a denim skirt that fell just above the knee. Sexy, yet understated, leather heeled boots completed the ensemble.

"Now if you come home at all tonight, I'll be grossly disappointed in you, Lacey."

The smell of roasted garlic wafted into the stairway as Lacey made her way down the steps. Bess, in her usual sweats, was hovering over the kitchen counters, chopping and dicing herbs and vegetables that Lacey didn't even recognize.

"That smells wonderful. What is it?"

Bess didn't even turn to Lacey to speak, concentrating on the task at-hand. "A little experiment. Sort of a lasagna with a little of this and that." She finally glanced over her shoulder. "Wow! You look fantastic."

"Thanks. Maeve's doing, of course. The only thing that's mine is the bra."

"I'll keep that in mind," a male voice said behind her.

Lacey blushed from head to toe at the sight of Mick standing in the entryway. "Bess, why didn't you tell me he was here?"

"I'm sorry," Bess said innocently, with palpable amusement. "I thought you heard the doorbell."

"I couldn't hear a thing over Maeve's lecture about my lack of style and colorless wardrobe."

Mick gave her an obvious once-over. "I'll mirror Bess's compliment and say you look fantastic."

"Thanks. So do you. I haven't seen you in a suit since—" She stopped suddenly, not wanting to remind him of the circumstances of their meeting.

"Doc's funeral," Mick finished casually for her. "Yeah, I bet you're getting sick of seeing me in jeans or in uniform."

Never, Lacey thought. "Ready to go?"

Mick wrapped his arm around her waist and whisked her out the door. "I can't imagine that what they're cooking for us tonight will be any better than whatever Bess is whipping up," he commented as they stepped into the crisp fall evening.

"I've never been to Eagle's Point, but I've heard it's incredible. I can't believe Edith managed to secure it for the fundraiser. She has such a way of getting people to do things she wants." Mick opened the car door for her, and as she sunk into his leather seats, she noticed his double-take as her skirt slipped further up her thigh. *Good,* she couldn't resist thinking.

He slid into his seat and put the key in the ignition. Glancing at her again, his finger lightly traced the exposed skin just above her knee. "Goosebumps," he commented. "Are you cold?"

"A little," Lacey murmured, a sinful thrill racing up her spine from his touch.

"I'll turn the heat up then," he said, giving Lacey the hope he might lean in and touch his warm lips to hers.

She fought disappointment when he pressed a button on the dashboard and she felt hot air blowing through the vents. "Thanks," she said half-heartedly.

When they arrived at the end of a winding road lined with fiery maples, the sight of Eagle's Point was nothing short of spectacular. The building was a stately historic mansion converted into a restaurant on the bottom floor with hotel suites above it, each with views of the Bay. Lacey silently fantasized about detouring past dinner and right up to one of the lavish suites with Mick.

As the maître d' seated them beside a floor-to-ceiling window, the beaming chef practically floated in from the kitchen to greet them, grinning from ear-to-ear.

"What a delight to have you here!" the chef said in an airy tone, enthusiastic hands fluttering in front of him as he spoke. "Edith told me that you have the final say on the selections, so I am preparing my personal favorites." He talked alternating English and French as appropriate, rattling off dishes that sounded delectable, if unrecognizable, to Lacey.

Within moments, the celebratory pop of a champagne cork summoned a parade of tantalizing appetizers.

Lacey cracked a smile at the sight of Mick's awkward grip on the champagne flute. He was much more comfortable drinking a beer, she mused, sinking her fork into a lightly encrusted crab cake drizzled with caper sauce. His strong hands looked as though they might crush the delicate crystal without even intending to. She couldn't help noticing their size and strength. As she licked the remains of the sauce from her fork, her mind wandered to the idea of those hands gently stroking her cheeks, her neck, her breasts, her stomach, her…

"Lacey?"

She blinked several times. "What?"

"Were you thinking about something?"

"No. I mean, my mind was just wandering. It's the champagne, probably."

"You looked like you were in the middle of a pretty interesting thought. I'll have to bring champagne to the next Scrabble night," he concluded with a meaningful grin.

His smile took her breath away. The way his perfectly white teeth were framed in such tempting lips, so soft and gentle. Such a contrast to his hard body, she thought dreamily, taking another sip.

"Any plans for Thanksgiving?" Mick's controlled tone snapped her back to reality.

"Going to Chicago to my parents, like always. I wish I could stay here."

"Why don't you want to go to Chicago?"

A wry smile crossed Lacey's face. "It's stupid. Remember my fantasy about announcing the sale of my first waterfront home at Thanksgiving dinner? Right now, all I have to announce is that I still have fewer sales than anyone else in the office."

"But you're the newest," Mick pointed out.

"I know. But still." Lacey shrugged, her thoughts drifting to Vi and whatever grand announcement her sister was plotting to unveil this holiday. Lacey knew something was up, and there were probably plenty of dollar signs attached to it. "How about you? Are you going away?"

"I thought I'd make Thanksgiving dinner for Edith. You know, turkey, stuffing, the standard fare. It's her first holiday without Doc, you know. And I'll be inviting any of the mids who aren't going home for the holiday. There are always a few who don't have plans. No family. Or one not worth going home to."

"That's nice of you."

Mick laughed. "Why do you always sound surprised anytime I do something nice?"

Because I'm thinking of all the naughty things I'd like you to do to me, Lacey thought, shrugging innocently in response.

"I had a CO do that for some of us when I was stationed in Hawaii. It meant a lot. This is the first time I'll actually have the space to be able to have some people over." He reached for his champagne again, but then quickly set it down, opting to chug a half-glass of water. "Got a friend and his wife coming up from Norfolk, too. We were stationed together in Tampa for a while. So tell Bess and Maeve they're welcome to join us if they want. It should be a good crowd."

Lacey burst out laughing. "I'm sorry. I'm just picturing Maeve in a room with a bunch of young, vulnerable mids."

Mick winced. "Oh. Yeah. Maybe that wouldn't be a good idea."

"You think?" She eased back in her chair, feeling the

effects of the champagne tap dancing through her veins, and imagined for a moment that they were here together. Really together. To be able to reach out and take his hand, knowing that the warmth he offered through his touch would also be hers when they were alone later. To be able to look out at the lovely moon picturing their future together, filled with a perfect mix of comfortable companionship and sizzling passion.

She let out a slow breath to steady herself. Not with this man. He had no interest in settling down. He had made that clear.

But right now, seeing the intensity in his eyes as he looked at her, she considered that maybe something temporary with him might be worth the heartbreak that followed.

CHAPTER 13

Pushing open the door to the hotel suite, Mick drew in a sharp breath at the sight of Lacey's perfectly formed backside bent over a fallen stack of cardboard boxes. God, she had perfect curves. The image would fuel his fantasies for at least a week. He cleared his throat. Lacey jumped at the sound.

"Whoa, Lacey. It's just me."

Mick grinned when Lacey's breath caught at the sight of him in his dress blues for Edith's fundraiser. He hated looking like a recruiting poster, his chest full of medals. But he did appreciate the effect it had on the opposite sex.

Her expression dimmed as she looked down at herself. Dripping with sweat, she peeled her dress from her soaked chest, and flapped the silky fabric in a futile attempt to dry herself. "You scared me. I thought I was the only one with a key."

"Mrs. B got me one from the front desk. She said you might need some help."

"Yes!" She nearly exploded at the offer. "I desperately need help. We were supposed to have at least five more volunteers here by now, but no one's shown up yet."

"They'll show up when the food's being served, I'll bet."

"If they even try to take a bite of food without putting in the work, I will personally murder them."

"You know, this dress uniform comes with a sword. Should I go back and get it?"

Lacey half-laughed and half-cried, tossing herself backward onto the king size bed. "Oh, God. Look at me, Mick! I'm a mess. It's the hottest November day in recent history and I've been unloading boxes for an hour."

Mick did look at her. A sheen of perspiration had covered her chest, making her dress cling to her. In the daylight, Mick could make out the perfect curves of her breasts and see a slight outline of her ripe nipples. She withered into the bed, sinking deeper into the lush down comforter with every passing second. He ached to lie on the bed beside her, and lick every inch of her moist body.

Shit, he thought as his body reacted. There had to be a Navy regulation against appearing in dress blues with a raging hard-on.

Focusing on the look of sheer misery on Lacey's face, he regained his composure. "You look beautiful. That dress is gorgeous. Just a little…wet." He choked on the last word.

"Maeve picked it out. Damn her. Leave it to a woman who has never lifted anything heavier than a credit card to send me here in a silk dress to do hard labor." She rolled over and punched a pillow, apparently unaware of her tempting position.

Mick's knees buckled in reaction, and he grabbed a bedpost to steady himself.

Lacey rolled onto her back again, staring gloomily at the ceiling. "It's not her fault though. I thought the hardest thing I'd be doing today is lighting a few votive candles. But there's a line of minivans a mile-long downstairs with silent auction items I still need to unload. I have to bring them up here until the extra tables are set up."

"Well, I'm here now. I'll take over any lifting." Averting his eyes from the inviting image of her on the bed, he offered a hand to pull her up. "Why not change into something else so your dress can dry out while we're setting up?"

"I didn't bring anything else."

Mick scoffed. "I'm a SEAL. I've got at least five sets of PT gear in my car."

"PT gear?"

"Workout clothes. Sit tight. I'll be right back."

Her head still spinning, Lacey punched in the numbers to Maeve's new security system, hoping not to wake anyone. She pulled off her shoes first. Then she unsnapped her bra, sighing with relief. Unable to make it up the staircase to her room, she collapsed onto the sofa.

The family room had that wintery scent of burning logs, and Lacey imagined Maeve must have had a fire in the fireplace tonight. The slight chill told Lacey she might need to shut the flue. But later. Right now, all she could do was elevate her aching feet and try to wind down.

The night had been exhilarating. Things went so smoothly after Mick had arrived, saving the day with his PT gear and strong arms. He had all the boxes unloaded in a quarter the time it would have taken Lacey.

Her dress had completely dried by the time she slipped it back on, and Maeve had been right. It was perfect—festive enough to be fun, yet subtle enough to be taken seriously as an up-and-coming real estate guru. She had handed out more business cards than she ever thought she would.

But it was Mick's presence that Lacey found to be the

most exhilarating part of the night. People had been attracted to him like moths to a candle, and Lacey was one of them. The sight of him in his dress uniform, shaking their hands, and accepting their thanks for his service to their country. Then he'd subtly encourage them to make a donation to the hospital. Laced smiled at the memory.

The guy would make a killing in real estate sales.

She wanted him.

Desperately.

"How was it?" Bess's drowsy voice drew Lacey reluctantly back into the present.

"Oh, no. Did I wake you?"

"I was already awake. I fell asleep at five, would you believe? My sleep patterns are so screwed up." She sat down beside her. "So?"

Lacey shook her head slowly, dreamily. "It was amazing. I couldn't have imagined it going more perfectly. I passed out so many cards. I really think I'm going to get some serious business out of this."

"So that's the only reason you're glowing? The business you'll get?"

Lacey was silent for a few moments, and then answered honestly, "No. It was Mick. The glow is definitely from Mick."

"Why aren't you doing something about that then, Lacey? He's not going to wait around forever for you to become some real estate giant, you know. I'd hate to see you let him slip through your fingers."

"I know. But being with Mick would just end up hurting me in the end."

"Mick would never hurt you."

"Of course he'd hurt me. He as good as told me he would. He said he's not looking for anything long-term. That would break my heart if I got too involved."

"Men always say that, Lacey. They change their minds."

"Men don't change. You of all people know that."

Bess frowned. "Men don't change their nature. But they do change their minds." She shifted her belly weight and put her feet up on the coffee table. "Do you know something?"

"What?"

"I didn't like Mick when I first met him."

"You didn't?"

"No. A build like that scares the hell out of me. And there's just no hiding it under the clothes. I met him when he was taking you out to dinner that first time. He showed up in his uniform—the brownish one, you know?"

"His khakis."

"Yeah. And it does nothing to camouflage a man's muscles. All I could think was how a guy like that could do some serious damage. I was so scared for you, I actually wrote down his license plate number."

"Is that why you slipped your pepper spray in my purse?"

"Yep."

Lacey turned to her intently. "Mick would never hurt me, you know that now, right? He'd never hurt any of us. He'd die first."

A smile crept over Bess's face. "I'm sorry, what did you say?"

"I said, he'd never hurt me."

"You said he'd never hurt you?" Bess repeated.

Lacey was a tad frustrated. "Yes. That's what I said." She paused, the realization suddenly apparent. "Oh, I get it. He'd never hurt me."

Bess rested her hands stoically on her belly and smiled. "Thanks for finally agreeing with me. Now what's holding you back?"

"You want to grab a beer?" The way Mick barked it into the phone made it sound more like a direct order than a question.

Jack's muffled voice came through on other end of the call. "It's past midnight and you want to go get a beer? What are you, in your twenties again?"

"I need to unwind," Mick grumbled. What he needed was to erase the image of Lacey in that damn dress from his brain. Even worse, he had to shake this unfamiliar feeling he had as he had watched her happily handing out her business cards, making contacts, building her dream.

He should be picturing her naked right now. Sprawled out on that big bed in the hotel suite, begging for him to take her.

He shouldn't be thinking of how adorable she was with that hopeful look on her face, her career finally taking shape.

Naked and panting. That's the way he should want her. Right?

Instead, his best sex fantasies about her were taking a back seat to imagining her joy at her first waterfront house sale. Or picturing her pride as she moves up the ladder within the real estate company. Hell, he wasn't even planning on being around for that. He'd be long gone.

This just wasn't natural. If it kept up, he might start thinking he was in love with her.

Not possible.

What had he been thinking? That Lacey would suddenly decide that she was content to have a fling? She wasn't that type. She wasn't *his* type. And he couldn't become *her* type—not with the life he had planned for himself.

"Come on, Jack. We can make it down to O'Toole's for last call."

"I'm in bed."

"It's a Saturday night," Mick insisted. "You always tell me you're never alone on a Saturday night."

"Technically, it's Sunday morning. And who said I'm alone?"

Mick heard the soft laughter of a female voice in the background. It pissed him off even more. Everyone in Annapolis was getting laid right now except him. "You shouldn't have picked up the phone then."

"I had to find out how it went tonight. You wore your dress blues, for God's sake. Don't tell me you still didn't get lucky."

"Then I won't tell you that. You can just assume it."

"You must be dying. Don't get me wrong. I think Lacey's great, but you better start meeting some other women or your dick will shrivel up and fall off."

Mick winced. "That's why I called. I need to get out. Now."

"You're out of luck, bro. I'm in some hot company, and you're not invited."

Mick heard the rustling of sheets and envisioned the lusty shifting of flesh over flesh. Envy simmered inside his veins. "Next week then."

"Can't. Got too much to do before the brigade leaves for Thanksgiving. And so do you. But the week after, you're on."

Mick shut his phone with a sense of finality. After Thanksgiving then.

He grabbed a beer from the fridge and tried to shake the idea that looking for another woman was somehow wrong.

Lacey and he were just friends. She made that clear.

And he had to stop thinking of her somehow, didn't he?

PART II

TWENTY-ONE YEARS AGO

Till today, Lacey had never seen her sister in pigtails. Even at nine years old, the sweetness of pigtails seemed incongruous with Vi's sharp business sense.

Hearing her sister approach, Vi didn't even glance over her shoulder as she stirred the lemonade. "Are you coming or what?" she asked Lacey.

"I guess so. Why are you in one of my dresses?"

Vi owned no dresses of her own. She preferred pants or shorts. "I'm selling lemonade. Goes with the territory." She carried the large thermos of lemonade out to the wagon. "Grab those cups and that sign, will you?"

Lacey did as she was told, as always, accepting her role as Vi's assistant in this business venture rather than a full partner. “But no one ever drives up our street, Vi. We’ll never sell any lemonade.”

“That’s why we’re mobilizing our lemonade stand,” Vi explained, heaving an impatient sigh as she taped the sign to the wagon. It read:

“Ice-Cold Lemonade. Just 99 cents a cup!”

“A whole dollar for a cup of lemonade?” Lacey gasped.

“Not a whole dollar. 99 cents,” Vi corrected.

“But they’ll never pay that much for a cup of lemonade. I was thinking maybe we’d ask for a dime. I don’t know.” Lacey floundered, as usual, in matters of business.

“They’ll pay a dollar a cup where we’re headed,” Vi said with a scheming glint in her eyes. “I saw they were laying tar about five blocks away. Nothing more refreshing than a cup of lemonade when you’ve been laying tar on a hot August day, I’ll bet.” She began pulling the wagon down the driveway with resolve.

Lacey trudged behind her in the scorching heat. Her eyes watered as the smell of tar eventually began wafting in their direction.

Vi’s voice was laced in sugary-sweetness as she locked eyes with the first man in a hard hat she saw. “Hi! Want to buy a nice, refreshing cup of ice-cold lemonade?”

“Kid, you’re charging a dollar for a cup?”

“Just 99 cents, sir,” Vi responded, unwavering. “It’s really good and I paid for the ingredients out of my own allowance.”

Lacey just stood there, pasting a grim smile on her face, with no idea what to say.

“Hey, Bob! Get a load of this!” one of the workers called out, attracting the attention of at least five more. “The kid’s selling dollar-cups of lemonade. Paid for it all out of her allowance.”

“Cute.”

"Sure, what the hell," another man said, despite the company of such young girls. "I'll take a cup. Here's a buck. Keep the change."

"Thank you very much, sir!" Vi chirped.

"I'll take one, too. Looks good."

"Can't resist the pigtails. I'll take two, kid. You got chutzpah."

Within minutes, the thermos was emptied, and Vi's pockets bulged with dollar bills.

When they arrived home, Lacey watched Vi rip the infernal pigtails from her hair with a scowl. "What are you gaping at?" Vi snapped.

Lacey shook her head, comforted by the return of Vi's sharp tone. "Pigtails and a dress?"

Vi rolled her eyes and flapped the stack of singles in front of her sister's face. "A means to an end, Lacey."

CHAPTER 14

TODAY

A tidal wave of slush cascaded against the curb as a cab pulled up, catching Lacey's eye. Armed with a glass of Chardonnay, she headed to her parents' front window for a better look.

Sometimes when Vi arrived for holidays, Lacey half-expected her to emerge from her cab or rented Volvo wearing pink Reeboks and sweats, hair pulled back in an efficient ponytail, five-foot-eight of gangly youth.

The years had raced by, and the changes in her sister were more dramatic than those in herself—as Lacey was reminded when the cab's door opened and the first designer boot stepped onto the snowy driveway.

If Maeve were here, she'd be applauding Vi's choice in footwear right now.

Umbrella snapping open, Vi stood from the cab, her unbuttoned coat revealing a tailored pantsuit that probably cost the equivalent of an average real estate commission. Definitely not the sweats of Vi's youth. Lacey glanced down at her borrowed clothes, thanking God for Maeve's open closet policy.

Over her shoulder, Lacey looked into her parents' great room, already brimming with holiday guests. Thanksgiving was never restricted to family in the Owens' household. It was an opportunity for Lacey's parents to call a caterer and invite fifty or so of their "closest" friends. The crowded room, mostly people her parents knew through work, would be a receptive audience for Vi's news about her promotion—or whatever work-related triumph her sister was poised to reveal.

Lacey waved through the window, and a smile spread across Vi's face when their eyes met. A warmth tugged Lacey's heart that could only come with thirty years of sisterly mischief, rivalry, and love. Suddenly excited to see her sister, she sliced through the crowd to get to the front door first.

Vi beamed when Lacey swung open the door, a certain glow about her that Lacey imagined must come from huge success. "Welcome home, Vi." Lacey's voice cracked with emotion as she reached for her sister and squeezed her tight.

Vi pulled out of the embrace first, her eyes sweeping over Lacey. "You look fabulous."

Grinning at the first compliment she had received since she had arrived, Lacey felt compelled to hug her sister again. "Thanks. You look great, too."

"Amazing what having a personal shopper does for my wardrobe, huh?" Vi winked, sliding her arms out of her coat.

Lacey lowered her voice. "Thank God you're here. All

these people speak in ticker symbols. I need you to translate." She reached out for Vi's coat and paused, waiting for her sister to remove her gloves. Right one first. Then the left...

...when she saw it. A strange flash that streaked across the image of her sister as Vi raised her hand to brush a lock of hair behind her ear.

The thin stream of illumination was bright, like a meteor shooting across the sky.

Or a diamond catching the light of the midday sun.

A diamond?

Instinctively, Lacey reached for Vi's hand, half to investigate and half to steady herself from sudden vertigo. "What the—"

"I'm engaged!" Vi looked giddy with delight. For a brief moment, Lacey wondered what was more shocking: the idea of her sister engaged, or the sight of her giddy. Vi was never giddy. Even when Vi was five and they were visiting a litter of playful puppies for sale, Vi hadn't been giddy. She had been calculating the pet shop's profit margins.

Dumbfounded, her sister's hand in hers, Lacey stared at a rock the size of a grapefruit. Or at least it looked like it to Lacey in her semi-delirious state.

"Can you believe it?" Vi's voice filled the silence. Behind her, Lacey could feel the presence of her parents closing in, followed by an entourage of their well-dressed guests.

"Oh, honey." Lacey's mom pulled Vi into a hug.

Honey? When was the last time her mother called anyone "honey"?

Vi was quickly passed from her mother's embrace to her father's, and then lost to Lacey in a string of handshakes that slowly pulled Vi to the other side of the room. It was for the best. Lacey needed to catch her breath.

Vi. Engaged.

Gazing at her sister now standing next to the fireplace, a glass of Champagne magically appearing in one hand and showing off her ring with the other, Lacey wondered why she hadn't considered this possibility. She knew something had been up. But with Vi's strict rules about focusing on work till she had her own show on CNN or an equivalent feather in her cap, Lacey never would have thought *this* was the big announcement Vi had planned.

So where are those rules now, Vi?

Sensing a burning in her chest that was probably that last chunk of Brie she had devoured, Lacey tried to edge out the jealousy from her mind and just be happy for her sister. Vi was glowing in a way that even the most expensive makeup couldn't replicate.

Just as a warm feeling crept into her heart, Lacey was struck by an image of Vi's inevitable future—a seemingly effortless balance of family and work. Vi'd move to the suburbs, buy a newly renovated historic house on a sizable lot, and have two perfect children. She'd hire an au pair from France and Vi's kids would speak two languages fluently by the time they were three-and-a-half.

It's was Lacey's dream… on steroids.

Meanwhile, poor Auntie Lacey would be crashing funerals, struggling to make a sale.

Broke.

And sexless.

Sexless? To hell with that.

"I can't believe you're leaving early." Poised to take a sip, the vapor from Vi's breath mixed with steam rising from the mulled wine in her two-handed grip.

Hot spiced wine on the front porch after Thanksgiving

dinner had become a tradition for Lacey and Vi the past few years. It wasn't just the comforting feel of warm wine touching their lips against the chill of early winter. It was an excuse to escape the guests and the suffocating small talk of post-dinner coffee. No one in their right minds would follow them outside in Chicago's bitter November cold.

Ordinarily, Lacey looked forward to this quiet time alone with her sister. But not tonight.

"Real estate emergency," Lacey offered evasively. "I'll fly stand-by tomorrow morning."

Vi's eyes were wide with disbelief. "Emergency?"

Lacey shrank down in the chilly cushions on the wicker chair. She hated lying to her sister.

Vi shrugged at Lacey's silence. "Well, okay."

Taking a sip of wine, Lacey decided it safest to change the subject. "Good turkey, huh?"

"Dad said they tried a new caterer this year."

Lacey tilted her head. "You know, I don't think I've ever had a home-cooked turkey in my life."

"Who'd want to? Everyone says they're always dry."

"One of my housemates is cooking Thanksgiving dinner back home. I'll bet hers isn't dry. She's a great cook." Thoughts of sanctuary in Annapolis had Lacey wishing she could call a cab for the airport right now.

"Handy having her in the house, I'll bet."

"Yeah. She makes homemade pizza every Scrabble night. The dough's even from scratch."

Vi's face scrunched, and for a moment she looked surprisingly similar to the awkward twelve-year-old she once was. "Scrabble night?"

"Yeah."

"You play Scrabble with your friends?"

Lacey met her sister's disbelieving stare. "Yeah. So what?"

Vi tossed her shoulders up casually. "I just didn't know

people really did that." She stared into the night sky, as though picturing it. "So you do this at parties or something?"

"No. Just every week. Our friends Mick and Jack come over and we just hang out on the back porch or have a fire in the fireplace and play games. Scrabble mostly. But sometimes Monopoly."

Apparently bewildered, Vi cocked her head, gazing at Lacey. "Sounds like something people do on TV, you know? Like in a sitcom. Kind of—I don't know—quaint."

"Now you're being insulting."

"No, I'm not. It's cute."

Lacey heaved a sigh. "So. What do you do with your friends?"

Silent, Vi frowned, swirling the cooling wine in her mug. For a moment, Lacey didn't think her sister would answer. Vi finally took a sip and shrugged. "Work."

"I should get you and what's-his-name a Scrabble game for Christmas."

That made Vi laugh, almost too much. "There's something I can't imagine. Josh playing Scrabble."

"Josh." Lacey repeated. "Josh. Trying to remember that name, but seeing as today's the first time you ever mentioned him, it might take a while. I can't believe you never told me about him till now. And here you are. Engaged."

Vi grinned. "You know me. I don't even talk about a stock till I'm ready to buy."

"How romantic." Lacey tossed back the rest of her drink, hoping the alcohol would fortify her. "So what happened to the whole 'work before love' mantra?"

"What do you mean?

"You used to say that relationships took too much energy and time. Too much conflict with a career."

"When did I say that?"

Lacey stared at her in disbelief. "*Always*, Vi."

"I guess I just met the right man."

"The right man," Lacey repeated, an image of Mick flashing in her mind—hard, rippling muscles beneath his too-sexy uniform. How more "right" could he be? Despite the cold, Lacey felt a hot, tingling sensation tiptoe across her skin as though she had just stepped into a steamy hot tub. She glanced at her watch. How many more hours till the first morning flight out of here?

"Late for something?" Vi's voice hinted of sarcasm as she looked at Lacey, eyeing the time.

You have no idea how late. "Just wondering when the guests will start leaving." Peeking into the window, Lacey was disappointed to not see any guests gravitating toward the coat closet. "So do I have to wait till the wedding to meet this Josh guy?"

Vi's lips formed a thin line, and she tucked her free hand into her coat pocket. "You might. He works a lot. Working this weekend, actually, or he'd be here."

"Well, at least he has his priorities in line."

Vi glared. "Don't be a bitch. Not everyone gets to take the holidays off."

Lacey shook head, hating herself. "You're right. I'm sorry. I was just joking," she offered, even though she knew she hadn't been. What was it about her sister that made her feel twelve years old again?

Vi narrowed her eyes. "I thought you'd be happy for me."

Of course Vi had thought that. It had been Lacey who decorated the kitchen in balloons when Vi was accepted to Columbia University… popped the champagne cork when Vi got an internship at the most prestigious brokerage in New York… gathered her friends to watch Vi's first appearance on TV.

Did she have any happiness left to offer her sister?

Angling her head, Lacey looked at Vi. Behind her sister's

department store mascara, Vi's eyes were uneasy, as though desperate for Lacey's approval, though God only knew why.

Lacey painted a smile on her face. "I *am* happy for you."

Vi took Lacey's hand and squeezed. "I'm glad," she said, and Lacey could have sworn she heard her sister's voice catch.

CHAPTER 15

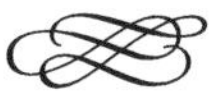

Goody-two-shoes Lacey had never had a speeding ticket in her life.

Today, she was willing to risk it.

Tightening her grip on the steering wheel, she sped down the empty highway heading into Annapolis, knowing that her destination was not Maeve's house.

It was Mick's.

She wanted him, damn it. And whether or not the distraction of having him in her life would derail her career didn't matter anymore.

As for the broken heart that likely awaited her in the future, she couldn't care less.

For once, now was what mattered to her. No eye on the future. Just grabbing today, as enthusiastically as she had grabbed that box of condoms at the drugstore en route.

She only hoped that he was still interested in her. Even a little.

And if he wasn't, she had worn the sexiest bra and panties she could buy beneath her sensible traveling clothes in case he needed some enticement. Who would have known there would be a Victoria's Secret right at the airport? That had to be a sign, right?

Slamming her car door behind her, she darted toward the Naval Academy security gates, barely stopping to show her ID as she walked briskly toward his home.

All smiles and slightly breathless, she rapped on his door.

When a woman answered it, Lacey could have sworn she heard the earsplitting sound of her own heart shattering to bits on his front door step.

Of course a gorgeous guy like Mick wouldn't wait around for her.

Lacey struggled to regain her voice. After all, Mick was nothing more than a friend. She had no claim on him. "I'm sorry. I was looking for Mick. I should have called first."

"No, please come in. He's just in the kitchen," the woman said with a comfortable smile.

Lacey was already backing down the stairs. "No, thanks. Really. Just tell him Lacey stopped by and to have a great weekend."

Turning on her heel, she headed down the street, her walk somehow transforming into a full-blown sprint. She was almost at the security gate when she heard a voice behind her.

"Lacey!"

She groaned knowing the dampness on her cheeks was likely accompanied by streaks of dripping mascara and smudged eyeliner. Oh God, how humiliating all this was. She didn't break stride and prayed he would give up the chase.

Damn that SEAL physical training; Mick was a lot faster. His hand touched her arm and he whipped her around to face him. "Lacey, what's wrong? What happened?"

"Nothing, Mick. Really. I'll talk to you later about it."

"Did something happen at your parents? You weren't coming home until Sunday, I thought." He wiped her tears with the bottom of his sleeve. Even in the brisk autumn wind, she noticed he smelled like onions and chili powder.

"No. It's nothing important. I'm so sorry I interrupted your date. Please go back to her."

"My date?" Mick looked baffled. "Oh, you mean, Kristine? She's Rob's wife. My friend from Norfolk, remember? We were watching the game and making chili."

Lacey stood there, confused and mortified. This wasn't what she had pictured. She had envisioned him opening up his door, her planting a sensual kiss on him as she proceeded to rip his clothes off of him. Then he would carry her upstairs and they would make mad, passionate love for at least the next three or four hours.

She wasn't sure how to improvise her planned seduction, drenched in tears, standing in the middle of a street with armed Marine guards only a few feet away.

"I—" she began, searching for a way to begin. "Vi is engaged. I guess it was a shock, that's all. It upset me."

"Engaged. Really? Who to?"

"Some producer. Probably get her own show out of the deal, too, knowing her."

"Her own show. I'm even jealous of her," Mick said, trying to get Lacey to smile.

Only more tears came. "It's not that, Mick. It's that she's engaged. All this time I thought the key to a successful career was putting everything else on hold. I thought that's what she did. But now, just look at her. She has it all."

Mick gently stroked her quivering bottom lip with his thumb.

Lacey melted at his tenderness. "I've been such an idiot—depriving myself of what I really want. Thinking that it might help me focus on some stupid career that probably isn't even right for me anyway."

He brushed his fingers across her cheek. "What *do* you want?"

A cold breeze blew over them, sending the last of fall's leaves floating to the ground. Lacey slid her hands into her pockets. She couldn't look him in the eye.

"You," she answered quietly.

Mick's mouth curved into a smile as he framed her face in his hands. Her lashes low, she looked up at him. Uncertainty clung to her, and her heart felt exposed, vulnerable—till he angled his face toward her, lifting her chin gently with his hand.

Lowering his lips near to hers, he paused only a moment, and she felt his breath caressing her lips before they finally touched. Then, at the sweet pressure of his kiss, warmth turned to fire as her lips explored him tentatively, then desperately, seizing the passion that burned red-hot in her veins.

The feel of his lips on hers was so satisfying and yet not nearly enough. She urged him on, pressing her body against him, sliding her palms up his arms and across his shoulders, then raking his cool hair with her fingertips. Her lips parted, and she tasted him. Timid at first, then hungry with desire. He moaned in response, a thoroughly masculine sound. There was no turning back.

Mick glanced up and saw they were attracting a few toothy grins from the nearby Marine guards. Firing them a deadly look, he pulled his cell from his pocket and dialed his own number. "Rob, I'm three blocks away. You and Kristine have exactly forty-five seconds to evacuate the premises."

Lacey heard a laugh on the other end of the phone. "WILCO," she heard the voice reply.

"Wilco?" she asked as Mick snapped his phone shut.

"Will comply." He knitted his arm with hers and hurried her up the street.

Darting up the stairs and stepping into his home, the click of the lock behind them sent a thrill down Lacey's spine. Mick checked the kitchen to make sure they were alone. He returned to her, grabbing a fistful of her hair and eagerly planting his lips on hers again.

"So what happens now, Lacey?" he whispered, making a searing path of kisses down her neck. His warm breath set the tiny hairs on her back on end and the gentle trail of his tongue ignited her senses. "Do I take you out on an official date or two before I try to seduce you?" Unfastening her buttons as he spoke, his mouth reached the skin between her breasts causing her breath to quicken. "Or would you prefer to have the seduction first? It's up to you."

Breathless, Lacey thrust into his hands the convenience store bag she had been holding tightly in her clutch. "Um, this might give you a clue."

He looked inside and grinned. "I see you bought in bulk. We better get started."

Smothered in a kiss so thorough she could feel its impact down to her toes, Lacey went slack in his firm embrace. "Just take me right now. I'm dying here."

He scooped her into his arms and carried her up the stairs. "Oh, I'm planning on torturing you quite a bit first. Payback for what you've put me through the last few months."

Lacey felt the air sizzle with anticipation as they entered his room. Her body dissolved into the soft, cool sheets when he lowered her onto his unmade bed. "You've really wanted me?" she asked, watching him pull his shirt over his head revealing his exquisitely sculpted chest and pecs. His jeans hung low on his hips and a light trail of chest hair led her eyes down his tight abs to his zipper. "All this time?"

As he pulled off his jeans, the full length of him all but

sprung from his boxers. "Uh, yeah, Lacey. I think there's your answer."

She splayed her hands across his well-defined chest, and traced the rippling of his abs on a journey downward. She had longed to touch him like this for so long that she savored the experience. "I was afraid it was just me." She touched him timidly first through the thin cotton of his boxers, then grabbed him more forcefully, gaining confidence at the feel of him fully erect in her hand.

He practically whimpered. "You're killing me, lady," he said in a strained voice as he ripped off his boxers.

Lacey found herself intimidated by the sight of him now, the perfect naked male form. A man who looked like Mick must be used to supermodel partners in bed. Certainly not barely-B cup real estate agents who go to the gym once every third full moon.

He must have detected her wariness as he undid the final button on her shirt and moved his attention to the red lace bra she had worn just for the occasion. His fingertips traced the outline of her nipples through the tantalizing lace. "So beautiful," he said, their eyes meeting as he pulled away the lace and took her in his mouth.

"Oh, God," she moaned in ecstasy, arching toward him as both breasts were freed from the tight lace. Sucking and caressing, his slick tongue moved in intricate patterns over her nipples. His mouth moved lower on a path down her belly, pausing to dip his tongue into her navel. Her vision suddenly foggy, she only heard the sound of her zipper lowering and felt him pull her pants gently from her legs.

He groaned, trying to maintain control as he saw the small red triangle of lace that greeted him. His hand journeyed to her butt and he smiled at the feel of his hands on nothing but flesh. "You wore a lace thong the entire plane trip for me? I'm indebted."

She let out a small laugh. "It's itchy on a long trip, too."

"Let me help your itch then," he said, kissing her mound as he pulled the tiny fabric from her.

Now lightheaded, her soft purr turned more to a cry while his fingers toyed with her, finding her moist and throbbing. His tongue teased her as the light graze of his teeth against her clit made her breath catch in her throat. "Please, Mick. *Now.*"

He gave only a slight shake of his head. "Payback, remember?" he said as he slipped a second finger into her moist heat.

No longer able to suppress the climax, her body spasmed, starting at her heated core and radiating outward in powerful waves, till even the tips of her fingers were alive with sensation. She threw her head back and cried out his name, wondering how she ever could have preferred a pint of Ben & Jerry's to this.

Lacey thought her body might relax for a moment. But it didn't, immediately climbing to new heights as Mick's hands and mouth kneaded her, moving over her, up her, and down her again. She cried out again, almost in pain from her own uncontrollable need. She wanted him inside her desperately.

"I need you. Please, Mick. Now."

At last, he gave in to his own lust, quickly reaching for a condom and then sliding into her, joining his passion with hers. He thrust inside her slowly at first, her own body adjusting to accommodate his size.

Nibbling on her breasts, his thrusts quickened against his own will, and he became even harder, causing her to cry out from the tantalizing pressure. Digging her fingers into him, she tugged on the maze of muscles on his back to pull him deeper into her.

Twisted in the sheets, they rolled to the other side of the

bed—her on top, then him again, and one more roll that sent them tumbling to the ground.

Their bodies slick with moisture, eyes wild with raw need, Mick was on top again and Lacey's body responded, climbing again to another peak. She met his rhythm, rocking her hips urgently, demanding satisfaction. She cried out a final time and felt her own release as he exploded inside of her.

Mick collapsed on top of her for a moment, and then moved them both to their sides, brushing a small lock of hair from Lacey's eyes.

"You okay?" he asked.

"Mm," she murmured quietly, pliant as Jell-O, with barely a trace of breath left in her body. Despite their awkward location on the floor, she had no interest in moving a muscle.

"If I had any idea we'd end up like this, I would have vacuumed," he laughed as he shifted his arm to prop up his head.

Lacey grinned lazily. "You don't hear me complaining."

Mick traced the line of her jaw with the top of his hand. "God, you are beautiful."

"I'd return the compliment, but I don't think I could adequately come up with one word to describe your body," she said, stroking the curved muscles in his shoulders and arms appreciatively.

He smiled, cupping her chin in his hand. "No. I mean you are beautiful in *every* way." He kissed her gently. "Your body, yes." Another kiss. "But also your face." A kiss. "Your smile." Another.

His kisses moved slowly from her mouth to her shoulders, making a seductive path along her collarbone, as he continued to list every attribute he could think of. Lacey was surprised by how many he could name.

"There's the way you care about your friends and family. Also beautiful." He kissed her again.

"Your laugh," he continued with the light touch of his lips now moving toward her breasts. Her back arched. He smiled at the way her body reacted so automatically. "The way you look in those stilettos."

Their bodies pressed together, she felt him harden at the image. Lacey's eyes widened. "Already? I didn't know that was even possible."

He ignored her comment, silencing her with his lips. "The way you make my body respond. Beautiful…"

CHAPTER 16

A beam of light peeked through the drawn curtains and passed across Lacey's closed eyes. She awoke confused by her surroundings, half melted into an unfamiliar bed, her body still humming from a night of lovemaking.

Remembering, she smiled with what little energy she could muster and reached over to the still warm part of the bed where Mick had left his impression. And what an impression.

Wishing he was still there, she rose to search for something to wear. Granted, Mick had familiarized himself with every square inch of her body the night before, but she didn't have the confidence to display it so easily in the unforgiving morning light.

She gave the room around her a quick appraisal, something she hadn't had a moment to do while Mick was stealing her full attention all night. Neat as a pin except for the unmade bed, but stark. Some pins and medals were left on top of the dresser, as well as two hardcover books that seemed to be about naval battles of some sort, from what she could gather from the titles.

There was no excess here. He was a man who could move across the country in the blink of an eye without looking back.

Her smiled faded at the thought of time wasted, as she peered out the window to the Academy's parade ground. Touching the glass, she felt an unseasonable warmth that seemed more fitting for September than for late November. But she knew it would not last. Annapolis's weather was a constant tease, and the harsh chill of winter was around the corner.

Why had she wasted an entire season fighting her feelings for Mick? She felt foolish for all the times she had longed to be held in his arms, but had pulled herself back, thinking that her career would somehow blossom if she deprived herself of any pleasant distraction.

Time passed too quickly, and Mick would eagerly leave Annapolis given the right opportunity with the Navy. She had to enjoy each moment with him while she could.

Daring herself to venture into his drawers, she discovered a neatly folded stack of his familiar PT gear. She pulled on a t-shirt and cinched his shorts so that they hung low on her waist. She jumped at the sound of her cell phone, and dug for it in the pocket of yesterday's jacket. "Morning, Maeve."

"Hey, Lacey. On your way to the airport?"

"Well, not really. I flew standby yesterday and came home early."

"You're upstairs? God, I didn't even hear you come in. Get your lazy butt down here. Bess made coffeecake."

"I'm not in my room."

Pause. "Okay. Well, where are you?"

"At Mick's."

"Oh my God!" Maeve shouted into the phone and then called out to Bess, "They finally did it, Bess!"

Lacey heard Bess's unmistakable "Woohoo!" in the background.

"Oh, come on, guys. You're acting like you're in high school," Lacey admonished.

"Shut up. We need to have some fun over here. So how was he?"

Lacey exhaled, low and slow, trying to come up with the right words.

Maeve didn't give her the time to answer. "That good, huh? I figured he would be. I think the career can take a backseat to skills like that."

"My career's not taking a backseat, Maeve."

"Fine, then, you can put Mick in the backseat. Hm, there's a thought."

"Seriously, Maeve, I'm counting on you and Bess to help me stay focused. I just realized that depriving myself of someone I'm this attracted to might not be helping my career at all." She filled her in on the details of Vi's surprise engagement and finished with a sigh. "So that's it. And Mick is the perfect relationship for me, if you think about it. He's out of here in a year or so. Knowing that will help keep my head out of the clouds."

"Hey, do you think he'll keep mowing the lawn next spring if you guys are still together?"

Lacey didn't dignify that with a reply. "Later, Maeve. Oh, and save me a piece of coffeecake."

She turned off her phone just as she heard Maeve mutter, "In your dreams."

Behind her, the floor creaked and she turned to see Mick, looking formidable and adorable at the same time, wearing nothing but boxers and holding a breakfast tray. Her blood stirred. "Hi," she said breathlessly.

Mick emitted a low whistle at the sight of Lacey in his PT

gear. "Morning. I wanted to serve you breakfast in bed, but I guess I wasn't fast enough."

Lacey's eyes danced. "I can remedy that." Tossing her phone onto a heap of yesterday's clothes, she jumped into the center of his bed.

Raising an eyebrow, he set the tray on the bedside table. "The eggs will keep." Lowering his body over hers, his kiss was full of hunger as he grasped her hands to her sides so that she was barely able to move.

She loved the taste of him. The feel of his mouth on hers filled every crevice of her soul.

He pulled back and gazed at her warmly. "God, you're beautiful in the morning."

"You must be kidding."

He dove into her mouth again and angled his body on hers so that she could feel his rock-hard response against her. "Obviously, I'm not kidding," he murmured as his mouth left hers and traveled down to the gentle curve of her neck. Slowly, patiently, his fingers traveled to where she was already moist and aching for him. He probed gently into her heat.

Lacey drew in a sharp breath from the welcome invasion, and her body arched sharply to meet the pressure of his hand against her.

"That's it, baby," he whispered in her ear. "I love seeing you this way." When his finger pulled out, she let out a small protest, but then his hands pulled her legs apart, and his mouth tasted her.

Something about the morning light pouring in made Lacey feel so exposed. "Oh, Mick. Not now. It's just—"

She couldn't complete her thought as her body writhed in involuntary ecstasy. His fingers and tongue sent her soaring upward until she cried out in a release that had her floating, free-fall, back to reality.

He smiled in satisfaction.

Her body flushed, she purred, "Somehow starting my morning with just coffee won't be quite as satisfying as this."

"Fortunately for you, I'm available most mornings," Mick replied, deftly pulling off his boxers and reaching for the box of condoms.

Lacey smiled and pressed her hands against his shoulders, urging him to lay back and let her straddle him. He groaned as she grabbed him and sank down onto the full length of him. Still fascinated by the hard ripples of muscle, she traced her hands down his chest, and he throbbed in response to her light touch, aching for release. Watching her hair fall upon him as she rode him, she quivered when his mouth grabbed her breast. His hand reached for her other breast and he kneaded, gently at first, then with force, until her eyes fell to half-mast.

Swiftly he flipped her onto her back and thrust, consuming her with each passing moment, until finally he claimed her again, sending her senses reeling with release.

It could have been minutes that passed in silence, or it could have been hours. Their bodies, slick with sweat, had melted into each other, lost in a tangle of limbs and sheets. It was Mick who first lifted his head to notice the absence of steam rising from the coffee that awaited Lacey.

"I think I'll have to get you some fresh coffee."

"Don't worry about it. It was worth the sacrifice," Lacey said, her hands sliding up his sinuous arms and then tracing the contours of his body.

"No, really," Mick insisted, pulling back. "I'll bring you some more. And I'll make some fresh eggs."

She felt a chill in the room as his warm body left hers. Suddenly feeling awkward, she pulled a sheet over her, sensing tension in the room. He slipped his boxers back on and reached for the breakfast tray.

Heading out of the bedroom, he glanced over his shoulder. His eyes were guarded, but his smile was warm. "Come to think of it, maybe you better come downstairs to eat. Or we might be sacrificing a few more eggs before noon."

Stepping into the kitchen, Mick had to consciously slow his breathing. He gripped the arch of the entryway to steady himself.

What the hell was happening to him? Sure, his body had been quick to respond to women before, but this was different. Much more disturbing. He liked feeling in control in relationships. But with Lacey, he was powerless.

He couldn't be in love with her, he thought, remembering his conversation with Jack. Love was not part of his life plan. At least not for five years or so.

How could he let himself get in this position? She literally had him by the balls. And what was even more endearing was that she didn't even know it. Just moments ago, he could see the questions in her eyes as she lay there in his bed. It killed him that he couldn't give her any answers. There was a part of him that wanted to climb back into bed with her and assure her that he would be there for her every morning of her life with such a satisfying wake-up call.

But he couldn't tell her that. There couldn't be a happily-ever-after for them.

He knew what happened to women like Lacey after sex. Suddenly, the hormones kick in and they start tearing out pictures of wedding gowns, cooing over babies, and sizing up minivans. Mick couldn't give her any of that. He had seen too many marriages fail and families shattered by the stress of Navy life, much less that of a SEAL. Some won the battle, but too many were casualties.

Until now, he had never considered that the risk might be worth taking.

No. Lacey deserved better than a high-risk relationship.

Venting his frustration on a half dozen eggs, he smashed them against the side of a bowl full-force and beat them mercilessly with a whisk.

How ironic that he stands in front of classes of mids every day droning on about honor, duty, integrity. What the hell was the honorable thing to do in a situation like this?

Break it off now?

Break it off in eighteen months or so?

Above the sizzle of the eggs cooking on the stove, Mick heard Lacey behind him. "I think you've beaten any life out of those eggs," she said awkwardly.

Glancing down, Mick saw spatters of egg on the wall alongside him. Silently, he slid them out of the pan and onto a plate. His eyes couldn't meet hers.

"So what's on your mind, Mick? Was this was a mistake?"

Tentatively, he turned to her and took her hand. Her fingers were like ice. "Is that what you think?"

"You tell me."

Mick drew in a breath, and then involuntarily let out a little laugh. "I can't imagine sex that great could ever be a mistake."

Lacey smiled, and Mick saw some of the tension leave her body.

"Lacey, I'm just terrified that I may have used you."

She burst out laughing.

Mick was puzzled. "That's funny?"

"Yes. I show up on your doorstep begging for sex, and you think you used *me*?"

Relief washed over Mick at the memory. "You *were* the instigator of this, weren't you? That makes me feel better." He shook his head in reprimand. "No. I'm your friend and you were vulnerable. You were upset about your sister and maybe you really just needed to talk it out."

"Uh, no, Mick. If I had wanted to talk it out, I would have gone home to Maeve and Bess. What I needed—whether I knew it or not—was to have at least fourteen sequential orgasms in the span of one night of sex."

Mick actually felt his face flush. "Fourteen? I guess I must have missed one or two."

Lacey just smiled in answer.

He cleared his throat. "So I guess the only question is, how frequently you might need this service again?"

"Are you volunteering?"

"Hell, yeah. Look, you know the deal with me better than any woman I've ever known. You know where I'm headed and just how little I can offer you in the future. But right now, you have me." He took her face in his hands. "You have my full commitment. If you want it, that is."

Lacey's eyes shone brightly against the smudges of yesterday's mascara. "I want it. My career is still the first priority to me. Maybe a relationship with you—with the full knowledge that it's leading nowhere—is the only kind I can handle right now."

Mick pulled her onto his lap and enjoyed the feeling of having her so close.

She snuggled into him. "God, I'm trying to build a real estate career here. I'd be the last person to want to have a long-term relationship with a Navy guy who is only going to expect me to move. I'd be kissing my career good-bye."

Mick felt the oddest mixture of relief and disappointment at her words. He had dreaded the idea of her broken heart, but hadn't fully considered the possibility of his own.

He soothed his confusion by pressing a firm kiss against her lips. "Then we're okay?"

Biting her lip, Lacey nodded.

"Good, because I'm not sure which I'd miss more. The friendship or the sex." Mick kissed her again thoroughly, tangling his hands in her silky hair and felt his own body respond. "Mm. I think I know which now."

The subtle movements of her lithe body as she sat on his lap nearly sent him over the edge as she pulled his mouth back to her own. One eye open, he glanced at the plate of eggs on the counter.

Hell with it, he decided. The eggs could wait.

Again.

CHAPTER 17

Cozy in front of Maeve's fireplace, Mick watched Lacey carefully place her T, E, and R tiles on the game board. "Wetter," she said, her eyes locked on Mick's.

"Mm." Mick responded, his knowing eyes glimmering in the firelight. He pulled three tiles from his own stash. "How about this one? Suck." His meaning was apparent.

Lacey practically purred a response, ignoring the presence of their friends.

Maeve groaned. "Oh, *God*. Will you two stop?"

Jack took an angry chug of his beer. "Suck. Yeah, this sucks all right. If you want a room, go upstairs, will you? Some of us are trying to play a serious game here."

Mick looked at Jack innocently. "I don't know what you're talking about."

Maeve glanced down at the board, reading some of Lacey and Mick's latest additions. "Suck. Wet. Big. Lucky. If I wanted to play Scrabble with a couple teenagers, I'd call the kids down the street."

"Okay, okay," Lacey conceded. "We'll keep our hidden meanings to ourselves."

"Yes, puh-lease," Jack said with vigor adding E and T tiles to the word "ball."

Mick shook his head. "*Ballet*? Okay, Nancy-boy. Guess that girlfriend of yours took your balls with her when she left."

"You're not dating Lisa anymore?" Maeve asked lightly.

"*Lissa*," Jack corrected her pronunciation for the umpteenth time. "She dumped me last week. She thought I was dating someone else, which I wasn't. Total paranoid."

"Why would she think you were dating someone else?"

"I talk in my sleep. Guess I said a name that wasn't hers."

Maeve snorted.

Mick rose to check out the snow falling outside, and leaned against the doorway leading to Maeve's addition. The room's paned windows looked out to a winter-blooming magnolia, and Mick could picture Bess's child seeing her first snow fall here next year. For a brief moment, he dared wonder what it would feel like to have a home of his own, one he intended to fill with a lifetime of firsts for a child, rather than the kind of home he left without looking back.

His eyes wandered to Lacey, and a strange tug gripped his heart. The Navy was the only family he could have right now. "You better watch that sleep-talking with your security clearance, Jack. Don't want to say something you shouldn't."

Jack shrugged. "I don't think Lissa would understand anything I said about nuclear engineering, anyway."

"She didn't seem too bright," Bess agreed.

"When did you meet her?" Lacey asked.

"I bumped into them at The Buzz once."

"I've never been there," Mick said blankly.

Lacey grinned. "You're too old. It's where twenty-something singles go to get coffee. I don't think they let you in if you're over thirty."

Laughing, Bess patted her belly. "Yeah, I'm the only pregnant woman I've ever seen there. I can't even drink the coffee —it's way too caffeinated for me now—but I love just smelling it." She added a P to "lucky."

"Plucky," Jack nodded solemnly. "Not bad."

Lacey sighed as she finished off a two-letter word. "I should tell you that I had the letters to make the word 'hard,' but I'm sparing you all since you're overly sensitive tonight. Does anyone need anything from the kitchen?" she asked, waggling her empty soda can.

Bess reached over to hand her an empty glass. "More juice, please."

"As if she doesn't pee often enough," Jack said with a sidelong glance to Maeve.

Still leaning on the doorframe, Mick gave a little backwards nod toward the addition with its bare drywall still exposed. "Your office is really coming along, Maeve. But when are you going to paint it?" He would never let it slip around Bess that the space was destined to be a surprise nursery. Still, he couldn't help tease Maeve.

"Still can't decide on a color," she responded, sending him a cryptic glare. She kept her eyes locked with his until Lacey was out of the room. "Choosing a color is a commitment, Mick. What color are your walls?"

Mick's stony expression made it clear he heard Maeve's real meaning. "My walls are white. Same color as they were when I moved in. Guess I have a hard time making a commitment."

Maeve's eyes drilled holes into Mick as he sat back down on the couch. "I don't want to see Lacey get hurt."

He picked up three letter tiles. "I don't want that either."

"Look. I think you're great. I think you're great together. But I love her like a sister. She needs something lasting, and you know you're not it. Don't lead her on."

"I'm not, and I won't." Raising his head, he looked at her pointedly.

Jack's cheery voice broke in. "You know, in his defense, officers aren't actually allowed to paint the rooms in those houses in the Yard."

Mick looked down at the tiles in his hand, seeming to hesitate before adding them to the board. Then, giving a nearly imperceptible shrug, he placed them on the board.

Maeve, Bess, and Jack looked down at the board at the three tiles Mick had added to the L. The tiles spelled "love."

Maeve and Bess glanced at each other, their eyes wide.

"Interesting word choice," Bess said in a near whisper.

"Damn. That V's on a triple letter square," Jack commented.

Maeve shot Jack a look. "You're so oblivious."

"No, he's so *right*." Mick rose to help Lacey in the kitchen. "Fifteen points, Maeve. And stop thinking so damn much."

Stepping through the doorway, Mick saw Lacey stooped over an open dishwasher, steam already frizzing the hair that had fallen from her ponytail. "Let me help," he said, stacking several clean plates from the washer and putting them in the cabinet.

"Thanks." Lacey passed a handful of forks to him. Mick reached for them, and held her hand for a moment, frozen, wondering how the simple act of emptying a dishwasher could seem to intimate.

"What?" Lacey's eyes met his.

He held her gaze, at loss for words, then shook his head. "We should have gone out to eat again tonight."

"Why?"

"Call me selfish, but I'd rather be alone with you."

Laughing, Lacey nudged him aside as she reached for the refrigerator door. "You've taken me out three times this week already. I'm gaining weight from all the restaurant food.

Besides, we've been neglecting our friends." She poured orange juice into Bess's glass. "And call *me* selfish, but sharing you with a restaurant full of people is a lot less private than playing Scrabble here."

Standing behind her as she put the juice back in the refrigerator, Mick rested his hands along her waist and pressed his body to hers, hoping she could feel just how deeply he wanted her right now. "You're right. How about I make you dinner tomorrow night? It will have to be chili. Extra spicy." With a devilish grin, he turned her by her shoulders and pulled her close again.

Standing tiptoe to raise her lips less than an inch from his, her eyes sparkled. "The hotter, the better," she whispered, and tasted him.

Amid a sea of pillows, Lacey rested her head on Mick's chest, listening to the slow beating of his heart as he stroked her hair.

Pure bliss, Lacey decided, savoring the simple pleasure of having her skin pressed against his. Almost as satisfying as the sex she had been enjoying just moments before.

Almost.

Mick traced the skin along her collarbone and down her arm, and then lifted her hand to his lips. "Maeve's worried about you and me."

Lacey raised her head. "Did she say something?"

"Mm, yeah. Earlier tonight. Told me I better not lead you on. I'm not doing that, am I?"

"God, no, Mick. You've been completely straightforward. I'll talk to her." She eased back into the center of his broad chest and caressed the muscles that spanned out to his arms.

"I know you're not wanting anything that extends past this job and I'm fine with that."

"You are?"

"Of course."

Beneath her, Mick shifted his weight in the plush mattress. "So you wouldn't want to try to extend this after I get orders to go someplace else? You haven't thought about that at all?"

"Not a bit."

"Okay." There was a brief silence. "I need something to eat. Want something?"

"Some water would be great," Lacey said, suddenly anxious to be alone to gather her thoughts. She watched him pull on some shorts and leave the bedroom.

Liar! she thought the moment he walked out the door. *What a liar I am!* She drew up her knees and hugged herself, somehow needing the comfort of the human touch, even if it was only her own. She could hear the creaking of the staircase as he went downstairs, and found herself feeling more alone with each step he took.

Liar.

A life with Mick was *all* she had thought about from the moment their bodies had first joined. Every moment spent with him, she was wondering in the back of her mind how she could possibly stand the emptiness when he left her.

Was this love? Lacey knew she loved him as a friend, but was it the type of love that two people built a life—a world—around?

Was it that elusive love that seemed to reach beyond definition? The kind that made two people grow old together, watching sunsets and holdings hands, blind to the gray hairs and wrinkles, like Maeve had always described her grandparents?

Lacey let out a little snort. What did it matter? He was leaving anyway.

She was lying to herself and to him every time she promised that she'd be fine after he left. She'd be a basket case. Lacey slapped her thigh. This was exactly why she had told herself not to get into a relationship while she was building a career this time. Because everything would fall apart when Mick left.

And he *would* leave, she thought remorsefully, even angrily, as she looked over at the medals he always left scattered on his dresser. It was the Navy first with Mick.

Fine. Two could play at that game. If she was going to fall apart when he left, then she better build a hell of a strong career before then so that it could survive the blow of his departure.

Maybe it was time for her to overcompensate a bit—work even harder at her job just to prepare for future pitfalls. She knew just how to get started, remembering the funeral tomorrow morning that Bess had read about in the obituaries.

She grabbed her clothes and started getting dressed just as Mick walked into the room.

"I thought you were staying the night."

"I can't, Mick. I remembered something I have to do for work tomorrow morning. I'm sorry, but it's really important."

"Is it something I can help with?"

"No. But thanks." She kissed him, savoring the feel of his lips against hers.

Yes, she might not survive when he left her. But, by God, her career would.

CHAPTER 18

Alone in the kitchen, Bess clicked the button on Maeve's phone and looked at the caller ID.

Unknown name. Unknown number.

Not that unusual, she consoled herself. But something about the voice had sent a chill down her spine. It wasn't Dan on the other end. It didn't sound like him. Besides, Dan wouldn't be asking for Lacey.

She gave herself a little shake and dipped her spoon again into the brown sugar bag. She swore that she could feel the enamel on her teeth rotting away, but she didn't care. When she saw the fresh bag in the cabinet, it was calling her.

Giving in completely, she moved her sugar feast to the kitchen table wishing she had thought to get a glass of milk before she sat down. Getting out of a chair was getting harder these days.

Lacey walked into the kitchen, face curled up in revulsion. "I've never seen anyone eat raw brown sugar before."

"Cut me some slack. I'm pregnant."

"I'll bet you used to do that before you were pregnant."

Bess grinned. "You're right. Hey, someone just called for

you. I offered to take a message, but he said he'd call you on your cell."

"Huh." Lacey pulled out her phone and checked for messages. "Didn't get any calls. What's the caller ID say?"

"Unknown name. Unknown number."

Lacey shrugged. "Oh well. He'll probably call later. You're home early today."

"My afternoon house cancelled because one of the kids is sick. They didn't want me to catch something. Would you mind getting me some milk?"

Lacey pulled a glass from the cabinet. "That was nice of them to tell you."

Bess nodded, patting her belly. "Yeah. Gotta stay as healthy as I can."

"Eating nutritious things like raw brown sugar," Lacey finished for her.

"Hey, no additives. A pure snack."

Lacey sat down and kicked off her heels. "Explain that to your dentist."

"How about you? Why are you home early?"

"I was at a funeral. Didn't make sense to bother going into the office after."

"That's your second one this week," Bess noted.

"A lot of rich people seem to die in the winter." Lacey sighed. "But it looks like I got a waterfront listing out of a funeral I went to last month."

"Really? That's great!"

Lacey pulled her hair out of its clip. "Not just great—fantastic. It's right on the Bay in a gated community. If I can sell this one, it will be more than I've made in an entire year in my life," she said, putting particular emphasis on the last three words. "I'm meeting with the homeowner tomorrow morning to sign the papers. It was her mom that passed away —ninety-seven years old, and she had been living with her for years, taking care of her. So now she's selling the house and moving to Hawaii."

"Hawaii?"

"Yep. It's been her lifelong dream. She's so excited. Nice to sort of see a happy ending come from a funeral I crashed for a change." She stretched out her legs in front of her. "Mick is taking me out to celebrate tonight. What are you up to?"

"I'm going to the mall to buy a crib, if I can just get the energy."

Lacey's face froze. "Really. Hmm. Well, which one did you pick out?"

"The most utilitarian one," Bess said with a bit of a scowl.

"Oh, you mean the cheapest."

Bess sighed. "Yeah. But it will do the trick."

Lacey's voice was strangely uneasy. "Um, why not join us for dinner instead? Mick's buying, you know. You can really soak him."

Bess laughed. "Thanks, no. I have to get this done. I have so little energy after a day of work, and it's only going to get worse."

Lacey all but physically blocked her path out of the kitchen. "Well, if you know what style you want, why don't you just show me online, and I can pick it up for you?"

"It's too much trouble."

"It's no trouble at all, Bess. Really. You need to get rest when you can."

Bess paused. They really were too protective of her. But her puffy feet stretching her old Nikes to capacity prodded her to say, "You really wouldn't mind?"

"I love any excuse to go shopping. Besides, I have to go check out the baby stuff if I'm going to find something cute for the little girl when she gets here."

"You guys really don't have to get us anything. We'll be fine on our own."

Lacey rolled her eyes. "Will you quit it? You've already made us swear we won't throw you a baby shower. You better not deprive us of doing a little baby shopping."

Tears filled Bess's eyes. "I really don't deserve you guys."

"Oh, honey," Lacey said, her voice catching. "Yes, you do. Yes, you really do."

"So tell me all about the possible listing." Mick's grin was wide, as he took her hand in both of his.

Sitting side by side in the secluded high-backed booth of a dimly lit restaurant, they were hidden enough from other patrons that Lacey was tempted to curl up on his lap.

"It's gorgeous. Waterfront. Gated community." Lacey shook her head, still unable to believe her own good fortune. "People will be clamoring for it. The properties in this community just don't come on the market that often."

"So how did she find you?"

Lacey's heart nearly stopped. "I'm sorry. What?"

"How did you get the client? Was it a referral or something?"

Unable to lie, she blurted, "You know, I really shouldn't even talk about it until the contract is signed tomorrow. I might jinx it."

Mick shook his head with a smirk. "You're so superstitious."

"Can't help it." Lacey attempted to smile.

"Well, contract or not, you should be proud she even called you. Your name is obviously getting out there."

And you have no idea how, Lacey thought grimly, fighting the urge to come clean.

"Your career is really taking shape," Mick continued, rubbing her hand with pride, apparently unaware of the moral war waging in Lacey's head.

"And how about you?" Tugging her hand free and reaching for her wine glass, Lacey tried to divert attention from herself. The guilt was suffocating. "How are your plans shaping up to get you back on the road to San Diego?"

Mick gave a slight nod of thanks to the waitress as she put the cheese fondue in front of them. "Actually," he began, refilling Lacey's glass from the half-empty bottle of wine, "I may have some good news myself before the school year is out."

"Really?"

"There's an Admiral I knew when I was stationed in Rhode Island. He's in Qatar now, but heading to the Pentagon in a couple months to do some briefs. We've got dinner on the schedule." Mick took a sip of his drink. "I'm hoping he might be able to pull a few strings and get me out of this job early and into something better for my career."

"Like in San Diego?" Lacey's heart was sinking.

"Not likely there right away. But he needs an EA in Qatar for the rest of his tour there. And that will look a hell of a lot better on my résumé than what I'm doing now."

Lacey pressed her lips together. She knew he'd be going. This shouldn't come as a surprise to her. "That would be great, Mick," she said, forcing a smile. "I have to admit. I was getting pretty used to having you close by, though."

He took her hand. "Qatar wouldn't be long. No more than a year. Then I'd be back stateside, hopefully on the West Coast. We could—"

She pulled her hand from his. "Stop, Mick. We both knew where this was going. I don't need patronizing. I'm going to be so busy with business, I'll barely notice you're gone."

Mick frowned slightly. "I hope you'll notice a little."

"Of course I will. We'll still email and get together anytime we can. We promised we'd keep the friendship going, right?"

"Right," Mick responded, his brow furrowed as he reached for a chunk of bread. "Besides it's too early to think about it right now. I haven't even talked to him yet."

"Exactly," Lacey agreed. She took a hearty sip of her wine, as though to fortify herself against the feelings welling up inside her.

He's leaving. A timely reminder. Just as she was debating whether to confess the funeral crashing scheme that had brought him into her life.

That would have been foolish, she could hear Vi's voice saying. Even though Mick would not vindictively undermine her career, he would feel obligated to at least tell Edith. And one slip from her to one of her well-connected friends, and Lacey's entire career could shatter to pieces.

Maeve glanced up when she heard the door open. "I thought you were staying the night at Mick's."

"Changed my mind," Lacey said, trying to sound indifferent.

Maeve raised her eyebrows. "Trouble?"

"No. Just confusion."

"Ah. That I can relate to," she said, turning so that Lacey could see the oil painting she was holding in her hands. "What do you think of it?"

Lacey struggled to not cringe. "Um. What is it?"

"Well, I was so inspired by that ultrasound—excited, really. So I commissioned my favorite artist to do a rendering in pink to match the room."

"That was... thoughtful, Maeve."

"But it's hideous. Go ahead and say it. I mean, God—it looks like a pink alien swimming in plasma." Maeve cracked a smile and burst out laughing as her eyes met Lacey's.

"It is disgusting. You aren't going to give it to her, are you?"

"Not a chance. It might throw Bess into premature labor or something. I feel a migraine coming on just looking at it. I'll probably store it until the kid is a teenager. When she's sixteen she'll think it's cool." She set the painting down on the ground with a sigh. "At least that crib I ordered is a show-stopper. It arrived at Jack's place this afternoon. It'll really be the centerpiece of the room."

"So Bess is asleep, I take it?"

"Out like a light." Maeve sat on the couch and held out a plate of chips. "So, you want to talk about it?"

Lacey sat, accepting a handful. "I think it was easier just being his friend."

"That's not how I remember it."

"You're right. It was never easy with him was it?" Lacey sighed. "Every time I'm around him, I feel like I'm losing sight of what's important."

"So? What's important?"

"My career, right now," she replied as though trying to convince herself. "But after just ten minutes with him, I feel tempted to throw away my career and follow him wherever the Navy sends him next. Or beg him to take me along, in my case."

"I don't think that would be a hard sell."

Lacey shook her head, reaching for another chip. "He's made it clear that his career comes first and settling down is not in the picture for him right now."

"Sounds like the same thing you keep telling him."

Lacey looked at her blankly.

"So *maybe* he's as conflicted as you are, Lacey."

Exasperated, Lacey threw her head back on the couch's down pillows.

Maeve shook her head and laughed. "Oh, Lacey. Stop over-thinking and just enjoy today. You don't know how lucky you are to have it."

CHAPTER 19

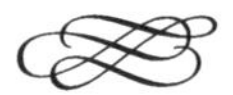

It was too cold for a tour of the Naval Academy, Lacey was reminded again by a gust of cold air as Mick held the door open for her. But, catching a sideward glance of him, she decided spending the afternoon with Mick made it worthwhile. Even the slight brush of her bare hand against his uniform as she passed warmed her to her toes.

"So his dead body is really in there?" Stepping out of John Paul Jones's tomb, Maeve curled her lip.

"It's no different than in a graveyard," Lacey noted, linking her hand in Mick's offered arm as they walked around the side of the Chapel.

"Well, it's something I could have lived without seeing. What's with the dolphins on the casket?"

"Symbolic of the sea. He was a great Navy hero, Maeve," Mick explained with clearly diminishing patience. He gave a salute as a Captain walked past them.

Maeve perked up visibly, giving the passing man an appraisal as she started up the long staircase to the Chapel doors. Letting out a heated breath, she leaned into Lacey's ear. "What is it about those uniforms? Do they starch them in pheromones?"

Lacey laughed, finally realizing the real reason Maeve had begged for a tour of the Academy. Lacey should have known it had nothing to do with interest in architecture or history. She glanced over at Bess, trailing behind them. "You okay, Bess? You're so quiet."

Mick stopped at the Chapel doors and shot Lacey a questioning look.

"Her blood pressure was up a bit at her last check-up," Lacey explained.

"We can stop here and do the rest of the tour on another day," Mick offered.

Bess wrapped her coat tightly around her as a breeze whistled through the barren limbs of the tall oaks on the Yard. "I'm just tired. Is there someplace I can get some juice?"

"Of course. We can head to the Officers' Club."

Bess glanced down the daunting staircase she had just climbed. "Well, let's see the Chapel first, since we're already here."

Mick swung the door open just as a young man in uniform was leaving the building.

"Sir." The man offered a quick salute.

"Cadet Griffon," Mick greeted him.

"Glad to see you, Sir. I enjoyed your class on mixed martial arts last week. I plan to enter Ranger School when I graduate, so was happy for the training by someone in the SEALs."

"Excellent. I know several Rangers. Stop by my office next week, and I'll get you some contacts."

"I'd appreciate that, Sir."

"Forgive me, ladies." Mick's tone was formal. "This is Cadet Tyler Griffon. He is a visiting cadet from West Point for the semester."

The young man flashed a smile and shook their hands.

"Griffon, this is Lacey Owens, Bess Foster, and Maeve Fischer. Are you headed by the Officers' Club or steerage?"

"Yes, Sir."

Mick reached into his pocket and handed the Cadet some bills. "Would you mind bringing back Bess a bottle of orange juice? She's a little peaked."

"My pleasure, Sir," he responded amicably, glancing down at Bess's belly. "Ma'am, congratulations. My sister is pregnant now, too."

Bess just smiled weakly in response.

"So how far along are you, Ma'am?"

"Closing in on six months."

"Wonderful. I'll be back with some orange juice before the Commander is finished with your tour of the Chapel."

"Thank you, Griffon," Mick said, dismissing him with a salute.

Entering the quiet warmth of the Chapel, Bess let out a soft sigh that only Lacey seemed to hear.

"Mick, why don't you give Maeve the tour? Bess and I can sit down here and catch our breath," Lacey suggested.

"You're sure?"

Lacey nodded.

"Just give us the heads-up if you want to go home, Bess," Maeve said, eyeing her friend.

"No, I'm fine. Go." Bess said quietly, sitting in a nearby pew. She glanced at Lacey. "You should go too, Lacey. I'm capable of sitting here without a chaperone."

"Which is more than we can say for Maeve in this place," Lacey noted, tossing her chin in Maeve's direction as they witnessed her head turning appraisingly every time a sailor walked by.

Both women shook their heads.

Lacey's eyes rested on Bess. "You okay?"

"Just tired, like I said."

"No, I mean, you seem a little down suddenly."

Bess let out an awkward laugh. Then she quickly looked away, her eyes welling up.

"What is it, Bess?"

"I don't know. He was probably my age, you know? That cadet. Or close to it." She paused, reflecting. "And well, he's really cute, isn't he? So here I am, wishing a guy like that would ask me for my number—and instead he asks how far along I am. How could I not be depressed by that?"

"You won't be pregnant forever."

"But I'll be a mom forever. An unmarried mom. Let's face it. I'm not like other people my age. They're all out meeting people and going to parties and dating. And here I am, hiding out from an abusive ex, scrubbing floors for a living, and worrying about stretch marks."

Lacey shifted fully toward her. "Look, I know it might seem like everyone your age is having a blast. But believe me, they aren't. When I was your age, I was too busy job-hopping to be at parties or do much dating. That's how *I* spent my twenties."

Bess wiped her nose unapologetically on her coat sleeve. "You're right. I just keep feeling like everyone my age is having a decade-long party that I'm not invited to."

"I used to feel the same way." Lacey glanced over her shoulder to make sure the cadet had not yet returned. "You *are* right, though. That guy is smoking hot. Too young for me, so Maeve is obviously not rubbing off on me."

Bess laughed quietly, glancing at Maeve's dumbfounded expression in the distance. "Look at her, Lacey. She's bored out of her mind right now."

Lacey nodded sympathetically. "Mick's droning on about some naval history thing or another. He'll chew her ear off for hours if we let him. He's such a history buff."

Bess gave her arm a playful slap. "But you think he's adorable, everything about him. I can tell."

"Yeah, I do. It's cute how excited he gets. His eyes sort of flash and he rubs his hands together when he is on a topic he really loves." She waited, watching him closely. "See? Like that."

"You know him well."

Lacey watched him move to the next stained glass, Maeve grudgingly in tow.

"Why don't you join them, Lacey? I'm really fine here."

"No. I've been in here before for a funeral."

"Yikes. Better not let that slip out in conversation."

Lacey grimaced. "Don't I know it?"

Bess sat thoughtfully. "Do you ever think you should just fess up about it? I mean, I'll admit, when I first heard what you did, I thought it was a little—um—what's the word?"

"Predatory?"

Bess winced. "Not the word I would have chosen."

"But it's the right word, isn't it?"

Bess ignored the question. "But now that I see all that you do for people at such a difficult time in their lives. All the patience you give them. It's more like you're just offering a specialized type of real estate service. It really might not bother Mick at all. It would be horrible if he found out by accident."

Lacey stared into the distance, surrounded by the guilt-inducing religious images in the Chapel's intricate stained glass windows. It would be easier to have this conversation sitting at the bar in O'Tooles. Slumping in the pew, she knew she couldn't risk the best marketing strategy she had for a man who would only be leaving her, especially now that it was finally paying off.

It was as though Bess had read her mind. "Or maybe you could just take a break from it, Lacey. You know? Until Mick leaves for his next job. Because right now crashing funerals is just making you feel miserable at a time which should really be perfect for you."

"Take a break," Lacey repeated thoughtfully. "Until he leaves me."

"Or however long you want. If business slows down again, you can always go back to it."

"You know, I never really thought of that option. I always just think about whether I should give it up completely. And if I took a break, I could have more time to do some more volunteer work with Edith. It really has been helpful getting my name out there in the right circles."

Bess smiled. "And you could enjoy your time with Mick without this nagging guilt about the way you met."

Lacey's eyes met Maeve's in the distance. They all but screamed, *Rescue me.* "I think we better save Maeve. Her head looks like it's going to explode." She turned to Bess. "You know, you were right about one thing. You're not like other people your age. You're a hell of a lot wiser."

Mick walked briskly across the campus to his office. He hadn't meant to let the day get away from him like that. But they had obviously been so interested in naval history, he might have gotten a little carried away.

He was definitely feeding off their enthusiasm.

It was a shame they had to end the tour on account of Bess's exhaustion. He shook his head, hoping Lacey and Maeve would talk her into cutting back on housecleaning jobs.

For that matter, he wished he could get Lacey to cut back on work, too. It seemed like every weekend she had back-to-back showings and open houses. He kept quiet about it, knowing how important her career was to her. But he couldn't help imagining how nice it would be to spend a lazy Saturday morning with her in bed, or enjoying an afternoon watching mindless television together in front of the fireplace.

It was the holiday season, for God's sake. They should be decorating the house or picking out a tree. Or shopping together.

Shopping together? Did he really just think that? He hated shopping, holidays or not.

He bristled. What was happening to him? There must have been something about seeing Lacey walking up the aisle of the Chapel to him at the end of the tour. The way the light beamed through the stained glass illuminating her dark hair, and making her eyes sparkle. She seemed to glow with a radiance more befitting a…

…bride. He stopped in his tracks, shaking the image of Lacey in white.

Yes, he should definitely avoid walking into that Chapel with her anymore.

He swung open his office door to see Jack hammering away at his keyboard. Jack let out a weary grunt in greeting, a far cry from him snapping to attention as he had once greeted Mick several months ago. "I didn't expect to see you in today, Jack."

"I'm behind in paperwork," Jack responded brusquely.

"Just got done giving the girls a tour."

Jack grumbled something inaudible.

"Had to stop early because Bess got a bit worn out."

No response from Jack.

Mick raised his eyebrows. "She's okay, though. Just some minor blood pressure issues."

Jack answered only with the clicking of his fingers on the keyboard.

Mick sat at his desk. "Then on the way out, Maeve mooned the statue of Vice Admiral Stockdale."

Jack abruptly stopped typing and turned to Mick.

"Had to see if you were even listening." Mick smiled. "Well, you should have come. It was a good tour. They were hanging on my every word."

A snort came from Jack, his face sullen and his fingers pounding keys with a vengeance.

"Are you really backlogged with work, or are you pissed about something? I can't tell."

"Pissed about everything, really. Got a ton of work to get done before we get out of here for the holidays and now my whole damn family wants to have a freaking reunion in Disneyworld this Christmas, which seems like a nightmare to me. Why the hell would I want to waste my time at Disneyworld when I have no wife, no kids, and no interest in talking mice?"

"Might be fun seeing your nieces and nephews enjoy it."

"Then *you* go."

Mick threw his hands up. "Okay, I'll back off."

"Thank you," Jack said with mock gratitude.

Mick sorted through a pile of mail that had accumulated on the desk. He sliced open an envelope that didn't look like the standard military mail. "Huh. What's this?"

Jack glanced over. "Some ball invitation. Don't get excited, Cinderella. I got one, too."

"You going?"

Jack grimaced. "Why the hell would I want to go to another military ball?"

"I hear you there. What's the occasion?"

Jack shrugged. "Who knows? Probably some Four-Star's wife bought a new ball gown and needed someplace to wear it." Sarcasm laced his every word.

Mick shook his head. "You're in a hell of a mood."

Jack grunted.

"So why don't you take that girl you started seeing?"

Jack looked at Mick as though he had grown a horn in the middle of his head. "Why would I do that? A woman goes to a military ball and she suddenly starts thinking she wants to be a military wife. Before you know it, she's dropping hints about her ring size and whether she prefers platinum or gold."

"You're right about that," Mick noted, pondering whether or not it would be a smart idea to invite Lacey. "But then you'd be closer to having those kids to take to Disneyworld with you."

Jack glared, clearly displeased that Mick had figured out why he was really pissed.

Mick stared at the invitation, then tapped it on the side of his wastebasket, debating whether or not to toss it in.

"Are you asking Lacey?" Jack asked, frowning.

Mick set the invitation aside thoughtfully and let the question hang in the office unanswered for the remainder of the afternoon.

CHAPTER 20

Lacey wasn't much of a cook, but with a little coaching from Bess over the phone, even she would admit that the Chicken Parmigiana looked tasty. The aroma of fresh roasted garlic and sautéed onions that hung divinely in the air would be the perfect greeting for Mick.

She felt a familiar charge of anticipation when she heard his key in his front door. Silly, she thought, to still respond that way.

His voice called in from the foyer. "Lacey? You here?"

She appeared, wooden spoon in hand, wearing a tidy apron over her work suit. "I hope you don't mind. I wanted to surprise you with dinner."

"You here is the best surprise I could ever have named. Dinner or not." He loosely wrapped his arms around her waist and met his lips to hers.

"How was your day, dear?" she asked playfully.

"Perfect now." He groaned a bit as he pulled her body full against him. "So what did I do to deserve this, so that I can be sure to do it again?"

Lacey's eyes danced. "Oh, I think it was all those salutes

you got during our tour yesterday. Something about watching people salute you gets me a little…"

"Turned on?" Mick offered helpfully.

"Mmm…"

"So, um, how much longer does it have to cook?"

"It's ready now."

"Damn," he said. "Because so am I. But not for dinner." With that, he kissed her again deeply, tracing his tongue lightly along her teeth and gently teasing her breasts with his light touch as his hands pushed past the apron. "This is like a Doris Day fantasy, you know."

"Really? Aren't you a little young to know anything about Doris Day?"

"Are you kidding? Every guy has his Doris Day fantasies," he said, nimbly untying her apron and lifting it over her head. "The woman was timeless." He planted a trail of kisses down her neck. "She was an icon." He unbuttoned her top three buttons. "She was…" he cupped her breast in his hand and kissed it, "…not nearly as sexy as you are right now."

Lacey whimpered, completely lost to him. Giving in to her own yearnings, she struggled to unbutton his uniform with her one free hand.

The sudden harsh sizzle of water boiling over into the flames had her rushing into the kitchen on pure instinct with Mick following.

"Pasta's ready." Laughter was in Mick's voice.

Lacey let out a sigh of relief seeing her dinner was not ruined. "That was close. Now no more distractions, Commander," she pointed the wooden spoon at him then licked the remains of the sauce from it.

"Then you'll have to stop doing that."

"What?" she said, taking another sample of the sauce.

"That." His eyes were shaded with lust as he eyed the spoon she was lifting to her mouth.

Lacey figured it out. "Oh, you mean this?" Batting her lashes and tracing her tongue along the side of the spoon, she then sank the spoon full into her mouth and let out a seductive purr.

Mick's lashes fell to half-mast. "Now I know why they call it a wooden spoon."

Lacey grinned. "Bad joke. Now sit back and let me serve you."

They managed to get a few bites of the meal in them before Mick swept her into his arms and took her on the rug in front of the fireplace at Lacey's suggestion. The bedroom upstairs seemed too damn far at the time. She had needed to have him inside her, to feel his hands stroking her, caressing her, manipulating her into positions that made her blush even as she lay naked alongside him moments after.

They put another two helpings of the meal on plates and ate them—well, part of them—in front of the fire. But their meals grew cold again as he tempted her once more.

Hours later, they lay satiated in front of the fireplace, keeping warm despite the fading embers.

"I should put another log on," Mick murmured, his face still buried in Lacey's hair.

"Don't go," she objected, not anxious for their bodies to part. She locked her gaze on his in a plea and found herself lost in his steel blue eyes. There was a kind of soft joy in them tonight that made her wonder, even hope, that he was growing to love her, too.

Because yes, she loved him. She laughed a little, imagining Maeve and Bess rubbing it in that they were right. They had known before she did.

Mick smiled, a little warily. "What?"

"Hmm?"

"What's funny? You were laughing a moment ago."

Lacey shook her head dismissively. "Nothing. Just funny how life is sometimes." She adjusted her body to nestle her head against his chest. The reassuring rhythm of his heartbeat lulled her.

Relishing the feel of her skin moving against his, she reached above their heads and pulled the shirt from his uniform closer. She traced the edges of the emblems and ribbons that were a mystery to her, just as he still was in so many ways. "What do all these mean, Mick?"

"Hmm?"

"These bars and symbols. What do they all mean?"

Mick pulled the shirt over to him and started naming them off as though they were menu items. "Well, these oak leaves on the collar tell people my rank is Lieutenant Commander. And these two ribbons are for expert pistol and expert rifle." He adjusted his weight as he took the shirt in his other hand. "This is my Sea Service Deployment ribbon with bronze stars for the number of tours, and then this is my Overseas Deployment Ribbon with a silver star for five tours and a bronze star for one more. This is for Southwest Asia service three separate times."

Lacey's eyes were wide. "Wow. You've been busy."

Mick let out a slow breath coming to his personal awards. "This one here," he started, pointing to a ribbon near the top, "is a purple heart."

"You got a purple heart?"

"Two," Mick answered casually. "The first was for this knife wound in hand-to-hand combat with an insurgent who was trying to toss a grenade at my team." He turned on his side, revealing a well-healed scar on his side that was camouflaged amid his rippling muscle tone.

"My God."

"The gold star on it means I got a second purple heart for getting shot in the shoulder on my last mission." He lifted himself up a bit and pointed to a scar just below his shoulder.

Lacey paled.

"And these are just some more personal awards. Bronze Star with combat V. Joint Meritorious Service Medal. Navy Cross from my last mission with the SEALs."

She touched her hand to her mouth, and he must have seen the uneasiness in her eyes, because he rushed through the last.

"And these ones are Navy Commendation and Navy Achievement Medals, and some Unit Commendation Medals."

With Lacey at a loss for words, the silence between them was broken only by the faint crackle of dying embers.

Mick tried to lighten the tone. "So, all in all, we call it chest salad."

"Chest salad?"

Mick just smiled and nodded.

"I call it impressive, myself."

He shook his head dismissively. "It's not much, really. It's just my job. We pin things on for everything. It's like wearing your résumé on your uniform."

Lacey stroked his shoulder where the worst of the two combat scars seemed to tell a story of its own. "First time I saw this one, you were mowing Maeve's lawn." She smiled at the memory, feeling as though a lifetime had passed since then. "I always wondered what it was from, but was too afraid to ask."

"You shouldn't have been afraid to ask me. You can ask me anything."

Leaning closer, she kissed the scar meaningfully. "That's not how I was afraid. I was too scared to hear the truth. I sometimes try to forget what you did, and what you'll do again. The risks you take. The thought of something bad happening to you…"

Mick took her in his arms. "Hey. I'm not letting anything happen. There are always risks in life, but I'm one of the best trained out there."

Lacey's smile was brief as she tugged the shirt from Mick's grasp, this time to wrap it over her naked body. Her fingers reverently touched the many emblems pinned to his shirt that now had so much more meaning to her. "So this is why everyone salutes you when you walk by?" she asked with a coy smile.

"Or tells me when I'm supposed to salute to someone else."

"Exactly. But that's not as much of a turn-on."

Mick laughed. "Okay, then. Back to the image of people saluting at me..."

His laughter was buried beneath her kiss. She let her hair fall onto his chest as she tasted him, the hint of tomatoes and onions reminding her of the leftovers on the stove. She groaned. "I forgot to put the rest of the chicken in the refrigerator. It's probably bad by now."

"Honey?"

Lacey's expression warmed at the endearment. "Yes?"

"No offense to your dinner. But it doesn't hold a candle to what you offered for dessert." He wrestled her back underneath him and stroked the side of her face affectionately. Leaning over her to kiss her, he stopped, brow furrowed.

"What's wrong?"

"Nothing. Just wondering something actually. Do you like balls?"

Lacey's eyes widened. "Uh, I like yours. Is that what I'm supposed to say?"

Mick laughed. "No, I mean the kind where you dress up in a gown and dance and all that."

"I haven't been to one."

"Well, the Navy is having a big one in February. Do you want to go?"

Lacey glowed at the invitation, and for a fleeting moment pictured herself sweeping across a dance floor in Mick's arms. She sighed, wriggling out from under him. "No. Thanks, though."

"No?"

"Mick, it's a really sweet offer. But I don't have a ball gown, and I doubt even Maeve has one I could borrow." Frowning, her lips formed a tight line. "And I'm a bit tight on money till I sell one of these listings."

Mick shrugged. "So, I'll buy you one."

"No way. I really wouldn't feel comfortable with that." Grinning, she added, "Besides, you are way too masculine to be playing fairy godmother."

Mick feigned offense. "I have a feminine side."

Lacey laughed, tracing her full palm down his sculpted chest, along his abs, and then grabbing the length of him, already standing at attention. "Oh, yeah? I'd be interested to see where you keep it."

Mick drew in his breath at the aggressive touch. "Keep grabbing me like that and I'll buy you a whole closet full of ball gowns."

Her laugh was low and seductive as she reached for the condoms, grateful to find one left in the near-empty box. She pushed him over onto his back and straddled him. "I'm not interested in buying out the gown section at Nordstrom's," she said as she toyed with him. "I've got what I'm interested in right here." With him in her firm grasp, she lightly touched the tip of him against her own moisture, without letting him enter her. Stroking him, she teased him, dipping him slightly into her heat, and then pulling her body away.

"You're killing me, lady."

She smiled at the control she had over him now.

Or so she thought. Within a split-second she found herself flipped over and pinned to the ground.

"All that Special Forces training finally comes in handy," he said, smiling at her whimper of surrender as he plunged into her.

Kissing her savagely, he wrapped her legs completely around him, and brought himself to his full height, still joined with her. Her eyes shone with surprise at being carried up the stairs with him still pulsing deep inside of her.

She was on the bed now, she realized in a dizzying confusion, feeling herself sink into the lush duvet. He kissed her more gently now, as though being surrounded by the softness of the bed had somehow softened him. But it wasn't gentleness she craved now, grabbing his thick arms and digging her fingernails into him. "Don't hold back with me this time, Commander," she practically growled, capturing his lips with hers. Fiercely, she raked her hands against his chest, her body almost sizzling as her fingers touched his scars. Now that she had glimpsed into his world, she found herself desperate to be taken by the warrior in him.

Mick's hands seized her hips now, and his teeth grazed along her delicate skin, urgently needing to finish what he began.

With Mick's headboard ramming against the wall in a desperate rhythm, their lithe bodies tumbled and twisted in possession. At last, they gave themselves to each other completely, melting into each other.

Lacey's eyes were glazed over. "Wow," she said in a drawn-out breath, swearing she could see steam rising from their melded bodies.

His chest still heaving from exertion, his eyes met hers—mellow, half-opened, and filled with satisfaction. She could feel the rawness of the skin around her lips from his kisses, and glanced down to see pink marks on her arms revealing where he had gripped her too tightly.

"Dammit, Lacey. I shouldn't have been so rough with you. You'll be bruised tomorrow."

"Mmmm. I hope so," she purred. "Why are you apologizing? This other side of you is sexy. Real primitive."

"Yeah, that's one word for it. Something about the way you mounted me like that. Grabbed me. Teased me. Made me want to..."

"Give me a spanking?" Lacey laughed playfully.

Amusement crept into his eyes. "Okay, so obviously my apology is unwarranted."

"And unnecessary. Mick, it's nice you have all these different sides. Sometimes you're so sweet and gentle like a big teddy bear..."

Mick let out a laugh.

"... and other times you are so protective—very alpha male. And this time, I could see the warrior in you. It's like getting a glimpse of the you who goes into battle. You never share that side of you with me." She bent over him and kissed him deeply. "I love all the different aspects of you."

Damn! Her eyes suddenly widened. Did she really say that word out loud? It was too early to use the "l" word lightly. 10. 9. 8... She could hear the countdown begin till he ran screaming from the bed stammering some excuse about a place he needed to be right away.

In desperation, she backtracked. "I mean, I love all those aspects of you, in the enjoyment sense. You know, the way I love ice cream, and Scrabble, and Maeve and Bess. Not anything..."

He pressed a finger to her lips, obviously to save her from embarrassing herself further.

"You didn't answer me about one thing, Lacey."

She breathed a sigh of relief, eager to change the topic. "What didn't I answer?"

"Whether you will be my date to the ball. I'm buying you a gown and that's the end of it. I needed to figure out something to get you for Christmas, anyway."

"That's just too lavish a gift. I'll never be able to get you something that nice for Christmas."

"Tell you what. I'll get you the gown. And you get me whatever you wear underneath," He flashed a scheming smile. "I think I'd come out ahead in that bargain."

When she opened her mouth to refuse, he lifted a finger. "Lacey, it's just a dress. Besides, now that I've seen your wild side, I might get the urge to rip the damn thing off you at the end of the night. If I buy you the dress, I won't feel as guilty for ruining it."

"I wouldn't even know how to act at a ball. I barely got through Edith's fundraiser alive, remember?"

"You'll love it."

Lacey pursed her lips in thought. "Okay, I'll go. But promise me you won't let me make a fool of myself." Smiling, she pressed a kiss to his lips. "And thank you." She spotted his approving grin as she rose naked from the bed to find one of his old t-shirts to wear.

"My pleasure. And Lacey?" He gave her a playful smack on her bare bottom. "For the record, I love all your aspects too."

CHAPTER 21

Georgetown was magical in the snow with holiday decorations glimmering as they blew in the wind.

The traffic was a logjam with the streets barely plowed. Determined shoppers bustled along the streets, trudging through the snow in designer boots, their arms heavy with bags bearing the trendiest names in fashion. Scores huddled into coffee shops to thaw themselves with overpriced lattés while jabbering on their cell phones, their voices loud as they dropped the names of Washington DC's most prominent politicians.

Mick normally would have been annoyed by such a crowd—people who thought themselves so worldly yet had lived such sheltered lives. Something about war had hardened him, witnessing such suffering and poverty. When he had first set foot in Annapolis for his new job, he had no patience for people who did not value the lottery they had won simply by being born in the United States.

Having Lacey on his arm softened him, he realized as they walked along Wisconsin Avenue, already holding two shopping bags filled with holiday gifts. There was something valuable about just living in the moment and opening his heart to pleasure, rather than constantly planning for the next mission. Maybe he had learned to finally enjoy the freedoms that he worked so hard to protect.

She gave him that, he thought as he looked over at Lacey's rosy-cheeked face. He couldn't resist bending over for a taste of the tiny flakes of snow that were stuck to her forehead as he kissed her. "You're freezing," he noticed.

"I'm loving it. It snowed all the time where I was growing up. I don't get nearly enough of it here."

"Well, just the same, let's make the next stop that boutique Maeve recommended. I don't want you so worn out from Christmas shopping that you don't have the energy to find a dress for the ball."

They steered themselves off Wisconsin Avenue and onto the side streets, where slick modern townhomes were sandwiched in between picturesque brownstones that were nearly as old as the city itself.

Mick's toes felt a chill as the wet snow crept into his boots. "Your feet must be frozen," he noted, glancing at Lacey's inadequate shoes and making a mental note to buy her some more practical boots before the weekend was over.

"It's not so..." she began, but was unable to complete her sentence as Mick swooped her onto his back. "What are you doing?"

"You're riding piggyback the rest of the way," he said matter-of-factly. "And if you argue, I'll have to throw you over my shoulder which is actually easier on my back, but not nearly as civilized."

Lacey laughed as she bounced the rest of the way on his back, with her bags rattling in the wind. "I've never ridden piggyback in my life."

"Not even as a kid?"

Letting out a little snort, she scoffed. "You really have to meet my dad. And *then* tell me if you can picture him giving me a piggyback ride."

The thought of meeting her parents should have sent an uncomfortable chill down his spine. Yet it didn't. He even found himself intrigued by the idea.

Mick carried her down a narrow staircase into the lower level of an historic building. "This must be it," he said, putting her down so that he could press the doorbell.

Maeve had clearly called in advance, because the manager and an assistant greeted them at the door with two glasses of champagne and a selection of gowns in Lacey's size. Maeve was, apparently, a woman whose shopping aptitude was respected in DC's Georgetown.

Mick settled into a chair as Lacey was swept into a sea of silks, satins, and chiffons. It certainly was nothing like buying clothes at the PX on base or even at a civilian mall. The staff-to-shopper ratio must have been about five to one here. But all the fuss was worth seeing Lacey's face shining as bright as the moon that was already rising in the winter sky outside.

Twirling in front of him, she was showing off another dress just as her eyes fell to the price tag.

"No looking at price tags," he reminded. "That was what we agreed."

As the manager stepped away to find matching shoes, Lacey made a beeline for Mick. "This is really expensive."

"You don't like the dresses?"

"Of course I like them. But I can find something that costs a tenth of that at the mall," she said, price tag in hand.

A quick glance down and he shrugged. "That's doable, Lacey."

"Mick…"

"Stop," he said, planting a kiss on her lips. "You know all that hazardous duty I sign up for? There are certain pay bonuses you get with that. And when you're deployed as often as I was, there's not much opportunity to spend money. So this," he said, pointing to the tag, "is nothing. One minor indulgence that I think I'm allowed after all these years. You're not going to deprive me of that, are you?"

Lacey paused, her face softening. "You," she began, cupping his head in her hands, "are a very generous man."

I'm a very lucky man, Mick thought as the manager came back into the room carrying stacks of shoes in his arms.

Lacey felt slightly dizzy, and it wasn't just from spinning around in front of the mirror so many times, watching expensive fabrics swirl at her feet. And it wasn't the champagne that had mysteriously been refilled twice when her flute was running low.

It was Mick. It was the way he looked at her with such complete adoration. Lacey knew he wasn't the type to settle down with a family. But what she learned this day was that Mick was the type who could truly cherish someone.

That should be enough for her, shouldn't it?

After the shopping spree was deemed a success, Mick went to get the car so that Lacey would not have to walk any longer in the snow.

"It's picking up out here, isn't it?" Lacey said, sliding in beside him, a hint of sadness in her voice at the thought of the day coming to an end.

"They're saying at least six more inches tonight."

"Wow. We better get home before it piles up any more."

"Actually, we're not going home," he said, pulling up to the front door of an historic hotel just a few blocks from the White House.

The doorman opened Mick's door first. "Are you staying with us, sir?"

"Yes, we are. Reservations are under the name Riley," Mick said, popping the trunk and handing the keys to the doorman.

Another doorman quickly opened Lacey's door. She looked at Mick, confused.

"Mick, we're not staying here, are we?"

"Surprise," he said, taking her hand and leading her out of the car.

"But we can't. I—I didn't even pack anything, Mick."

"Bess and Maeve took care of that for you," he said as Lacey looked over her shoulder and recognized her own overnight bag being pulled from the trunk by the bellman. "I thought you needed a little spoiling."

"As if you didn't spoil me enough today."

He swallowed her up in his huge arms. "That's not all the spoiling I have planned for you." He traced a finger across her chin and met his lips with hers.

The shades open, the morning sun glared through the hotel window. Stark naked, Lacey rose quickly from the bed to draw the shades shut, hoping not to give the people in the office building across the street too much of a show.

"Mmm," Mick murmured, half awake, as she slid back into bed with him.

"Shh. Go back to sleep," she whispered, gently kissing his lips as she nuzzled back onto his chest.

He mumbled something inaudible as she stroked his hair. His jaw slacked a bit and he started to snore. She gently adjusted him so that he could breathe more easily, and the quiet returned. Lying silently beside him, she let her mind drift to the memories they made together the evening before. Mick had indulged her every fantasy, starting with a horse-drawn carriage ride down The Mall toward the Capitol Building where the grand architecture of the Smithsonian Museums were lit up in the night. Cuddled beneath a blanket with him, all of Lacey's senses forever etched the experience into her mind: the storybook clip-clopping of the horse as it trotted down the busy street; the way the street lamps seemed to magnify each perfect snowflake as it cascaded toward the ground; the feel of Mick's warmth alongside her with the scratchy wool blanket shielding them from the frosty air.

Room service was awaiting them when they returned to the hotel, and they ate wrapped in the sumptuous bed linens, with the lights off and the drapes open so they could watch the city being blanketed with snow. As the city noises abated outside, they comfortably melded together enjoying the sweet sound of each other's slow, contented breathing as they drifted off to sleep.

Now as she watched him, Lacey felt him twitch every once in a while, and wondered what he was dreaming about. Was he here, dreaming of yesterday's carriage ride, or of making love with her? Or was he on the battlefield, dreaming scenes she could never even imagine? She stroked his arm that was outstretched on the bed and traced the outline of the scar on his shoulder.

Worry furrowed her brow as she imagined the things that this man had seen and done in his life. She wondered where his career would take him next, and prayed silently he would be kept out of harm's way.

Not long from now, the Navy would move him far away again. Far away from her. Far away from the safe, simple life they were leading in Annapolis.

The last twenty-four hours had been something of a

fantasy for her, a magical moment in time that she hoped would comfort her when he left.

And he would leave.

What if she were to follow?

Looking again at the scar and imagining the mission he was on when he was injured, suddenly her flailing real estate career didn't seem nearly as important.

She would follow him anywhere, she realized with a start. Give up her career, start fresh in a new town, maybe on the other side of the country. Other women did it. Why couldn't she?

Squeezing her eyes shut, she tried to imagine what Vi would tell her right now. But the only thing she envision was Mick a year from now. Two years. Ten. Forever. She wanted to be the one waiting home for him every time he deployed. She wanted to watch his grey hairs come in and that hard six-pack slowly dissolve into a softer, decidedly average belly after he left the SEALs. Smiling at the thought, she tried to picture a few more wrinkles defining his face, and knew that she wanted to see them slowly appear over the years. If he wanted her to, that is.

If only he wanted her to.

They both jumped when they heard Lacey's cell phone ring. She cursed softly, running across the room to dig it out of her purse before Mick completely awakened.

Too late. Mick's eyes were wide open, and a smile spread across his face as he looked at Lacey in the nude, frantically fidgeting with her phone.

Lacey saw Maeve's number on the caller ID. "Maeve?"

"No, it's Bess, Lacey. I'm so sorry to call. I held off as long as I could."

"It's okay. Are you all right? Is the baby all right?"

Bess's voice was tight on the other end. "We're fine. But, well—your car was broken into."

CHAPTER 22

Swallowing a groan, Mick adjusted his position in the soft sofa, feeling the ache in his lower back shoot ripples of pain up his spine and across his ribs.

He couldn't believe he was this sore from just shoveling two driveways. It was almost embarrassing, and he'd be damned if he'd ever admit to it.

Maeve's had been a simple, short span from the garage to the street. He had the mission completed well in time for Lacey to race out the driveway to her Saturday meeting with a new client.

When he volunteered to do Mrs. B's, he really should have considered its size. The massive driveway seemed to stretch from her three-car garage to Buffalo, New York.

Why not just offer to shovel Highway 50 while he was at it?

Still, it needed to be done. He certainly wouldn't have let her call a professional when he had two perfectly good arms to shovel snow. And the exercise would do him good. While he worked out regularly at the Academy gym, he missed the raw, genuine ache that came from hauling a ninety-pound pack across a sandy desert.

Or shoveling a driveway.

Besides, he was getting paid with the best hot cocoa he had tasted in his life, he thought contentedly, as Mrs. B brought him a second steaming cup of liquid indulgence from the kitchen.

"Had she left her car unlocked?" Edith continued their conversation.

"No, it was definitely locked. The window was broken. All the doors were opened; the trunk was popped. But then, that's it. They didn't take anything. Not even her GPS."

Edith shuddered. "It can't be a coincidence. It is so similar to what happened to Maeve's house. I hope the police are taking that into consideration."

"They are. And they said they'd send a patrol car over regularly to keep an eye on the place. But they have no leads."

"Any footprints in the snow?"

"It kept snowing after the break-in, so they're hard to make out. And any car tracks were plowed over."

"Did Bess or Maeve hear anything?"

"Maeve's room is on the other side of the house, and Bess sleeps like a log. A bomb blast wouldn't wake her since she entered this last trimester." Mick set down his mug. "One of the neighbors says he heard glass breaking, but figured it was just someone throwing out their glass recyclables."

"I don't like this at all. If this is the same person that broke in before, then the girls are obviously a target."

"Most likely Lacey is the target since it was her car," Mick pointed out, his gut clenching into a tight knot. "I'd feel better if Lacey stayed with me until this thing got resolved."

"They do have that alarm system now."

"It's useless to her after she steps out the door. If she were on base with me, she'd be safer. No car gets past those guards at the gate without a DoD sticker and military ID."

"Mick, if you want Lacey to move in with you, I don't think this is the way to go about doing it."

"I'm not asking her to move in with me."

Edith raised her eyebrows.

Mick relented. "Well, I am—but just temporarily 'til they catch this guy."

"Which could be never. And what is Lacey supposed to do when you get orders and leave Annapolis?"

Come with me! a voice shouted in Mick's head. But he kept the idea to himself, knowing it was absurd.

Edith sighed. "If you are thinking of moving forward with your relationship, you should do it because you love each other. Not because Lacey is frightened or you are concerned for her safety. Good intentions aside, it's not a healthy way to start a life together."

"I didn't say we were starting a life together. I just would feel better knowing she was safe."

"And would you keep her safe when she's in her office? Or at the grocery store? You can't protect her all day. So I wonder if it's just an excuse to have her closer to you."

Mick shifted uncomfortably.

"Think about your intentions toward her truthfully before you suggest her moving in with you. It would be unfair to play upon her insecurities or fears to get her to uproot her life. Because if you aren't proposing to start a life together, she will be left high and dry when you leave here for your next post."

Mick stared down at the mug of hot chocolate, suddenly finding it less appetizing.

Mrs. B was right. Mick hated that.

Lacey stomped the snow off of her new boots at the door, punching the security code into the alarm. "Anyone home?"

"In here," Bess's voice called from the kitchen.

When Lacey joined her, she couldn't suppress a laugh at the sight of a pile of stuffed animals heaped onto the kitchen table. "What happened in here? It looks like Disneyworld exploded."

"That's about what happened. Jack came by saying he had picked up a couple things for the baby when he was in Florida. I had no idea how much."

Lacey picked up a Daisy Duck and tossed open a princess blanket, shaking her head at the pile. "That was so sweet of him."

"It was," Bess said tentatively, "but it's just too much."

"Jack loves kids. You know that. He just got carried away. Let him have his fun."

"I feel awkward accepting all of it."

"Oh, get over it. Just accept gifts graciously," Lacey said in a Minnie Mouse voice, her hand shoved up the dress of a puppet.

Bess's brow creased. "It's not just that. It was the way Maeve acted."

"What do you mean?"

"I don't know. I couldn't figure it out. It was like maybe she was jealous."

"Of what?"

"Maybe of me, you know. Of the attention or something. I'm not sure."

"Well, they definitely had a fling. Maybe all those times she said she didn't want something more than friendship with Jack she was lying. Where is she now?"

"Said she had to go to the store. She left before Jack even did. I wish you had been here. It was weird."

"Did Jack say anything?"

Bess snorted. "You know Jack. He's not one to pick up on anything. The man's clueless. Should I mention something to Maeve when she gets home?"

Lacey picked up a Tinkerbell that had rolled off the pile of toys as she sat at the table. "No. Not unless she keeps acting weird. You know how she likes keeping her feelings to herself."

"Wish I could do that as well as she does."

"Me, too. She's the master."

Bess started piling all the toys back into shopping bags. "So how did your client meeting go?"

Stretching her legs out in front of her, Lacey rolled her eyes. "Well, I took them to five houses, and every one wasn't perfect enough. They're very high maintenance."

"Where are they moving from?"

"DC. Chevy Chase area."

"Well, that explains the high maintenance part. Those homes there are gorgeous."

"Yeah. They got my name from Edith, actually. He's a doctor who just started working at the hospital."

"Nice," Bess said, scrunching her face as she touched her belly.

"You okay?"

"Just something I ate. Maeve tried making French toast for breakfast."

"Ah, no wonder Mick didn't linger when he was done shoveling."

"Yeah. She's a hell of a designer, but not the best cook." Bess struggled out of her chair. "I think I'll lie down until the effect wears off."

Lacey watched Bess head out of the kitchen, and a sudden panic tore through her, knocking her nearly breathless when she saw blood on Bess's pants. "Oh, God." She rose quickly to

Bess's side. "Oh, God, Bess, honey, let's get your coat. You're bleeding. I'll drive you to the hospital."

Maeve knew she couldn't cook to save her life. Today's breakfast certainly confirmed that.

But as she stood in front of the butcher's department at the grocery store, she could at least take pride in knowing one cut of meat from another. Grabbing the best-looking shoulder roast from the pile, she felt gratified to take part in tonight's dinner preparation in some small measure.

Glancing down at the list Bess had given her, she headed to the spices and frowned, remembering her odd reaction to those damn toys this morning. She hoped no one had noticed. Well, certainly Jack didn't. A bulldozer could come careening through her dining room wall and he wouldn't notice.

But why had she reacted like that? Was it jealousy? Most likely. She'd been doing a pretty impressive job of concealing her own yearning for a child as she watched Bess walk the waist-expanding path to motherhood.

Every time Bess took Maeve's hand to share a kick, one half of Maeve's heart leapt and the other half shattered to bits.

But today, seeing those toys that Jack brought, something snapped. Was it because it was Jack showering gifts on Bess?

Was there some part of her that wished Jack would do the same for her, for the baby she would never have?

The baby *they* would never have, she dared to take the thought one step further. Maeve had to admit having a fantasy or two from time to time about settling down with Jack, sharing in marriage the same contented relationship they shared as friends.

Add to that, the hot sex she still remembered vividly, even though it had been nearly a decade since they went down that road. The guy was a freaking gymnast in bed.

Maeve frowned at the array of spices. Absurd idea. Marrying Jack.

She couldn't deny the attraction. It was there, just as it was seven years ago. But this morning she had been reminded why she was determined to steer clear of him. Some men were meant to have kids. Broods of kids. Jack was one of them. She only had to look at the mountain of toys he had bought for Bess's child to see it.

One eyebrow raised. And really, she thought, why couldn't it be with Bess? She was young and obviously fertile as a rabbit. He had a big enough heart to care deeply for the child Bess already had. Maeve knew that for a fact. The guy's heart was the size of Montana.

So was the size of his…

Maeve gave herself a shake. Mustn't let her mind wander in that direction. No, Jack wasn't for her. But Bess? It would be nice to know that Bess's baby had a father Maeve approved of. Someone strong enough to kick the ass of that ex-boyfriend if he ever reared his ugly head in this town.

It might be an idea worth pursuing—if, that is, she could stand to watch Jack settle down with someone other than herself.

Which she'd have to do eventually anyway.

She shook her head ruefully. God, it was hell being her these days.

She plucked her ringing cell from her purse. "Hey, Lacey. How'd the showings go?"

"Maeve, I'm at the hospital with Bess. She started bleeding."

Maeve froze in the middle of the produce aisle. *"What?"*

"They've already admitted her, and the doctor wants to do lots of tests. So far, the baby looks fine."

By the time Lacey made it through the sentence, Maeve had abandoned her grocery basket in the middle of the aisle and was halfway out the door. "How is Bess?"

"Really upset, as you can imagine. Scared. But I think she's doing better now that we've heard the baby's heart beat."

Maeve couldn't help the lump in her throat. "My God, that little tike. She's got to hold on a little longer before making her debut."

"Exactly."

"I'm at my car now and on my way."

CHAPTER 23

Jack carried a cold six-pack of Cokes in from the kitchen, and tossed cans to Maeve, Lacey, and Mick. "You know, after smelling hospital smells all last night, this paint actually smells good to me."

"You don't like the smell of paint?" Feeling a wet drop on her cheek, Lacey wiped, smearing pink halfway across her face.

"No, do you?"

Lacey took a deep breath. "Oh, yeah. I love the smell."

Mick laughed, opening Lacey's can for her, and then using the bottom edge of his sleeve to wipe the paint from her face. His hand rested on her cheek one second longer than it needed to, and the simple touch sent a warm tingling down her neck. "You learn something new every day. Remind me to skip the perfume for a Valentine's Day gift and give you a gallon of this instead." He poured more Pink Paradise into her roller pan.

Appreciating the view as Mick bent over, a smile crept up Lacey's face. The contours of his muscular back and arms through the thin Henley had a way of making the simplest action as sexy as hell.

"And this is the no-VOC paint," Maeve added. "Imagine her with the hard stuff."

"Oh, quit it and get back to work. We only have one day to get this done."

"*If* Bess gets out of the hospital tomorrow," Mick reminded her.

"If. But I'm optimistic. All the tests came back fine."

"Need a hand here, Mick," Jack said, holding up half the changing table. "Think you can handle some man's work?"

Mick set down his pink-saturated paintbrush and shot him a glare. "If I were putting that thing together it would have been done an hour ago." He picked up one end of the half-assembled piece. "All that nuclear training, and you can't even put together a diaper changing table." Letting out a slight grunt, he sat on the floor among the pieces of finished wood.

"A little trouble sitting down, old man?" Jack teased.

"Back's a little sore from yesterday."

Jack tossed Lacey a smirk. "Well, well. Now we know what you two were up to when you got back from the hospital."

"It's from shoveling, dumb ass. And I didn't see you out there helping me with Maeve's. Scared of a little hard labor?"

"If I throw my back out for Maeve, it'll be doing something completely different from shoveling, believe me. Besides, it's not that big of a driveway. Never would have imagined you'd need help. I could have had it done in a half hour."

Lacey sighed. "Oh, boy, here we go."

"Hmmm?" asked Maeve, her back facing them as she streaked her roller up against the wall.

"It's the dick measuring contest again."

Maeve turned immediately, then shot Lacey a disappointed look. "Damn, I thought you meant literally. They're still clothed."

Lacey laughed, glancing out the window as another cloud passed in front of the sun. "Hope those clouds don't build till the electrician comes to install the chandelier. We really need the light."

Maeve glanced at the clock. "We'll be fine. He'll be here in a half hour. Shouldn't take him long either, if we stay out of his way."

"Don't see why you need an electrician for that. I've installed light fixtures before," Mick offered.

"So have I," Jack piped in, always in competition. "I've even installed dimmers."

"Boys, boys. I'm sure you both could do it. But I'm not risking anything. Last place I need faulty wiring is in a baby's room. Besides, the electrician is the hottest number since that lawn boy."

Lacey made her face light up in feigned interest. "Really?"

Mick definitely noticed.

"Really," Maeve answered. "Gay as a maypole, though, unfortunately. But still great to look at. Definitely a 10. What a waste."

"Depends on your perspective. I'm sure his boyfriend doesn't think it's a waste," Jack suggested diplomatically.

"Can't wait to see what a 10 looks like," Mick grumbled.

Lacey snickered. "Well, remember that lawn boy? He was a 9."

Mick's eyes met Lacey's. "So what am I?"

Lacey and Maeve glanced at each other, and said in unison, "9 ½."

Mick punched Jack in the arm. "Better than lawn boy," he pointed out.

"9 ½?" Jack fired a look at Maeve. "Then what am I?"

Maeve eyed him discriminately and shrugged. "A 7, I guess."

"*He's* a 9 ½," Jack said, pointing at Mick, "and I'm just a 7?"

Maeve's eyes widened innocently. "What? I've seen Mick with his shirt off. It's been years since I've seen what's beneath that packaging. Things tend to sag with time."

Jack's eyes flashed in challenge as he ripped his shirt over his head, revealing a tight abdomen rippled with muscles, and sculpted arms that didn't need flexing to look impressive.

The temperature in the room increased by ten degrees.

Lacey snickered quietly, fanning herself.

"So what do you think now?" Jack asked, daring Maeve.

Maeve just grinned. "I don't know yet. Keep going."

Rolling over, Lacey frowned at the feel of cool sheets alongside her. She wished Mick would have spent the night, but they all needed to catch up on their sleep since the night in the ER.

It was still dark, but Lacey could hear the first song of morning coming from a lone bird outside her window. Not many sang in the winter's wee hours, but there were always a few who were tenacious.

Lacey reached toward her lamp, the soreness of a day spent painting spanning from her shoulders to her fingertips. Her thoughts flew to the beautiful baby's room downstairs. Her grin wide, she envisioned the tiny crystals in the chandelier that glistened in the light, scattering colorful rainbows onto the walls. The heirloom quality crib was fit for a princess, and the shades of pink were as sweet as cotton candy.

As excited as a five-year-old on Christmas morning,

Lacey jumped out of bed, suddenly needing to take just one more look at the magical space.

Bess was going to love the room, Lacey thought, stepping quietly down the stairs, not wanting to wake Maeve.

Flicking on the switch, the winsome chandelier shone its light on Maeve—not asleep in her room at all—but curled up on the floor of the baby's room, her face streaked with tears.

Lacey's felt the air rush out of her lungs. "Maeve. What's wrong?"

Maeve wiped her face. "Oh, shit, Lacey. I thought you were asleep."

Lacey paled. "Oh my God. Did you hear from the hospital or something?"

"No. No. That's not it. Bess and the baby are fine. This is…nothing. Just forget it. Go back upstairs. Everyone is entitled to have their little breakdowns, right? It's probably PMS."

Lacey sat on the floor beside her. "What is it?"

"Nothing," Maeve scooted a couple inches further from her friend.

"I'm not leaving till you tell me what's wrong."

Maeve reached for another tissue, and blew unceremoniously. "It's nothing, really."

Lacey crossed her arms. "I can sit here waiting all morning."

"Dammit." Maeve rolled her eyes. "It's just, this," she said, throwing her hands up to the room. "It's just—hard."

"Hard," Lacey prodded, bewildered. "Why?"

Maeve let out an exasperated breath. "Because I can't have kids."

It took a moment before it sank in. "You can't have children?"

"No. All that bullshit about hating kids is just that, bullshit. I just can't have one."

"Oh, Maeve, I'm so sorry. Are you sure?"

Maeve nodded. "A few years ago, I was diagnosed with breast cancer."

"My God. That's too young."

"Yeah, that's about what I said to the doctor when he told me. No one ever thinks about the women who get it that young, you know? It's just not that common, but it happens."

"Are you okay now?"

Maeve reached over and knocked on the doorway. "Knock wood. Anyway, the doctor had told me I'd be smart to harvest some eggs before chemo if I wanted to have kids because it can do damage."

"But you didn't?"

"No. That dick I was married to gave me some crap about if it's in our destiny to have kids, then we'll have them." Maeve shook her head. "I can't believe I ever listened to him. But I was too scared of losing him right then to question him. I didn't want to face cancer alone." Combing her hand through her hair, she sighed. "He actually stuck by me through the surgery and the chemo. But then he moved on to someone else. It didn't help that he found her while we were still married."

"Son of a bitch."

Maeve leaned her back against the doorway. "Really, I can't blame him much. He's just in his thirties like me, you know? Having a wife with breast cancer isn't something he was prepared for."

"That's bullshit. As if *you* were prepared for it? Any guy with balls would have stuck with you. He was your husband, for God's sake."

Maeve shrugged. "It's funny. I thought I was okay with all of it up till recently. I kept telling myself how lucky I was to be alive. Nothing else should matter, right?"

"You're still human, Maeve. You have a right to be angry."

"And I was, believe me. My family pulled me through it all. Gram especially. That woman's a rock. But then when Gram died, that just pushed me over the edge. You remember how I was at the funeral."

Lacey did remember. It was the first funeral she had crashed, but seeing Maeve grieve made her almost forget why she was there. Almost.

Maeve gave her a squeeze on the hand. "Then when you gave me the idea of moving in here rather than selling, everything just clicked. I needed a clean break from my life in Baltimore. I needed to be someplace where I wasn't surrounded by bad memories. This is where I always came when I needed a piece of calm. Serenity. And I know it sounds stupid, but I really feel like there's a part of Gram still here. Like anytime I feel a little weak, she's right there, holding me up."

Lacey settled her back against the wall and felt the warmth of the house surround them both. "It probably sounds even stranger, but I've felt that too here. And I never even knew her."

"She didn't hold me up tonight, though."

Lacey wrapped her arm around her. "Yeah, well, maybe she kicked my lazy butt out of bed so I'd find you here crying."

Laughing, Maeve let out an exaggerated curse. "Damn her! That sounds just like something she'd do."

"You don't have to go through this alone. You've been there for me in so many ways, and for Bess and that baby. You shouldn't feel all alone in this."

Maeve's eyes widened. "You can't tell Bess. I don't want her feeling she has to hold back her joys or worries or anything. Promise me you won't say anything to her—or to anyone."

Lacey pursed her lips together. She could see the logic in

keeping this from Bess right now. But Maeve needed to draw strength from her friends. "I guess it's not my story to tell, Maeve. But I hope one day you'll reconsider."

A silence hung between them.

The first beams of dawn peeked through the window and sparkled in the chandelier's crystals. Lacey gazed at the room again, seeing it in a different light. "This must have been hard all these months. With Bess pregnant, I mean."

Maeve smiled a little. "You have no idea. But really, this is the closest I'll come to having a baby myself, you know? I want to spoil that little girl a bit."

That was obvious, Lacey thought. "It sure is a pretty room, Maeve."

"You think so, too?"

Lacey nodded, squeezing her arm around her friend's shoulders. "And you're the most generous person I've ever known."

Maeve waved her hand carelessly and wiped another tear. "Yeah, yeah. A hard-boiled marshmallow, that's what Gram used to call me. Just don't tell anyone else that. I have a reputation to uphold."

CHAPTER 24

A terrifying tingling sensation blazed a path from Lacey's stomach, up to her heart, and then out to her fingertips at the feel of the ball gown tightening around her torso. She tried to inhale. "It's too tight, Maeve."

Maeve squinted as she struggled with the tiny hook-and-eye closures. "It's not too tight. It's strapless. That's the way it's supposed to be. If it were any looser, it would fall right off you. Not that Mick would complain about that."

"Yeah, but it would probably happen right as I was introduced to some Four-Star Admiral, with my luck."

"And the old guy would go to bed with a smile on his face. Turn around." Maeve took Lacey by the shoulders and turned her to face the mirror.

Lacey couldn't help it. She hid her mouth behind her hand and suppressed a girlish giggle. "Why do I feel like I'm playing dress-up? It doesn't even look like me."

"That's because you're not wearing black." Bess laughed, stretched out on Maeve's bed. It hadn't taken long for the color to return to her cheeks after her hospital scare, thanks to the beautiful surprise baby's room that awaited her. Now under strict bed rest orders from her doctor, she reclined in Maeve's room so that she could be a part of Lacey's excitement.

Maeve smoothed out a layer of silk on the bottom portion of the dress. "I have to say, I'm impressed with your choice. Never would have thought you'd choose green. Black is so understated and red is so overused." She tilted her head thoughtfully, the designer in her taking over. "And blue would be so trite at a Navy ball, I'd imagine. But when you told me you picked green, I worried you'd look like a leprechaun. This malachite is just divine, though."

Lacey opened her mouth to respond, but couldn't. Nerves were short-circuiting her vocal chords.

"What's wrong, Lacey?" Bess struggled to sit up.

"Stay laying down, Bess, I'm fine. Just nervous."

"Just follow Mick's lead with everything. You're not there to impress anyone."

"But I want to," Lacey confessed.

Maeve shook her head at her friend's worried expression. "You need a distraction. Jewelry," she concluded. "It's time to accessorize."

"Oh, I don't have anything that would look right with this dress."

Maeve searched through three jewelry boxes that sat on her dresser. "Here they are," she announced triumphantly, handing Lacey a set of earrings and then continuing to forage through her collection.

Lacey gasped. Each earring boasted diamonds encircling an emerald with white gold detailing. "These are gorgeous. I can't borrow them."

"Why not? They were Gram's. She'd love to know her earrings were seeing some action."

"I'd be too worried I'd lose them."

Maeve rolled her eyes. "That's why I have them insured."

She pulled a matching necklace from a velvet pouch and draped it around Lacey's neck.

Lacey's breath caught at the sight. "Oh, thank you."

"Gram got them for her twenty-fifth wedding anniversary. They were from Grandpa, of course. But Gram picked them out herself. She said it was about time he bought her something to remind her of Ireland, since he stole her from her homeland." Maeve's smile was rich with memories.

"She had amazing taste," Bess said, admiring the jewels as they glistened against Lacey's pale skin, "like her granddaughter."

"Just wish I had inherited her good taste in men," Maeve responded with a smirk.

The evening began in a giddy haze, more like a dream than reality. Lacey stood awkwardly next to Mick in a traditional receiving line waiting to shake the hands of people with more medals on their chests than even her date. Her ankles wobbled in the heels beneath her full-length gown. She stole another glance of Mick as she steadied herself on his arm. Wrong move, she realized when the sight of him nearly knocked her breathless… again.

Covered in medals and ribbons, and seeming even taller than his six-foot-three, he was a mouthwatering morsel of patriotic decadence.

Her smile brightened, and she looked away, blushing.

He noticed. "What is it?"

"Your uniform," she confessed. "I thought I had gotten immune to them, but now you pull out this one. It's not the formal one you wore to the fundraiser."

Mick laughed. "Yeah, we Navy guys have a lot of variations. This one is called Mess Dress. Or Dinner Dress Blue, though no one ever says that. The one you saw before was the Service Dress Blue uniform which is a step down from this one. We call them SDBs. I prefer that one—I can wear it with a straight tie and I don't feel like a valet."

"Everything is so confusing in the military. I'm surprised you don't have some kind of handbook that tells what to wear and say and do."

Mick grinned. "Actually, we do."

"Maybe I should borrow it for the night."

Taking her hand, Mick kissed her palm gently. "Honey, you're a civilian. All you have to do is enjoy yourself. Leave the saluting to me."

When they finally entered the hotel ballroom, the sweeping hall glimmered with candlelight reflecting on champagne flutes. Shaking hands and making introductions as they wove through the maze of white-clothed tables, Mick guided her to their seats where his name and rank were written in flowing calligraphy on a nameplate.

Everyone stood at attention as the flags were marched in perfect formation into the ballroom. A mezzo-soprano beautifully sang the national anthem followed by *Anchor's Away* and the *Marine Corps Hymn*. After rousing applause, a silence fell over the ballroom as the invocation was said, which nearly brought Lacey to tears with its eloquent remembrance of the military men and women who were risking their lives at that very moment.

Patriotism was more than a word here, she realized. She got chills at the thought, and hoped that Mick didn't notice the goose bumps on her bare arms.

Brief speeches, toasts, and a random array of traditions ensued which Mick did his best to explain quietly to Lacey. She wondered if she looked as overwhelmed as she felt.

Mick took her hand as salads were brought out to them. "Enjoying yourself?"

"Yes." She leaned in closer to him. "Just feeling out of my league, is all."

Mick smiled and gave her a good once-over. "Beautiful, in that dress, you are in a league of your own. I'm lucky I'm the one who gets to take you home."

"Or back to your home, I'm hoping."

He returned her mischievous smile. "I'm feeling even luckier."

Exhausted after the whirlwind of pageantry, Lacey was grateful to return to Mick's and snuggle in front of a relaxing fire. Her mind was still racing, the dazzling images of the night dancing in her memory. She hoped they would never fade.

Mick's gentle caress traced along the contours of her face. "What are you smiling about?"

"Oh, everything. It was a wonderful night, Mick. I was just blown away by all of it."

"How so?"

Lacey's gaze fixed on the tiny sparks that leapt from the logs and drifted up the chimney like tiny bubbles in champagne. "Everything was just so impressive. Almost otherworldly to me. And all the people I met..." Her face fell, feeling a hint of insecurity creeping into her heart. "The things they've seen and done just somehow make my life look really insignificant. I mean, did you read those bios of the speakers in the program? And what would *my* bio read? Lacey Owens, now on her umpteenth career attempt, barely makes a living while renting a room in her friend's house."

Mick draped his arm over her. "No. It would read, 'Lacey Owens, whose courage and ambition has her embarking on a new career rather than accepting the status quo. Lacey

Owens, whose kind heart has brought her a dedicated following of friends.'"

Lacey grumbled, not particularly impressed with herself.

He pulled her closer. "Lacey Owens, who has somehow done what no other woman could—making a hardened Navy SEAL fall in love with her.'"

Her eyes met his tentatively, wondering if he really meant what he said.

He put her mind to rest. "I love you, Lacey," he repeated so easily, it stunned her.

The smile on her face resonated from her soul. "I love you, too, Mick."

CHAPTER 25

"I shouldn't have answered the phone," Lacey muttered, walking arm-in-arm with Mick down Main Street with a quickly depleting chunk of fudge in her hand.

Mick grinned. "You say that every time your mom calls."

"You're right. I never learn."

"So, what subtly insulting things did she say this time?"

Mouth watering, Lacey devoured another bite of the fudge. "Just that Vi decided to do a destination wedding in Palm Beach at some five-star resort, and mom offered to pay for my trip because she knows my life is a financial disaster."

"And you're upset about this? Hell, I'd be packing my bags."

"Well, you can go in my place. All we need is to find a maid of honor dress that would fit you. Or would the Navy frown on that?"

"Hey, 'don't ask, don't tell,' you know?" Mick winked.

Lacey laughed, stopping in front of a store window sparkling with jewels and staring emptily at the display. "There's no way I'm taking their money. I can't even imagine all the remarks I'd have to survive from them if I did."

Mick brushed a lock of hair from Lacey's face and gently stroked her cheek. "That Miron property will probably sell by then and you'll be flying first class to Palm Beach."

"Good to know someone has some confidence in me." Popping the last morsel of fudge into her mouth without remorse, Lacey leaned in to press her mouth against his. She felt the flick of his tongue along her own.

He pulled back suddenly. "That fudge tastes great. You should have shared."

"I offered," she defended with a laugh. Nestling closer into the crook of his shoulder, she felt herself decompress in his presence as they walked along the quiet street.

Annapolis was all but vacant of tourists after the winter holidays, with little to draw people in except a smattering of good restaurants and local character. The quaint decorations that once made Main Street look like a scene on a Christmas card had been taken down, and the weather was too cold for anyone but the most devout sailors to be out on the Bay.

For residents, this was a wonderful time, a time when the streets weren't crammed with cars, and local pubs were filled with familiar faces. As a slow drizzle started to fall, Lacey and Mick ducked into one of them and were immediately greeted by a few people they knew, including one of Maeve's neighbors and a pair of fresh-faced seniors looking guilty sipping their beers. They quickly jumped off their stools, standing at attention as Mick walked past.

"At ease, gentlemen," Mick said, leading Lacey to a table on the opposite side of the bar. He pulled out her seat for her. "You sure you don't want some dinner?"

"Just a drink is fine. I downed a quarter-pound of fudge, remember?" Lacey shrugged off her wet jacket as she sat down. "And you better not eat too much. I promised to make you spaghetti tonight. Or are you trying to avoid my cooking?"

"Hardly. Just avoiding that rain." Mick took her hand and played lightly with her fingers, tracing with care along the freckle on her right knuckle, the practical sheen of each fingernail, even that tiny calloused bump on her middle finger that came from years of gripping a pencil too tightly. She caught his brief, devilish grin.

"What?"

"Hmm?" Mick asked innocently.

"You were smiling."

"Can't I smile when I'm in the company of the hottest girl in the pub?"

Lacey's eyes glanced around them. "Not too much competition out tonight, but I'll thank you for the compliment."

"I was actually just noticing how sexy your hands are."

Eyebrows raised, she cocked her head. "You must be joking."

Mick's eyes locked on hers. "You still have the whole weekend off?"

"Mmhm." Her body hummed at the idea of an entire weekend with Mick, free of appointments or open houses. Or funerals, she thought as her grin widened. Taking a break from funeral crashing had definitely been a good idea.

"Great. You'll enjoy meeting Admiral Casey tomorrow night."

Her serenity evaporated at the reminder that they would be having dinner with the visiting Admiral who might be able to get Mick's career back on track. How convenient that she had forgotten that. "Are you sure you think it is a good idea for me to join you? I might say the wrong thing."

He took both of her hands. "Honey, after seeing you work that crowd at the ball, I think the Admiral will be putty in your hands." He flipped over her hands and gently kissed both of her palms. "God knows nothing else turns to putty in your hands."

Lacey felt her temperature rise.

"Besides, I'm nervous as hell about it, Lacey. I've always relied on my own accomplishments to build my career in the Navy. I've never been one to pull strings to get where I want to go. This is foreign territory for me. It will be good to have you by my side."

It will be good to have you by my side. Lacey played his words over in her head as the warmth of his hands closed around hers again. With an ache in her heart, she wished she could hear him say that every day for the rest of her life.

Mick smiled when he opened his eyes, his first gaze of the day resting on Lacey, still asleep at his side. He brushed the hair from her face, and rested his hand on her cheek for a moment. She felt warm. Too warm. Gently, he pulled the blanket off her shoulders.

A good breakfast was what she needed, he decided, quietly rising from the bed.

By the time he returned with a breakfast tray in hand, Lacey was half awake, a soft moan coming from her.

"Morning," Mick said softly, sitting beside her.

"Mick?"

"I brought you breakfast."

"Not hungry." She shut her eyes again. "I don't feel right."

"You seem a little warm. I'll get you a cool rag."

Mick found a fresh washcloth in the linen closet and drenched it in cool water. He placed it on her forehead.

"Mom?"

"No, Lacey. It's Mick. You must have a fever."

"Mick?"

"I'm right here, baby."

"Don't feel well. I should go home."

"You'll stay right here and I'll take care of you. I'll be right back."

Mick raced into the bathroom. He must have a thermometer somewhere. He was mildly impressed to find one shoved into one of several first aid kits he had collected over the years.

As a man who rarely got sick, he knew nothing about treating a cold. If Lacey had a shrapnel wound, he was the right guy to have around. Or a scorpion sting, or dehydration. Heat stroke. Dysentery. Hell, he could even hook her up to a damn IV if she needed it, but he had no idea what to do for a common cold.

He put the thermometer under her tongue and watched the number rise to 104.3. Shit, that's bad, he thought, reaching for the phone.

"Hey, Maeve, it's Mick. Lacey woke up sick. … No, she's not hung over. … Like a cold kind of sick. Or the flu. … Of course, I won't send her home like this. I wouldn't want Bess to catch it either." He rolled his eyes. "I'm keeping her here, but I'm just not sure what to do for her. I never get sick. … Yeah, I did. It's 104.3. … Sure I've got that. I'll give her some. … No, I haven't noticed any coughing yet. She's breathing fine. … Asleep. … She woke up a minute ago, but went back out again. She thought I was her mom. … Yeah, cute, Maeve. That's really funny. … Do you think I should get her to the doc?"

Lacey murmured something, but Mick couldn't understand her.

"Okay, I'll give her the pills and see if that brings it down. … Yeah, thanks, Maeve. Try to dig up her doctor's number for me just in case it gets worse. They might have someone on-call. I'll call you in an hour or so." He set down the phone.

"Mick?"

"Yeah, baby. I'm right here."

"I think I'm sick."

Mick couldn't help but smile a little. "Yes, honey, I think you are, too."

"I should go home."

"No way. I can take care of you."

"But you have your dinner tonight with the Admiral."

"Don't worry about that right now. Let's just get you better."

"I should go home," she repeated.

"It wouldn't be good to expose Bess to this," Mick said, knowing that might be the only thing that kept her here in his bed.

"Oh no. You're right." Lacey sighed, her limbs relaxing into the sheets again.

Mick stayed watch over her nearly every minute that day, listening to her quiet breathing.

He went downstairs to heat up some more chicken soup and dialed a number into his phone.

"Sir, it's Mick Riley, Sir. I'm sorry to do this so last minute, Sir, but I'm afraid I'm going to have to cancel for tonight. … No, Sir, I'm fine, but my girlfriend woke up with a high fever. I wouldn't feel right leaving her alone right now. … Many thanks for understanding, Sir. I hope the opportunity arises again soon. … Yes, Sir. I will give her your regards." Mick laughed at something the Admiral said. "You're absolutely right, as always, Sir." He set down the phone and stirred the pot.

Hours passing, Mick grew restless. He had too much time to think, but couldn't lose himself in a book and was too worried the TV would wake up Lacey. He didn't want to leave her side.

He was more of an action guy, he decided, as he watched the sun drop lower in the sky.

Mick's mind wandered to the simple statement the Admiral had made. "Better take good care of her while you're stateside, so she'll be waiting for you after you've been away."

It was a nice idea, but just not possible. Deployments were hardest on the people you left behind. Mick knew that from seeing other couples and families suffer.

He couldn't do that to her.

And how could staying together even be possible? Lacey's place was here, where she was building a career and had the comfort of good friends.

It would nearly kill him to leave her one day. He knew that now. But if he loved her, that's just what he should do.

One day, he wouldn't be the one to nurse her back to health. Mick would be just a memory. Some other guy would be sitting here with her. Some other guy would be the one to celebrate each time a house sold.

Mick shifted uncomfortably in his seat. Some other guy would make love to her. Hold her hand as they brought a new life into the world. Grow old with her.

Mick was suddenly feeling sick himself.

He left the room, needing to breathe.

God, he loved her.

Leaning against the doorframe, he gazed at the framed commissioning certificate in the hallway trying to remind himself of what had been most important to him for more than a decade of his life. His eyes rested on the Naval Academy watermark behind the stylistic writing and the signature of the President of the United States at the bottom.

He looked at his own name printed on it, McMurphy Riley, named for his mother's maiden name because she had insisted, his father once told him. Mick wished he had known her better, had more than just fleeting memories of her. He wished he could remember the love his parents must have had for each other. Maybe then he'd better understand his feelings for Lacey. Love was unfamiliar ground for him.

Was it easier for civilians, he wondered? Or was it always this damn confusing?

Mick's gaze wandered to a photo of the first ship he served on, surrounded by signatures of his shipmates. Then to a photo of SEAL Team Six before they left for his first deployment.

These were the images that should bring him comfort right now, as he tried to rebuild his SEAL career. But they didn't.

Instead he found himself looking at the empty spaces on the wall and wishing he could fill them with photos of himself and Lacey. He wondered what she'd look like on her wedding day or holding a child in her arms.

Mick felt a tightness in his throat that was nearly unrecognizable to him.

He went downstairs and grabbed the newspaper off the coffee table and a beer from the fridge.

Looking around each room he passed, he noticed with a sense of disgust that everything he hung on his walls had something to do with the Navy. Even *Jack* had a photo of his sisters and their kids on his desk.

But no, not Mick. God forbid he try to balance anything else into his one-track life.

For a fleeting moment, he let himself wonder if it might be possible for him.

He sat down by Lacey's side again, and flipped through the paper, careful not to rustle the pages too loudly. A flier from a jewelry store fell out from the coupon section, packed with dazzling photos of engagement rings. His eyes rested on it for a few seconds, and then he laughed quietly at himself for even considering the idea.

Lacey stirred, and Mick set the paper aside to rest his cool hand on her forehead.

"Mmm," she murmured.

"Hey, baby."

Lacey's weak smile was dazed. "Mick? It's dark."

"Yeah, you slept the day away."

"Feel hungry."

"That's a good sign then. I'll bring you some soup."

Lacey's eyes flew open. "You're supposed to be at your dinner with the Admiral."

"I'm right where I'm supposed to be," he responded easily, stroking her hair.

The realization struck him, and he heard himself repeat it as though for his own reassurance. "I'm right where I'm supposed to be."

CHAPTER 26

A 104 fever can't be psychosomatic, can it? The thought drifted again into Lacey's mind several days later sitting in the office, still consumed by guilt.

Mick had been looking forward to that dinner with the Admiral for weeks, and she had ruined it. He kept reminding her that it wasn't her fault she got sick. But of course, he didn't know the absurd fantasies she had about sabotaging the evening just so he'd stay in Annapolis.

Her shoulders slumped as she stared at the dull gray wall that divided her cubicle from the next. She knew she would never actually do anything to hurt his career. Oh, why hadn't he just left her alone to fend for herself?

She jumped with a start at the sound of her cell, her daytime cold medicine putting her on edge. "Carolyn, I'm so glad to hear back from you," she answered, recognizing the number.

The older woman sighed on the other end. "I'm sorry I was slow to call you back."

"That's all right, but we need to respond to the latest offer on your property before it expires. I know you haven't lowered your price on the other two offers, but I strongly recommend you consider it."

"My son thinks that I'll get full price if I just hold out."

"There's always a remote chance. But the longer you have your house sit on the market, the lower the bids will be. I can draw up some recent examples, if you'd like."

"I just don't feel comfortable lowering my price."

Lacey had to grip the arm of her office chair to keep from smacking her cell phone onto her desk. "Well, the choice is yours. You don't want to counter their offer at all?"

The pause on the other end brought Lacey the faintest glimmer of hope. "I just don't know. I can't make any decisions right now."

Lacey could hear the anxiety in her voice. "Is everything all right?"

"I'm just a bit shook up. My duplex was broken into last week, and I'm trying to switch to a two bedroom apartment in their main facility now, the one with the front desk and better security. I think I'd feel safer there. My son told me I was too old to be living on my own, and I'm starting to see he's right."

"Oh, Carolyn. I'm so sorry. Were you home?"

"No, I wasn't, thank heaven. And they didn't even steal anything, oddly enough. Just made a mess of the place." She let out a little laugh. "I guess even my TV is too old for a thief to want."

"I'm so glad you are all right. If you'd like, I can explain the situation to the buyer and they might give you a little more time to think things over."

"Would you mind? I'm just so focused on trying to find a different home right now. They might have a vacancy coming up this week, and I'm on pins and needles."

"Of course. I'll contact the buyer's agent and see what I can do."

"Thank you, Lacey."

Frowning, Lacey clicked off her phone. She knew Carolyn still wouldn't counter the offer and was annoyed with herself that she even offered to buy her some time. Her first waterfront listing was slipping through her fingers. It was only a matter of weeks before her contract ran out on the property, and Carolyn's son would convince his mother to try a different agent. All the work she put into having the place staged was going to be a loss.

It was just like Vi always said: Lacey let people walk all over her.

Well, at least the woman wasn't avoiding her. After leaving three unreturned messages, Lacey was starting to wonder. Who would have guessed her duplex had been broken into? Lacey was all too familiar with that feeling—first when Maeve's house was broken into, and then her own car.

Funny how nothing was missing in those cases either.

Lacey leaned back in her chair thoughtfully. Three break-ins and all with nothing stolen?

Hell of a coincidence.

Heading to Bess's doctor's appointment, Maeve had the heat on high in the convertible and the top down. It was 55 degrees, which was balmy compared to last week, and she was going to enjoy this first hint of spring.

"Aren't we taking Spa Road, Maeve?"

"No, let's cut through downtown. You haven't been outside in ages. You need a little diversion. And it's actually nice out."

Glancing at Bess as they reached the stoplight on Main, Maeve smiled seeing her friend relaxed in the car's heated seats and enjoying watching people bustle in and out of the historic buildings that line Main Street. The poor girl really needed to get out more.

A man in a Navy uniform walking purposefully down the street caught Maeve's eye. "Is that Mick?"

"Yeah, that's him. Honk your—wait! Don't!" She rested her hand on Maeve's arm.

"What? Why not?"

"Isn't that a jewelry shop he just walked into?"

Maeve shrugged. "Yeah, so?" Realization washed over her face. "Whoa. You think?"

They exchanged a look as Maeve pulled up slowly to the window of the store. "Can you see him in there?"

"No. Too many reflections. Wait. I think that's him by the last counter. It's hard to tell."

"He didn't see us, did he?"

"I'm sure he didn't."

Maeve's eyes narrowed. "Should we turn around and take another pass?" she asked as they drove on.

"No. We shouldn't risk it."

Reaching another red light on Church Circle, they sat silently contemplating.

"I wonder why he's in a jewelry store," Bess finally dared to say aloud.

Maeve raised her eyebrows in silent answer.

"Do you really think, Maeve?"

"I don't know. Maybe he just needed to get a new watch battery or something. Or that graduation ring he always wears? Maybe he needed it cleaned."

"Or maybe he's looking for something for Lacey."

Maeve couldn't suppress a grin. "Maybe."

"Maybe even something sparkly for her finger."

Warming at the thought, Maeve looked in the rear view mirror in the direction of the jewelry store. "Maybe."

"But we don't know for sure..."

"...so we better not mention anything," Maeve finished for her.

"Right. Chances are, it was a watch battery he was buying. Right?"

Maeve's phone rang, and she pressed the speaker button. "Hey, we were just talking about you, Lacey."

Bess shot her a look.

Maeve clarified. "And wondering if you need anything at the store. We're headed there after Bess's doctor's appointment."

"Actually, I could use some dental floss."

"Mint, right?"

"Yep."

"Got it."

"Are you going into your office at all today, Maeve?"

"Yep. I have a client coming in at three."

Lacey paused. "Well, would you mind bringing home those boxes that I asked you to store?"

"The ones I put in storage? Sure. That Carolyn woman is finally ready to go through them?"

"No. I don't think she's given them a second thought. Neither did I, till today. I just heard that her duplex in the retirement village was broken into. But nothing was stolen. Just like my car."

"And the house," Bess chimed in.

"So I got to wondering if the three were linked. And I remembered those boxes. I know this is a stretch and I don't want to get all Nancy Drew on you..."

"...or Charlie's Angels. I think that works better considering there are three of us," Maeve interrupted.

"Right. But what if someone is after something in those boxes?"

"Do you think we should call the police?" Bess asked.

"I'd hate to hand over her property to the police on such a long shot. Don't you think we should take a look first?"

"Agreed," Maeve said. "I'll bring them home tonight."

Sitting on the living room floor surrounded by boxes, papers, and file folders, Lacey regretted ever calling Maeve. "This is just *so* not right."

Reaching to her, Mick squeezed her hand. "You did the right thing. Three break-ins and nothing stolen? There has to be a link. The police would agree."

"Well, maybe we should just call them rather than go through all this ourselves."

Maeve raised her eyebrows. "And tell your client that you handed over her personal papers to the police on a hunch?"

Bess's nose was buried in a stack of manila envelopes. "Honestly, Lacey, I don't know if there's really a right thing to do in this case."

The boxes were filled with exactly what Lacey expected: bills, legal documents, expired passports, photographs, even some of her children's report cards. From the look of it, Lacey didn't think Carolyn had touched the boxes in years.

"What's this?" Jack leaned back into the sofa looking at some black and white photographs he had pulled from a large white envelope. He cringed. "Oh. This doesn't look good."

Maeve settled into the couch beside him. "Holy hell. Who is this guy?"

Mick reached for the photos. "Is this Carolyn's husband?" he asked, handing Lacey the pile.

The first two were photos of a construction site in the middle of a city block. She could see two figures standing on the steps of a brownstone across the street.

The next two photos closed in on the figures, revealing them in an embrace. The next three were similar, though obviously taken later from the progress on the construction. The man was the same, but each one was with a different woman. Several more photos were taken from a distance through a window, revealing just enough to be able to guess what was going on behind closed doors.

Lacey shook her head. "It looks nothing like him from the photos she had on her wall."

"Well, whoever he is, he's a hell of a player."

Maeve moved to sit next to Lacey. "He looks familiar, though. Doesn't he? I just don't know where from."

Lacey massaged the knotted up muscles in her neck. "Okay, so let's just talk hypothetically here. These photos obviously might be incriminating to this guy—whoever he is. If he's married."

"You said Carolyn's husband was a contractor, right?" Mick pointed out. "That would explain why the photos were taken at a construction site. So let's say—again, just hypothetical—that Carolyn's husband happens to discover that this guy is screwing around on his wife with multiple women and decides to blackmail him?"

"Then Carolyn's husband dies, and this player guy decides he wants to get the photos back." There was a gleam of intrigue in Bess's eyes.

Maeve frowned. "But how would this guy know to look here or in Lacey's car?"

"Wait a second." Standing up, Lacey began pacing the floor. "Maeve, remember when I had Carolyn's open house and I had thought someone had been in the house?"

"But you found out that it was her son, right?"

"Right. So what if, now that dear daddy is dead, the son decides he wants to be cashing in on the blackmail deal. So he tries to find the photos."

Maeve snapped her fingers. "And his mom happens to mention that you are storing some of her stuff, so he decides to try here. Then in Lacey's car."

A brief silence fell over the room.

"Well," Lacey concluded, "I guess it's time to call the police."

Maeve practically purred. "I hope they send that cute detective again. The one with the green eyes. Mmm…"

CHAPTER 27

Lacey didn't know whether to laugh or cry.

Sitting in her car, the motor humming, she stared at the unpleasant stripes of yellow police tape that now blocked the entries to her first waterfront listing. Her masterpiece. A house that sparkled under her exacting eye, perfectly staged for sale. She had transformed it from a dated eyesore into a jewel with the barest minimum of seller budgets.

Now it was considered a possible crime scene, unable to be sold until the case was closed.

The past days had been tedious. The interviews with the police investigators. The removal of her client files. Curious looks from her co-workers. And the worst part of it—the difficult conversation with Carolyn after the police commenced the investigation.

But Lacey had made the right move, the detectives assured her. The man in the photograph turned out to be more than just your average Joe cheating on his wife. He was a Congressman, now retired, who had allegedly used federal funds to purchase, renovate, and maintain the brownstone in the photos solely for his personal use as a meeting place for several affairs, at least one of which was with a paid escort.

The photos Lacey had given to the police unleashed a maelstrom of questions about the death of Lou Miron. No longer convinced that his death was due to natural causes, the police had begun an investigation. His son was in jail without bond for breaking and entering, and under investigation for the possible murder of his father.

Lacey searched through her purse for her ringing cell phone, blinking back frustrated tears. She was a real estate agent, for God's sake. They didn't prepare her for this in any of her real estate courses.

"Hi, Mick," she answered it dejectedly.

"I thought I'd check on you. Maeve said you went to the Miron house."

Lacey sighed. "Yes, I had to take the contact information off the sign. I'm kind of tired of explaining the situation to interested buyers."

"I'll bet."

Lacey looked out the window again, bewildered. "They have police tape all over the house. I had to get permission from the police to just take down the stupid sign. It's surreal."

"I'm so sorry you're going through this. Just keep focused on your other clients."

"You're right. Frankly, I'm surprised that I haven't lost clients over this. I was afraid my name plastered all over that front page article in the paper would put the final nail in my casket." No pun intended, she thought ruefully, remembering how she had acquired this client in the first place.

"Don't they say that any publicity is good publicity?"

"You might be right about that. My phone has been ringing off the hook. It seems there's an odd subsection of the population who think it might be cool to have Lacey the Crime-Fighting Real Estate Agent sell their property."

Mick laughed on the other end.

"I don't know though, Mick. Maybe real estate just isn't for me, anyway."

"Don't say that. You're a great real estate agent."

"That's in question. But thanks. I don't know if I really enjoy it though. I love taking care of people, walking them through a process, holding their hands through the ups and downs. But you know? I really hate the sales part. Maybe I should go back to school. Get my masters in psychology or social work. If I can make enough in real estate to cover some night classes, it might be possible."

"That's a great idea."

Mick's enthusiasm bolstered her spirits. "You really think so?"

"Of course. You'd be a natural in that line of work." He paused. "Now, Lacey? Go home. Sitting there any longer can't be good for you. Besides, you happen to have an invitation to a movie tonight from a rather hot-looking sailor."

"Sounds wonderful. But tell Jack I'd prefer going with you." Lacey brightened at the deep laughter on the other end of the phone.

Mick put his cell phone back in his pocket.

"How's she doing?" Jack asked, tapping out something on his computer.

"Not great. I'm worried about her. She put so much work into that listing. I hate to see her lose it."

"She can't let it get to her, though."

Mick pushed himself back from his desk. "She actually mentioned the possibility of going back to school so she could do something else. Something people-focused, but without the sales."

"Like a psych, maybe?"

"Yeah, or social worker," Mick added.

"I could see her doing something like that."

Mick pulled his chair back into his desk and began clicking on his keyboard intermittently, his mind drifting.

From the corner of his eye, he saw Jack tilt his head in Mick's direction. "Might free her up to move, too. That is, if she ever wanted," he offered noncommittally.

Mick's back straightened. "Why would she want to move?"

Jack raised his eyebrows. "I have no idea."

"There's more keeping Lacey from marrying me than that."

The corner of his mouth edging up into a smile, Jack's eyes widened. "Who said anything about marriage?"

Mick bristled. "If I get back into the SEALs, Lacey would be miserable. She'd be worried all the time."

"Uh, Mick, hate to point it out, but she'd be miserable and worried whether or not she was your wife. She loves you. Goes with the territory, man."

Mick stood to look out the window, hoping some answers would spell themselves out in the clouds. Minutes passed in an uncomfortable silence, and Jack resumed typing.

"I actually looked at rings the other day," Mick suddenly confessed.

Jack's hands dropped from his keyboard, and he turned to read Mick's face.

Mick shrugged. "I might have even picked one out."

"No shit? Congratulations, man!" He rose to shake his hand and gave him a swift thump in the shoulder.

"I know she's going to say no, but—"

"Wow, great attitude, Mick."

"—but I had to let her know how I felt. She's doing a great job of building a life for herself here. And she's happy, and that's the most important thing. But I thought I should let her know how I feel. Tell her that maybe if she'd be open to a life with me, then maybe we could work something out."

"Very poetic," Jack mumbled.

"So I thought I'd throw the idea out there."

"Send it up the flagpole and see if she salutes."

Mick laughed feebly. "Yeah."

"You know, just having a conversation with her might have sufficed. The ring might be overkill."

"You think? I thought it might increase my chances."

Jack rolled his eyes.

"And it comes with a thirty-day return policy," Mick offered honestly.

Jack burst out laughing. "Very practical of you. Do me a favor and don't tell her that, okay?"

Mick's sigh was deep, almost painful. "Seriously though, what do I have to offer but a future of sleepless nights and moves across the country?"

"Uh, maybe your lifelong devotion. Maybe the possibility of having children if she wants. Maybe the idea of growing old together."

Mick was quiet as Jack's words settled in. "Well, keep your mouth shut till I get the nerve."

Jack nodded. "I swear it," he said, raising his right hand with mock solemnity. "Seriously, man. You have my word. I never go back on it. So how many days left?"

"What do you mean?"

"How many days left on the return policy? How long have you been sitting on this?"

Mick shrugged. "A week or so."

"And you were thinking of asking her… when? Before retirement?"

"When I get the nerve, asshole."

Jack held up his hands and turned back to his work.

"Sorry, man. I'm on edge." Mick raked his fingers through his hair. "I was actually hoping sometime before Spring Break. That way, if she actually does say yes, we might be able to fly out to her parents so that I could ask them a bit more formally."

"Nice touch."

"But then the whole police thing happened, and I didn't think the timing was right."

"True enough." Nodding sagely, Jack glanced at his watch and gathered some files from his desk. "Well, I'm off to tell three mids that they failed their last exam."

"Be kind, Jack. Nuclear physics doesn't come easily to most of us."

Jack smirked. "Apparently, it's easier than proposing to a woman."

CHAPTER 28

Shifting uneasily in her kitchen chair, Lacey gazed out into the morning rainfall watching the birds battling for seed on Maeve's feeder. "Mick, did you hear what I said?" she asked awkwardly into the phone.

"No, I'm sorry. I was thinking about something else. What did you say?"

"I offered to fix you dinner at your place tonight, rather than go out."

"God, no," Mick said too quickly.

"Is my cooking that bad?"

"No, what do you mean?"

Lacey heaved a sigh, getting up from the kitchen table to pour another cup of coffee. "Your refusal was a little too enthusiastic."

"I'm sorry. I just wanted to do something special tonight. That's all. It's been a while since I've taken you out."

"You took me out just a few days ago."

"Something nicer, though." His voice was grave. "No, we definitely need to talk."

His strange tone did not escape Lacey. "And we can't talk at your house?"

Lacey could hear him swallowing a curse. "No, Lacey. We can't." There was a lengthy pause. "We're going to Eagle's Point."

Frowning, Lacey's eyes met Bess's as her friend shuffled into the kitchen. "Okay. I'll see you at seven, then." Hanging up her phone, she stared out the window watching the thick drops of rain pound into Maeve's already battered lawn.

Bess touched her shoulder. "Why so glum?"

"Hmm? Oh, nothing. Want some more juice?"

Bess leaned on the kitchen table during her descent to the chair. "No. I've peed enough this morning. Are you and Mick still going to dinner tonight?"

"I think so."

"Are things all right with you two?"

"I have no idea, really. He's been acting so strange lately."

"How so?"

"He's so distracted. Stressed about something, but never says what. I don't know. Maybe he's just not comfortable in our relationship anymore."

Maeve walked into the kitchen. "Mick isn't? Why? What's going on?"

Lacey rolled her eyes, suddenly wanting to change the subject. "Nothing. Really."

Bess glanced over her shoulder at Maeve. "Lacey thinks Mick is ready to break up."

"I didn't say that, Bess. But there's something going on. I don't know. Maybe it's all in my head." Setting her coffee mug in the dishwasher, she tried to make light of the situation. "Well, if he is going to dump me, I hope he does it before Wednesday. I saw a hell of a funeral coming up in the obituaries. The guy owned four acres of sandy beach waterfront."

Maeve snorted. "Now you're sounding like Vi."

Lacey tried to grin, but the moisture welling in her eyes gave her away. Withdrawing from the looks of sympathy from her friends, she trudged out of the kitchen.

"We really could just go down to O'Toole's," Lacey said as Mick held the car door open. "We're not celebrating anything."

Mick shut the door behind her and hopped into the other side. "Sure we are. It's the start of Spring Break."

"Well, I guess that is something. But Eagle's Point? I'd be content celebrating anywhere with you."

Putting one hand on hers, he backed out of the driveway. "That's what I love about you." The words fell so easily from his lips now, so different from any other time in his life. He nodded inwardly, knowing that Lacey was right for him.

If he could just get the nerve to propose. Asking a woman to potentially end her career and follow him to who-knows-where wasn't an easy thing to do. It was a wonder anyone ever got married in the military.

At least Eagle's Point was the right setting for a proposal. His tightly knotted stomach churned. God, it would be so much easier to ask her in an email.

"Besides, Eagle's Point is special to us," he went on. "If you hadn't volunteered to help with the fall fundraiser there, I never would have seen you again."

"Oh," Lacey said so awkwardly it made Mick glance her way. She looked wary at the mention of the fall fundraiser, full of regret. But when their eyes met, she smiled brightly, making Mick wonder if he had imagined it.

Driving over the Naval Academy Bridge, Mick warmed at the sight of anchor lights bobbing in the creek below them.

Annapolis's waterways were filling with sailboats again, the surest sign of warmer weather ahead. The rain had finally stopped that afternoon and a spell of southern breezes cleared the sky for the full moon that reflected in the water. Mick felt oddly calmed by its presence, until he felt the pressure of the ring box in his pocket as he shifted into first gear approaching a turn.

The winding road that led to Eagle's Point offered a wealth of memories for Mick, remembering their two shared evenings at the historic mansion when they were both still fighting their feelings for each other. They had come so far since then. As he stepped out of the car and opened her door, he gazed momentarily at the starry skies above him. A line of clouds was rolling in low in the western sky. Don't rain, Mick ordered them silently. He wanted everything tonight to be perfect.

Lacey stiffened noticeably at the touch of his hand on her waist as he led her into the restaurant and to the table that waited for them, with a bottle of her favorite Chardonnay already on ice.

"This is the same table we sat at when we first came here together." Lacey's voice sounded distant at the realization.

"I called in advance. I figure the table might be lucky for me," Mick said with a grin, nodding thanks to the waiter as he poured their wine.

When the waiter left, Lacey tossed back her Chardonnay like it was Gatorade after running a triathlon. Mick eye's widened. "Want another glass?"

Lacey didn't answer, and her jaw clenched visibly. "Mick, can I ask you something?"

Mick shifted uneasily at her tone. "Of course."

"You've been acting a little odd lately."

Mick reached for his glass and wished desperately he had ordered Scotch. "How so?"

Lacey balked momentarily. "Just as though there is something on your mind."

"Like what?"

Lacey almost laughed. "You tell me."

Mick's shoulder's sagged. "Have I been that obvious?"

"I guess. What's going on, Mick? Did I do something to upset you?"

"You? God, no. It's not you at all." Lowering his hands, he nervously pulled apart a dinner roll without eating it. It was now or never. "You know I love you, right?"

Lacey hesitated, confusion glazing her eyes. "Yes."

Mick nodded. "Well, I do. And because I do, I can't help feeling like you deserve a lot better than me. A life with me is just filled with a lot of instability. And your life is here, in Annapolis, right?"

"I guess. I mean, my career is here. My friends are here. But I never really thought I'd stay here forever, if that's what you mean."

Mick brightened. "Really?" The ring box in his pocket was suddenly burning a hole in the side of his pants.

"Right now, it's just the only choice I really have," she continued.

Mick's palms were sweating like faucets. He hadn't been this nervous on his last SEAL mission. Almost laughing, he wiped them on his napkin. "Well, maybe you do have some other choices." He stopped again and shook his head, frustrated. "It's just that, Lacey—"

"Lacey?"

Mick stopped abruptly as a woman approached their table.

Lacey's expression immediately changed as she glanced up at the woman. Her game face was on, Mick noticed. It must be a client.

"Mrs. Templeman." Lacey extended her hand. "It's so

good to see you. Mick, this is Mrs. Templeman. I listed her property in Harbor's Edge community."

"Of course." Mick had already risen from his chair to shake her hand. "Lacey's talked about your property. It sounds stunning."

"Only because Lacey staged it that way. Almost makes me want to stay in the house, except that I'm so anxious to move to Hawaii." The woman beamed. "Meeting Lacey at my mother's funeral was the only good thing that happened that day."

Mick watched all expression fall from Lacey's face. She swayed a little in her chair, as though chugging that glass of Chardonnay had been a huge mistake.

Mick tilted his head in Lacey's direction. "You knew her mother?"

Barreling on, the older woman touched Lacey's shoulder in a maternal gesture. "It was so good of her to come that day. You know, not many people were even there. Mom didn't have many friends toward the end since she had outlived them all. And we really are a small family."

Lacey's smile strained. "I was glad to be there."

"Well, I don't want to take up any more of your evening together," Mrs. Templeman said with a brief nod to the waiter as he started to place their dinner entrees in front of them. "I just thought I'd say hello. Have a lovely evening. And you take good care of her," she finished pointedly at Mick. "She's a peach."

Looking nauseous, Lacey stared at the salmon in front of her.

"Are you okay?" Taking her hand, Mick made a mental note to remind Lacey not to drink on an empty stomach. Her face was ashen and her hands clammy.

"Fine." She pulled her hand away and grabbed her water glass.

"She owns that new waterfront listing you have, right? The gated one?"

Lacey nodded.

"When did her mother die?"

Lacey shrugged. "Oh, a few months ago."

"I didn't know that someone you knew had died. I'm sorry, Lacey. Why didn't you tell me?"

Still staring at her plate, Lacey's whisper was barely audible. "I didn't actually know her, Mick." Mick could see her throat caught in a long, hard swallow. "Back when I was really desperate for some good listings, I'd sort of go to funerals to meet people."

Mick was mystified. "To meet people? At funerals?"

"Well, um, yes. People at funerals sometimes end up at a place in their lives where they want to sell their property. You know, to find something smaller. Or cash in on their inheritance."

"Oh." Mick scooped some potatoes au gratin onto his fork. Something clicked in his brain. Loudly. More like a bomb going off than a click, actually. "You mean, to meet the widows?"

"Or widowers. Or remaining family members." Lacey wary eyes finally met his. "Like Mrs. Templeman. She had been living with her elderly mother when she died and was anxious to finally move on with her life."

Realization dawning, a burning sensation sizzled in Mick's throat. "Or like Mrs. B?"

Lacey just stared at him.

"Lacey, did you know Doc?"

She looked out the window. "I knew of him."

Pulse racing, Mick slammed his fist on the table causing heads to turn. "Don't give me that bullshit."

Lacey's eyes flared. "Let me finish. I did know of him. I read about him. That's the truth. But that's it. No, I never met him." She took a deep breath. "And yes, I crashed his funeral hoping that maybe Edith might be interested in selling her property down the line."

"You crashed Doc's funeral?" he repeated in disbelief. A chill tore through him. "All this time, acting like you were some sort of friend of the family."

"I never acted like that, Mick. I never led anyone on."

"Does Mrs. B know this?"

"No."

"So you swoop into funerals to prey on the heirs, is that what it is? Trying to catch them at their most vulnerable moment so you can make a profit off of it?"

"No. It's not like that. If they're not in a position to sell, I would never think of pressuring them."

Seeing her eyes well up with tears, Mick fought the urge to reach out and console her. He was a fool.

Her lip quivered. "You don't know what it's like—trying to get started in this business. I haven't had to do it since I started meeting people with all this volunteer work I've been doing."

Another devastating thought occurred to him. "My God, that's why you volunteered for her, isn't it? For Mrs. B? Gave all your time for the hospital fundraiser? It was just to get on her good side. To stay in her life just in case she wanted to sell her damn house. And all this time I thought it was because you had a good heart."

"It isn't," Lacey started, then her gaze dropped. "No, it is," she corrected.

"So is that why you slept with me, Lacey? Is that why you're here right now? Just circling around Mrs. B's scope of friends like some sort of vulture until she wants to sell?"

"No!" Lacey shouted, slamming her napkin down on the table and darting out of the room in tears.

Mick's face was a furnace. He felt the curious eyes of the

people around him in the restaurant. Let them look, he thought gravely. He didn't give a damn if they pulled up a chair.

Betrayal swelling inside him with each passing minute, he sat at the table alone until the waiter approached asking if he wanted dessert.

"Definitely not," he grumbled. "We'll be leaving as soon as she gets back from the restroom. Could you bring me the check, please?"

The waiter nodded, darting a somewhat confused look in the direction of the lobby. He returned minutes later. "Excuse me sir, but I felt I should tell you, the lady you were with left in a cab several minutes ago."

Perfect. Just perfect.

CHAPTER 29

"Open this door, you goddamn son of a bitch!"

After a nearly sleepless night, someone banging relentlessly on his door wasn't the best way to wake up.

Bang! Bang! Bang!

"Open this door, Mick, or I'll kick it in!"

Mick groaned at the recognition of Maeve's pissed-off voice likely waking up the entire row of townhomes along the parade field. His head throbbing, he threw the window open. "Shut up, Maeve, or the Marines at the gate will blow your head off."

She stood glaring, hands on her hips. "I'll just duck and let them kill you instead, you bastard."

Mick looked up and down the street to see how much attention she was attracting. He rolled his eyes and waved feebly at a Captain down the road staring at their scene as he hesitated to get into his car.

He charged downstairs to let her in. There was no other option short of calling the MPs.

He flung open the door. "*I'm* a bastard? I'm sorry, but I'm not really sure exactly what *I* did wrong here."

"You made the most devoted, caring person I have ever known cry her eyes out last night."

Mick fought the faint tug on his heart. As furious as he was, he couldn't bury the feelings he had for Lacey. "Well, I'm so damn sorry if I was a little taken aback when I learned that my girlfriend preys on the elderly for profit. I teach ethics, for God's sake, and meanwhile Lacey is trying to cash in on the most vulnerable people she can find. Even Mrs. B. When was she planning on telling me this? After I was old and grey and she tried to sell *my* house?"

"She tried to tell you. You told her that you didn't want to know what goes on during her work day."

"Never. *Never* did she try to tell me."

"Oh, yes, she did. When you jumped to the conclusion that Lacey was trying to sell Edith's house."

Mick sputtered an instant remembering, and then rallied his defenses. "And I see now that I was right."

"You are *not* right," Maeve fumed, grabbing a nearby mug and sending it crashing into the ground full force.

"What the hell do you think you're doing, Maeve?"

"I'm from the South. When we get mad, we throw things."

"Not in this house," Mick spewed back.

"Lacey never pressured her to sell her house. Ask Edith. Go ahead. If anything, she changed her mind, just like she did me."

That caught Mick's attention. "You?"

"Aha! Yeah, you don't know that either, do you, you know-it-all pain-in-the-ass? My Gram's funeral was the first one she crashed."

"*What?*"

"I was already going through hell in my life, but then Gram dies on top of everything else. You talk about vulnerable? I was the dictionary definition of it. I met Lacey and contacted her only a couple weeks later about selling Gram's house. She had nothing back then. She rented a cheap room in a house with a bunch of loud college students a decade younger than she was."

Mick was feeling sick, the image forming in his mind of Lacey struggling to get by.

"She needed that listing, Mick. She needed me to sell Gram's house so badly she could taste it. But you know what she did? She convinced me that the house was meant for me. She saw the vision I had for it, the memories there that I couldn't let go of. She flat out refused to list it." Maeve squared her shoulders. "You stand there judging Lacey's integrity? Well, maybe integrity has always been cut and dry to you. Maybe you've been so sheltered that you never had to find some gray area just so you could make ends meet."

Now Mick's temper flared. "Sheltered? I've been to war, for God's sake."

"That doesn't make you better than any of us. That doesn't mean you know what it's like in a world where no one salutes when you walk down the street." Shaking her head, she reached for the door. "I thought you'd be good for her. I thought you were one of the good guys. Maybe I was wrong."

She flung the door open to find the tall, broad form of a man on the other side. He stood there in uniform, his chest full of ribbons, and the tiniest hint of gray coming in around his temples.

Mick snapped to attention at the sight of the senior officer.

Still fuming, Maeve gave the older man an obvious head-to-toe appraisal and muttered, "Does everyone have to be so damn good-looking around here?"

She bounded down the steps.

Captain Joe Shey's grinning eyes followed Maeve as she blazed a path across the parade field, her feisty hips swaying as she darted along. Stepping into Mick's home, he bent to pick up a piece of broken coffee mug. "Making new friends in Annapolis, I see, Mick."

"Sir. I wasn't expecting you." Mick was poker-faced, but he seethed inside at the sight of the man who had stonewalled his career. A flood of memories of his last mission rushed back. The searing heat and the taste of sweat. Sharp winds thick with sand that cut into his face even as blood streamed down his side. The ache of Lieutenant Sully's body flung over his shoulder as he charged to the secondary extraction point.

Suddenly, he wasn't in Annapolis anymore. He was back in Afghanistan fighting for his life and the lives of his team.

Captain Shey's voice dragged him back to reality. "I know you weren't. We need to talk. You alone?"

"Except for you, Sir."

"Good. Got coffee?"

"Yes, Sir. In the kitchen."

Mick made himself and the Captain a cup of instant.

"Sit down, Mick," Captain Shey ordered, his hand gesturing to the kitchen table. "I know I'm not your favorite person right now."

Mick sat across from the man, bitterness tingeing the sides of his eyes and slowly spreading across his face. "Respectfully, Sir, how many calls did it take? To undo my San Diego orders and get me sent here?"

"Took more than I thought it would. You've got a few Admirals in your back pocket I wasn't expecting. And you're highly decorated. Navy Cross, for God's sake. Hell, you're a damn superstar." He laughed a little, at complete ease in the situation, and leaned back in his chair. "I put you in for the Medal of Honor, by the way, for your last mission."

Mick's stared in disbelief.

"It'll be forever before I hear back, and God knows they

probably won't give it to you seeing as guys generally need to be dead to get one these days. But I wanted it on record."

"Sir, if you thought so highly of my performance on that mission that you'd put me in for the Medal of Honor, then why the hell am I teaching in Annapolis?"

"Your performance on the mission was admirable. But afterwards…" The Captain crossed his arms. "…you fell apart, Mick. You were dangerous."

"To who? You?"

Captain Shey scoffed. "Hell, no. To yourself. To your team if you were sent on another mission." Leaning forward, he took a long sip of coffee. "You overstepped boundaries. If I sent you to San Diego in that condition, you would have ended up getting a month's worth of psych evals. You were too pissed off to be in black ops. We need level-headed men, not hot-headed SOBs who mouth off and question their chain of command."

Mick's eyes narrowed. "May I speak frankly, Sir?"

The Captain smirked. "You always did."

"You deserted us under heavy fire, for no reason I can guess, except that you were afraid of getting a dent in your Black Hawk helicopter."

"For no reason you can guess," the Captain repeated. "Will you listen to yourself? There are things that happen in the field that even you don't know. You may not have the clearance to know why we had to pull out the bird and risk your team. But you've served with me on five missions and you should have known that if I pulled out, then there were more lives on the line than just your sorry asses."

The Captain narrowed a steady gaze on Mick. "You and me, Mick? We're not friends. I don't owe you explanations. If you start thinking you deserve explanations from your CO then you better get out of the SEALs."

Mick shifted uncomfortably.

"Son, you better learn to stop jumping to conclusions in your life and give the people who have earned your trust a lot more leeway. Not everything's in black and white."

Mick's eyes dropped. "I've been hearing a lot of that lately."

The Captain gave a curt nod, ending that part of their conversation. "I'm not here for a social call or to put some salve on your old wounds. I'm here because we're recalling you for a mission."

Mick's eyes met the Captain's, stunned.

"You'll be briefed on the C-17 out of here. There's a car waiting outside to take you to Andrews. The Academy will be notified that someone will need to replace you."

"Will I be coming back?"

Captain Shey laughed. "You'd be crazy as hell to start asking that question now. But you might. Right now, I'm just interested in the next few weeks of your life. I could care less what happens to you after that."

"Sir, if you don't mind me asking, why me?"

"Because we're going back to that area outside of Kandahar. No one knows the terrain better than you and Lieutenant Sully. Sully's out, of course, on account of his leg." He stood from the table and reached for his cap. "I'll give you a couple minutes to grab your ID and tags. Might want to take out the trash," he suggested casually. "It'll be a while before anyone sees the inside of this place again. Welcome back, Mick. Don't call me a pansy-ass again."

Mick jumped to attention and remained frozen even after he heard the front door close behind the Captain. He felt a stirring in his blood that he hadn't felt in months, a surge of adrenaline that shook him from his stunned stupor and sent him up the stairs to grab his things.

ID and tags. Shaving kit. Desert cammies. He stuffed them into his rucksack, and glanced at the phone, feeling the need to hear Lacey's voice on the other end. But he knew he couldn't tell her he was going.

He put on his khakis to travel to the airport, knowing he would box them when he got to Andrews. Lacey would find out eventually, he knew. Rumors were quick to spread, and Jack would do some searching when he came back from Spring Break and didn't find Mick in his office.

Mick heaved a frustrated sigh. Why did he and Lacey have to fight now? Was it like Maeve had said?

Damn it, he loved her. Funeral crasher or not. He still loved her. She knew that, right?

Never let the people you love wonder how you feel. It's a waste of precious time. Mrs. B's words haunted him now. He could remember when she said it to him, only days after Doc died. He hadn't listened or understood.

God, I'm an a-hole, he thought, the reality of it killing him.

He glanced at himself in the mirror as he pulled his razor off the sink. He looked like hell. Of all the times to be pulled into a SEAL mission. He hoped he could manage some sleep on the fourteen hour flight to the Middle East.

Charging out of his bedroom, he stopped for a second and looked over his shoulder. The house was a mess. No matter. No one would touch his house while he was on a mission.

Unless he got killed.

Then it would be Jack, Mick imagined, who would pack his things. He just hoped that Jack would break his word in this one case, and tell Lacey that Mick had wanted to marry her.

Mick would want her to know he cared about her that much, admired her that much.

Loved her that much.

A curious lump in his throat, he darted toward a heap of

dirty clothes in the corner of the room and searched the pockets of the pants he wore last night. Pulling out the ring box, he opened it, and set it on his dresser.

There.

If Mick couldn't come home to her, she'd find out how he felt.

He could hear the hum of the motor outside his house as he turned off the lights, grabbed the kitchen garbage bag, and locked the front door behind him.

Her puffy eyes hidden behind sunglasses, Lacey trudged up to the door of Edith's house picturing the sweet, unassuming woman inside who had no idea she had befriended a vulture in Lacey.

Isn't that what Mick had called her? A vulture.

Hand outstretched, she paused a moment, her courage waning, before finally ringing the doorbell.

"Lacey! So nice to see you, dear." Edith's warmth resonated so naturally as she opened the door, making Lacey feel even worse.

She obviously didn't know. At least Mick had done the courtesy of letting Lacey be the one to tell her.

"Hi, Edith."

Cocking her head to one side, Edith took a long look at Lacey pulling off her sunglasses. "You don't look well at all."

"Edith, can we sit down and talk, please?"

"Of course." The older woman had already begun guiding Lacey to the sofa.

Lacey could remember sitting here the first time. Seeing Mick walk through the doorway with his confident stride. She remembered his surprise at seeing her. And that touch.

That moment when he shook her hand and she knew she never wanted to let go.

The tears poured from her eyes.

"My dear, what on earth has happened?" Edith took Lacey's hand in both of hers.

"I have to tell you something. Something awful. When I met you, it was completely under false pretenses."

"At Don's funeral?"

"I didn't know your husband. Not till I read his obituary. I —I used to look in the obituaries for potential clients."

Edith looked confused. "You wanted work from Don?"

"No. From you." Lacey withered slowly into the couch, spending the next painful minutes trying to explain why she was at Donald Baker's funeral all those months ago. And why if funeral homes offered frequent flyer miles, she'd never pay for airfare again.

By the time Edith understood, Lacey was slouched over the arm of the sofa from humiliation and exhaustion. Whoever said confession was good for the soul had obviously never confessed. "I just thought it might be a good way of getting my business cards out there to some people who might actually sell."

Edith raised her eyebrows. "But you practically turned down my listing when I called."

"That was because I didn't think you should sell. I'd never pressure someone into doing something like that."

Edith patted Lacey's hand, still in her gentle grip. "A good choice. So why are you crying?"

Lacey's face curled up. "Because it's a horrible thing to do —to try to benefit from someone's death like that."

Laughing, Edith's eyes sparkled. "I should show you the bill from the funeral home. That might make you feel better."

"It doesn't bother you?"

The old woman's smile was serene. "Lacey, I didn't know

half of the people at that funeral and I'm betting if Don had sat up in his casket he'd have said the same thing."

"Mick thinks it was unethical."

"It might be," Edith admitted noncommittally.

"He called me a vulture."

Edith rolled her eyes. "That boy always did have a flare for the dramatic. So he found out by accident?"

Lacey nodded.

"I can see why that might have caused him to be upset. No one likes learning things by accident. But he'll get over it. Now about your—um—career direction, dear. We must be able to come up with a better way of finding clients for you than attending funerals."

Lacey sighed. "I'm not even sure if I want to be in real estate anymore. I don't know. I'm thirty years old and I still don't know what I want to be when I grow up."

A knowing look swept over Edith's face. "Do you know who has the answer to that? Little children. Ask children what they want to be when they grow up, they don't even think about it. They just tell you."

"Not me. When I was a kid, I kept changing my mind."

"Yes, but that's just it. You ask them one week, and they say a ballerina or a fireman. The next week it's an astronaut or a teacher."

"I don't get it."

Edith tilted her head, her eyes shaded with years of wisdom. "You don't have to be one thing. Just be what feels right *now*. You don't have to commit to a career the way you do a husband or a child. Just follow your interests. Follow your heart."

A heron outside the window caught Lacey's eye as it gracefully landed along the shoreline. She pressed her lips together thoughtfully. "My sister Vi was never like that. She always had direction. She always had her eye on the finish line. My parents, too, I think."

Edith shook her head slowly. "Then I feel badly for them. Life should be a journey, not a destination. Because otherwise, you'll discover we're all pretty much going to end up in the same place." She suddenly laughed. "You should have at least learned that much crashing funerals, my dear."

"Life is a journey," Lacey found herself repeating. She smiled as she saw the heron dip his head into the water and raise it again, a hefty fish in his long beak.

Could it really be as simple as that?

CHAPTER 30

Bess eased herself into one of the soft leather chairs at The Buzz, her senses absorbing the lovely aroma of coffee beans. She looked at her tea steeping in front of her, and rubbed her belly. Thirty-seven weeks as of yesterday. Less than three weeks to go. Soon, she'd sit here with her baby girl and sip a cup of coffee.

"Mmm," she murmured quietly at the idea. How she missed high-octane coffee.

It was a slow day at The Buzz. With Spring Break underway, the usual crowd of midshipmen and local college students was replaced by a smattering of tourists.

She smiled a little. It was good to be alone. Much as she loved Maeve and Lacey, they hovered over her like a couple of mother hens since her stay in the hospital. It was endearing. Kind. Thoughtful. And a huge pain in the ass.

But today, Maeve had taken Lacey on a day trip down to Solomon's Island to get her mind off of Mick. She hoped some time away from Annapolis and a little shopping in the island's quaint local galleries might perk up Lacey's spirits.

Bess couldn't believe Mick hadn't called her yet. But then

again, Lacey hadn't called him either. They were at a stalemate.

A young couple entered the coffee shop, eyes filled with energetic laughter. Bess quickly slouched in her chair, recognizing the man as the visiting West Point cadet Mick had introduced her to months ago at the Chapel. She definitely didn't want to be recognized right now, with her huge belly and swollen ankles.

She watched him order for them both and pay. "To go," she heard him say. Thank God, she thought. They'd leave without seeing her.

Raising her tea to her lips, Bess casually gave the woman with him a quick appraisal. She was beautiful, of course. Perfect blonde hair and a trim little waist that had Bess longing for her own.

Bess wanted to hate her. She really, really did.

The cadet—she couldn't remember his name—turned around to peruse the place. His eyes landed briefly on Bess and continued on. She breathed a sigh of relief.

He turned back to the counter, and then glanced at Bess again, recollection in his eyes. After saying something to the woman with him, he headed in Bess's direction.

"Commander Riley's friend, right?"

Bess looked up and tried to act surprised. "Yes. Bess Foster."

He reached out his hand. "Tyler Griffon, Mrs. Foster. I met you a few months ago."

"Yes, I remember. And please, call me Bess," she said, unable to confess that she was the furthest thing from a Mrs.

"How are you?"

"Fine. Closing in on the big day, as you can tell," she said, self-consciously patting her belly. "Thirty-seven weeks as of yesterday."

"You must be excited."

"That's one word for it," Bess said, forcing a laugh. "So what are you doing back in Annapolis? I thought you were only here for a semester."

"It's Spring Break. I came down to visit my girlfriend. She's a student at St. John's College. We met when I was down last fall." He gave a nod in the direction of the blonde across the room pouring creamer into her coffee.

"That's nice."

"She's going to law school at Georgetown after she graduates this year. She's scary-smart," he said, pride filling his eyes.

Too smart to get herself knocked up by an abusive boyfriend, Bess thought dismally as his girlfriend joined them, a bag of scones in her perfectly manicured hands.

"Bess, this is my girlfriend, Bridget Needham. Bridge, this is Bess. She's a friend of Lieutenant Commander Riley."

"The one who gave you those contacts at the Rangers, right? Nice to meet you."

"That's the one." Tyler turned his attention to Bess again. "I don't imagine you've had any word from him yet?"

Bess's eyes widened. Had news of Lacey and Mick's argument actually spread through two branches of the military? They must be hard-up for gossip. "Um, no. We haven't heard from him since last week."

"His girlfriend must be concerned."

Okay. This was getting weird. "Concerned about what exactly?"

Tyler's face froze. He glanced at his girlfriend uncertainly and then back to Bess. "I'm sorry. I heard that he got recalled by the SEALs."

"What?" Bess gasped, gripping the side of her chair.

Tyler's girlfriend looked sympathetically at Bess. "Tyler, why don't I run to those shops on my own and we'll meet up in half hour or so? Give you time to catch up," she said, obviously not feeling at all threatened leaving her boyfriend with a pregnant woman.

"Bridge, that's great. I'll call you on your cell in a bit. Thanks, hon." He gave her a quick peck on the lips.

Despite Bess's current state of anxiety, she still felt a tug at her heart from the show of affection.

Tyler sat in the chair next to Bess. "I really spoke out of line. You know, it's just a rumor."

Bess felt her stomach cramp up. Great, Bess thought. Gas. *Just the thing to make me even less appealing to the opposite sex.*

"Are you all right?" He must have noticed her discomfort.

"I'm fine," she shifted in her seat, struggling for a better position. Her back was killing her. "What is this rumor, then, exactly?"

"Just that Commander Riley left the Academy suddenly for some SEAL mission."

Bess shook her head. "He would have called." Even after arguing with Lacey, Mick certainly would have called. Wouldn't he?

"Not if it's black ops. Those guys just disappear."

Bess took a deep breath and let it out slowly to relieve the pressure in her stomach. Why had she eaten that third egg this morning? Wincing, she tried to ignore his look of concern. "So, um, is there any rumor about when he's coming back?"

Tyler just shook his head. "Are you sure you're all right?"

"Not really. Too much stress, I think." Why wasn't Maeve here? She'd know what to do.

"Uh, yeah, or you could be in labor."

"No. I have three more weeks. This is just stomach pain." Unconsciously, she started rubbing her belly. "Is there some way we can find out for sure about Mick?"

"I wouldn't know. I could ask around, but I doubt I'll be

able to find out much at my rank. You could ask any Navy officers you know who are stationed here."

Jack, Bess thought immediately, reaching for her tea to calm her nerves. Where was Jack spending Spring Break? She wracked her brain trying to remember. "Ow!" A sharp pain sent her lurching forward, spilling hot tea all over her lap.

"Okay, that does it. I'm taking you to the hospital. My car's parked on Main."

She took his hand gratefully, leaning heavily on it, dignity be damned. The sudden pain had stolen all her energy. "I think that's a good idea. Thanks."

Charging down the hall of the maternity floor with Maeve, Lacey felt lightheaded. Her heart hadn't stopped racing from the moment she had gotten the message that Bess was being driven to the hospital by some guy named Tyler.

She wasn't due for another three weeks.

And who the hell is Tyler?

"Where have you been?" Bess barked when she saw them. She was walking down the hall with a death grip on a man who looked familiar.

"Oh, *you're* Tyler," Lacey said, recognition dawning. She shook his hand. "I remember you from that day at the Academy. Thanks for taking care of our girl. Well, *girls*, considering the one on the way."

Maeve hugged Bess. "Are you sure you should be walking around right now?"

"The doc said it would be good for her. Helps move things along, so to speak," Tyler offered, his attention never leaving Bess as she was passed from Maeve's embrace to Lacey's.

Lacey squeezed her friend. "We've been so worried. I'm so sorry we weren't here to get you to the hospital. Maeve got a ticket racing up here."

Still slightly stooped over, Bess angled her eyes at Maeve. "And a phone number, too, if I know your attraction to men in uniform."

"Ha! If I had a number, do you think I'd have a ticket? No. There was a ring on his finger, and that's one line I won't cross."

Bess managed a small laugh. "Tyler, I really can't thank you enough for staying with me while I waited for them. It really wasn't necessary."

"Of course it was. I wasn't going to leave you by yourself."

"You're really sweet. But you go on with your day now. Hanging out in the maternity ward for three hours is certainly not the way you wanted to spend your Spring Break."

Tyler glanced at his watch. "I figure I'm nearly three hours vested in this, and I'm not leaving till the mission is complete."

Lacey smiled at him, confirming her first opinion of the cadet. "The mission, huh?" She turned to Bess, "Translated from military-speak, I think that means he's not going anywhere."

"But your girlfriend—"

"—is touring the Museum for Women in the Arts with four of her sorority sisters right now," he said glancing at his watch. "You aren't really going to make me join them, are you?"

"No—ooooooh!" Bess completed her sentence with a low-pitched moan, her eyes rolling upward and her grip on Tyler intensifying.

Maeve and Lacey looked at him in alarm.

"Contraction," he explained, timing it with his watch. "Gone yet?"

There was a long pause before Bess slowly resumed walking. "Mmhm. That was a rough one. I think I want to lie down in my room now."

"How about I head to the nurse's station to get you some more ice chips? And you can catch up with your friends." Tyler's gaze fell on Lacey and Maeve. "Can I get you two something from the cafeteria? Maybe some coffee?"

"God, yes." Still bleary-eyed from lack of sleep, Lacey could have kissed him for offering. She reached for her purse.

"No, my treat," Tyler said, and strode down the hallway before Lacey could argue.

Maeve's mouth was practically watering. "Can we clone him?"

Bess started shuffling toward her room. "I'm in pain and you're planning a seduction."

Maeve laughed, opening the door for Bess. "We called Jack and he's catching an early flight back, but won't make it here till tomorrow. He really wanted to be here." She glanced hesitantly in Lacey's direction. "Do you think one of us should call Mick?"

"No," Bess spat out. "I need to talk to you first—*ooooouuuch* —" Gasping from another contraction, she gripped Lacey's hand. "—some other time." Releasing her grip, she saw dents from her fingernails embedded in Lacey's hand. "Oh, God. Sorry, Lacey."

"No problem." Lacey hadn't missed Bess's reaction to the mention of Mick's name. Curiosity gnawed at her, but she forced herself to not pry. Bess was in no shape to do much talking.

Maeve perched herself in front of an uninspiring view of the hospital parking lot. "I don't know why you're not getting an epidural. You don't have anything to prove. This isn't some sort of test you have to pass, you know."

"I know. I just don't want one. Maybe it is a test, for me, anyway. Maybe I want to prove something to myself." Bess let out a pain-mitigating breath. "I've been a doormat most my life, you guys. I've never been tough."

"Don't say that."

Bess shifted in the stiff hospital bed. "But it's true. I want to be tough now. I need to be. For her." She rubbed her belly. "I want to be strong. I want to be able to climb mountains for her if I need to."

Maeve's expression was grave. "You hear this, sister," she started, pointing her finger. "You don't have to be tough. You have us. You be whatever you want to be, and we'll stand by you. Both of you." She smiled, leaning over to talk to Bess's tummy. "You hear that, kiddo?"

Lacey's smile diminished and tears started pouring down her cheeks.

Maeve immediately rolled her eyes. "God, Lacey, you get so emotional when you don't get enough sleep."

Bess was more sympathetic. "What? What's wrong?"

"Oh, nothing's wrong. I was just thinking this is the last time it will be just the three of us. It'll be four now."

Maeve's abrasive shell visibly cracked, and her expression warmed. "Well, thank God. The two of you were getting so boring."

Bess winced at another contraction, and fought to get her words out. "You guys are the best friends I ever had."

It was Maeve's turn to let a tear fall. "Gram always told me that friends are the family you choose."

Lacey joined hands with Maeve and Bess, and they rested their hands on Bess's belly. Her voice was soft. "Then I choose you."

PART III

SEVENTEEN YEARS AGO

Lacey sat at the dining room table, which often doubled for a desk in the Owens household. Gripping her pencil tightly, she added another name to her list.

Nine, Lacey thought, tapping the pencil against her chin, making sure she hadn't forgotten anyone. A light going off in her head, she jotted down another name.

Vi snuck up behind her, peering over her shoulder to see the names on the list. "Kristen Jenkins? You're inviting her? I don't like her. She always smells like cat litter."

"Well, it's not your birthday party," Lacey snapped.

Vi shrugged, plopping her math homework down on the table and pulling up a chair.

"Besides," Lacey added, suddenly angry, "you're not

invited."

That was perhaps one of the few things Lacey could have said that could pull Vi's attention away from math. Math was her favorite subject at school. "What do you mean, I'm not invited?"

Lacey struggled to ignore the hint of rejection she saw in Vi's eyes. She had to stand firm on this. For once. "If you want to go to a birthday party, you'll have to wait for your own next month."

"You know I have Dad and Mom just give me the cash."

"Exactly. You take all the money that they would have spent on a party and save it. But then I'm the one throwing the party."

Vi tossed up her shoulders carelessly and looked back down at her homework. "So, take the cash instead of the party. They made the same offer to you, you know."

Lacey slumped in her chair, feeling her argument losing ground. "But I'd rather have the party."

Vi didn't look up from her work.

Irritated, Lacey squared her shoulders toward her sister. "But I'm not going to have you coming to my party and enjoying it when you're not going to throw a party next month that I get to go to. It's just not fair." With great flourish, Lacey picked up her list, pushed back her chair, and stormed into the kitchen.

Was that hurt she had seen in Vi's eyes? Lacey pressed her lips together. Well, it serves her right if it was, she decided as she stared into the fridge.

Truth was, she couldn't bear to hurt her sister.

She gave herself a shake. "Snap out of it, Lacey," she said to herself quietly. Vi was using her. That was what it was. Every year, Vi would happily deposit a check from her parents equivalent to the cost of the pizza, the cake, and whatever other expenses Vi had observed at Lacey's birthday party from the month before. She inventoried it all, everything from the party hats to balloons, hovering over the festivities like some sort of deranged accountant.

Then she'd eat Lacey's cake, sing "Happy Birthday" with her friends, and have the time of her life. All at Lacey's expense.

Literally.

Well, Lacey was almost thirteen now. Practically a teenager. She wasn't going to be the pushover she had been in earlier years. Vi might complain to their parents that she wasn't invited to her own sister's party, but Lacey knew they'd let her invite whomever she wanted.

Or *didn't* want.

They might even respect Lacey for laying down the law to her sister. For standing her ground. Wouldn't that be refreshing?

Looking sullen, Vi stepped into the kitchen. "You're right, Lacey."

"I am?"

"Yeah. I'll skip your party this year, if that's what you want." Vi's lip trembled just a bit. Or was that in Lacey's imagination?

"It's not what I want. It's just what's fair," Lacey said.

"Absolutely," Vi agreed.

Lacey wasn't expecting this. She sighed, watching her visibly deflated sister unwrap a Hoho and pop half of it into her mouth as solace.

Frowning, Lacey took the other half from her sister's hand. "Well, so long as we agree that it's not fair, then I guess you can come."

"Really?"

"Yeah." Lacey cracked a smile. "But you better get me a really good gift."

"Deal."

CHAPTER 31

TODAY

Baby Abigail stared up at Lacey, a perfect cherub, eyes locked on hers as her tiny bow of a mouth sucked happily on her bottle.

In silent awe, Lacey gazed down at the tiny miracle nestled on her lap. It seemed as though Abigail had nearly doubled in size the past month. The darker hair she had at birth had fallen out, and a crop of fiery red hair was popping up. Just like her momma, Lacey thought as she glanced at Bess.

Holding little Abigail, Lacey's worries melted down to a more manageable size. Over a month had passed since Jack had told her that Mick had been recalled on a black ops mission. Bess was still in the hospital at the time, but Maeve had sat with her on the couch that day, holding her hand as Jack confirmed what they had learned from Bess's new West

Point friend. Jack had promised to do all he could to find out details, but "no news is good news," he assured her, when it came to SEAL missions.

There were still so many unanswered questions between Lacey and Mick. For all she knew, he was still fuming about the deception she had allowed from the first day they met, and patting himself on the back for being rid of her. Oddly, even that thought comforted her, because it would mean that Mick was still alive. She gently stroked Abigail's forehead, the feel of the baby's soft skin somehow comforting her.

"You get completely lost in her, don't you?" Maeve's voice interrupted her thoughts.

Lacey glanced up. "That's it. That's exactly it. She makes life simpler somehow. If she's okay, then everything's okay."

Bess looked at the clock. "Shouldn't you be getting ready for your appointment? I can take over from here."

Lacey didn't lift her eyes from the baby. "There's nothing more important in my day than this. Carolyn Miron can wait, waterfront property or not." Lacey had no idea why Carolyn had asked her to meet for coffee. She had learned last week from the district attorney that Carolyn's son had changed his plea to guilty for two counts of breaking and entering. Lacey had thought that bizarre chapter in her life was closed now.

Maeve's forehead creased with worry. "Are you sure you want to go? Maybe one of us should go with you."

"She's harmless, Maeve. Maybe she just needs to talk." Lacey smiled at her protective friend. "I promise I'll call as soon as I'm done."

Jack burst in from the baby's room. "What is this?" he demanded holding a tiny shirt that had "Go Army! Beat Navy!" printed boldly across the front.

Maeve looked up. "Watch your tone around the baby, Jack."

He held up his hands in defense. “Okay, my bad. But who gave her this?”

“Tyler sent it for Abigail when he got back to West Point,” Bess said without compunction.

“That cadet?” His eyes flared. “It’s bad enough he was the first guy to get to hold the baby. But then this?” He waved the shirt in the air.

Bess rose to quickly snatch it out of his hand. “It was sweet. I promise I won’t have her wear it on Army-Navy game day.”

“Football,” Lacey explained in a whisper to the baby, “brings out the worst in men.”

As Jack moved to sit beside Abigail, Lacey saw him do a double take at something on his sleeve. It was brown and she’d bet it wasn’t chocolate.

“Crap,” he muttered. “That’s the last time I’ll change a diaper in uniform.”

“Shh,” Lacey said quietly. “I think she’s dozing.” Abigail smacked her lips a little, contented. Her tiny blue eyes flickered shut.

Under the warm spring sun as the new leaves waved happily in the breeze, Maeve’s little home seemed complete with this new life inside of it, even while another life was so uncertain.

Carolyn Miron stirred the creamer in her cup. “I want to thank you for meeting me like this. I feel horribly for all that my family put you through these past months.”

Lacey felt immediately relieved by the tone of the conversation. “Carolyn, I was just so sorry to have to hand over those personal belongings to the police.”

“You had no choice.” Carolyn shook her head. “I have to

admit, I always knew that my husband was up to something, though I never would have suspected he was blackmailing someone. Lou—" she sighed, "—was not a good man. But my son?" Her hand trembling slightly, she raised her cup to her lips. "After he decided to take the plea bargain last week, Jeffrey confessed to me that he was heavily in debt from gambling. His father had told him about the photographs a few years ago—probably bragging about it, knowing Lou. So when Lou died, my son thought it might be an easy way to make money."

Setting the cup down, the older woman stared emptily out the café's window. Her voice was hollow. "I never would have thought he would turn out to be so much like his father. Or maybe I just didn't want to see it."

Lacey wished she knew the right thing to say. "I'm so sorry for what you're going through."

Carolyn waved her hand dismissively. "At any rate, I've decided to move up north to be with my daughter and her family. I need the support right now."

"That sounds like a good plan."

"And now that the police have confirmed that Lou died of natural causes, they've taken the police tape down from the house." She took an uneasy breath. "So I was wondering if there's any chance you might relist the property for me."

Lacey felt conflicted, with all the trouble the Miron listing had already caused her. "I—"

Carolyn interrupted. "I give you my word that I'll take the first reasonable offer that comes this time. And if it's appropriate, I'd be comfortable in offering you a higher commission."

Cha-ching! The tug of profit prodded Lacey to jump at the offer just as her cell phone vibrated. Glancing into the depths of her purse, she saw Jack's number light up the screen. Jack calling in the middle of a workday was a rarity. Suddenly trembling, she grasped her phone. "Carolyn, this may be important. Would you mind if I took this outside?"

"Of course not. Take your time."

Lacey darted out the café's entrance, her pulse racing. "Jack? What is it?"

"Lacey." Jack's guarded tone did nothing to soothe Lacey's nerves. "I have some information on Mick's team. It's not good, but I'll tell you straight off that I don't have the complete picture yet."

Lacey leaned against the wall to brace herself.

"I heard from a contact at Bagram Air Base that they treated a few SEALs about a week ago. They were in critical condition, and flown to Landstuhl for more treatment."

"Landstuhl?"

"In Germany. They patch you up best they can in the field and then send you there if you're still in bad shape."

"I have to go there, Jack."

"I don't even know if Mick was one of them yet. I've called, but they won't release information to me. I know a few people there, but haven't heard back from them yet because of the time difference. I should know something tomorrow."

Lacey felt helpless. "I have to do something, Jack."

"They all may be fine now, or even headed back here to Walter Reed in Bethesda by now. I don't want you going anywhere until I find out more. I probably should have waited to tell you, but I knew you'd want to go to him if he is in Germany. I thought some extra time to make arrangements might help."

Lacey pressed her eyes shut, willing away the tears. "You did the right thing by telling me. I'll dig out my passport and get someone at work to cover for me at my closing tomorrow if I need to fly out before then." There was a brief silence between them, enough time for panic to grip her like a vise closing up on her heart. Control was slipping away. "I have to go, Jack. Please, please call me the instant you know anything more."

"You know I will."

Snapping her phone shut, Lacey wiped a tear from her cheek.

Her arms ached, desperate to hold Mick again, to feel his warmth beside her. Oh, God, to turn back time to that last night together and give her the chance to say how sorry she was, rather than run away.

She shook her head. Suddenly, his forgiveness—his understanding—wasn't nearly as important to her. She just wanted him alive.

She just wanted him *home*.

CHAPTER 32

Anyone who ever complained about flying coach should take a transatlantic flight on a C-17 military cargo jet.

Belted into his seat, the roar of the engine shook Mick's body like an industrial-sized paint mixer. Even with his noise reduction headphones, he was still certain he'd be deaf before they touched down at Andrews Air Force Base at 1700 hours.

Maybe that was for the best. If he were deaf, he wouldn't be able to hear Lacey when she told him to get lost. He could imagine her now, standing at her front door, her lips forming the words as if in a silent movie. "Take a hike, loser." After the way he had treated her, he wouldn't blame her.

Of course, she wouldn't be that callous, he thought. Not Lacey. She was too caring. Too protective of other people's feelings. She'd say how happy she was that he was alive, and thank him kindly for stopping by. Then she'd gently send his broken-hearted self on his way.

Sweet Lacey. Thoughtful, kind Lacey. Completely opposite from how he viewed her that last time they were together.

What a judgmental bastard he had been. Okay, maybe it was a little weird that she crashed funerals for a living. And he wished that she had told him on her own. But they would have worked things out if Captain Shey hadn't shown up on his doorstep the next day. That's what couples did, right? They had arguments, and then they worked things out.

He nodded to himself, then winced when his body jolted from turbulence.

There's something about a fourteen-hour flight home from a war zone that gave a man plenty of time to wish he had someone waiting home for him. He had never felt that way before. It used to be that after a deployment, all he had wanted was a soft bed, a change of clothes, and about eighteen hours of solid channel flipping on his TV. And a steak. God, yes. After nothing but freeze-dried MREs, a good prime rib would send him into ecstasy right now.

Most of his deployments had lasted longer than this one. He was lucky this time. He had lost a few days getting patched up at Bagram, but didn't have to go to Landstuhl.

He couldn't say the same for the other guys on his team. But they were stable now, and sounded in good spirits in their last phone conversations with Mick. That was enough good news for Mick to get the hell out of there.

And back to Lacey.

Now if he had only one ounce of luck left, he would use it up standing in front of Lacey, begging for forgiveness.

Then, his final luck spent, he'd be more than happy to leave the SEALs. After this last mission, he felt about ten years too old for this. He doubted it showed, but he'd rather leave before it did.

Hell, he'd leave the Navy if that's what she wanted. If that's what it took to win her back, he'd walk away from it all.

Anything to see her face waiting for him when he came home from work. He'd cup her sweet face in his hands and kiss her so gently she would beg for more. "Off your feet," he'd say with a smile, "so that I can massage them."

Then he'd make her dinner.

Then he'd make slow, sumptuous love to her as many times as his war-scarred body would allow.

Mick shut his eyes, savoring the image he was drawing in his mind. It had been so long since he'd seen her. What had it been? Five or six weeks, maybe? Short in terms of a deployment, but an eternity when you were forced to disappear after an argument without even being able to call or email. He would have given anything to just tell her he was sorry. To tell her that he had a ring in his pocket that last night together that belonged to her, no one else.

She probably moved on, he thought with a scowl.

Mrs. B might have even set her up with that damn doctor she had once mentioned. His eyes grew cold at the thought. If he ever mistreated her, Mick would tear him in half.

Ha! Mistreated her? Like he had, Mick remembered, questioning her ethics, even accusing her of sleeping with him to land a real estate deal, and then calling her—what was it he had said?

A vulture, that was it.

Real nice, dickhead.

If she'd only let him, he'd spend the rest of his life making it up to her.

Lacey stepped into the afternoon sun, grateful for its warm rays. The air conditioning had been on high in the settlement office, and she was nearly losing feeling in her fingertips.

Fortunately, the freeze hadn't kept the seller from signing on the dotted line, Lacey thought with a sleepy grin.

Lacey's first waterfront property was sold. Mrs. Templeman's stunning gated community property overlooking the Chesapeake Bay was now under the ownership of a former Oswego, New York couple, anxious to embrace the milder winters of Annapolis. At this very moment, Mrs. Templeman was in a cab headed to the airport to catch her flight to Hawaii and fulfill her lifelong dream.

Such a pleasant transaction. Lacey nodded, pleased with herself, despite the constant pressure she felt behind her eyes the past twenty-four hours.

A fat commission check in her wallet, she had already reserved the services of a photographer to take her picture for some full-color brochures. And she had signed up for a summer class that she could apply toward her Masters in Social Work. Taking Edith's advice, Lacey knew it wasn't a step toward a lifelong dream. It was just something worth exploring, something that piqued her curiosity.

It was another part of her journey.

She'd even have enough leftover to buy a last-minute ticket to Germany, she thought, checking her cell. Her face fell at the sight of no phone messages. She fought the urge to cry, not being able to share her success with Mick. Not knowing where he was.

Not knowing whether he was even alive.

No. Mustn't go there. She took a deep breath, trying to push Mick to the back of her mind until Jack learned more. Mick wouldn't want this moment stolen from Lacey. She had envisioned this day for so long, picturing herself telling her parents she had finally sold a waterfront property, placing Lacey among the elite top-tier of Annapolis agents. She had imagined their relief that their only biological daughter had inherited their business sense in some small measure.

This was the moment she had waited for—the conversation she had been rehearsing since the moment she received her real estate license. She'd allow herself that, and worry the rest of the day about Mick.

Phone in hand, she paused thoughtfully a moment, and then dialed.

"Lacey?" a voice answered.

"Hey, Vi! How are wedding plans going?"

Vi's harried voice was brimming with contempt. "Ugh! What wedding plans? Aside from picking the place, nothing has been done. I wish he'd listened when I said I wanted to elope. I'm flying to London tonight to do an interview. How am I supposed to plan a wedding?"

"Why not hire a wedding planner?" Lacey slowed her pace down the street, in no rush.

"I did. I had to fire her. She just keeps hounding me with questions like 'what are my colors?' My colors? What the hell is that supposed to mean? Am I a college football team?" Vi shifted her tone as easily as ever. "How are things there?"

Lacey paused, forcing herself to not cry on her sister's shoulder about Mick. There was no reason to cry yet, she reminded herself. "Well, I just sold my first waterfront property," she said, hoping the words would boost her own spirits.

"*Really?* You're actually done with closing and everything?"

Lacey found herself grinning. "And everything."

"That's great. Was it that crime scene one?"

Lacey laughed. "No, that's still in limbo. She did re-list it with me, though."

"So what house was it?"

"A house in a gated community just south of downtown."

"Waterfront *and* gated?" Vi let out a low whistle. "Bet that fetched a pretty price."

Lacey beamed, remembering the number of zeros on the commission check. "You'd win that bet."

"I'm proud of you, Lacey."

Exactly what Lacey had longed to hear. "At least *you* are. I'll have to remind myself of that when I call Mom and Dad. I can just hear it." Lacey did her best imitation of her mother's harsh tone. "'Oh, you finally sold something? I hope it will help pull you out of that credit card debt from those real estate classes you took.'"

"Ha! Don't feel bad. They do the same thing to me."

Lacey stopped cold in the middle of the street. "They do?"

"Oh, sure. Dad keeps telling me that I can't seem to decide whether I'm an economist or a journalist, and that if people really took me seriously, I wouldn't have to wear so much makeup on TV."

"Are you kidding? They brag about you to me all the time."

Vi actually snorted. "News to me. So have you picked out a maid of honor dress yet?" she asked, deftly changing the topic as easily as the winds change direction on the Bay.

"Was I supposed to?" Lacey leaned against a nearby parking meter.

"Don't tell me you're expecting *me* to. I haven't even picked my dress, and I'm the bride."

"Shouldn't I talk to the bridesmaids about it?"

"Oh no, it's just you."

"You don't have any bridesmaids? Why not?"

"I don't have time for friends. I have women I know through work, but I wouldn't want any of them to stand by me on my wedding day. Too personal. That's why I'm doing the destination wedding thing. I'm hoping he'll keep the numbers down on his side. I can't have just you standing up there by yourself if he has eight people standing up for him."

Lacey didn't know what to say. "Yeah, I can understand that, I guess."

"This whole thing keeps giving me flashbacks to all that birthday party cash I soaked Mom and Dad for. Remember? Who would I have invited to a birthday party except you?" Vi laughed.

Resting one hand on her hip, Lacey tightened her grip on her cell phone, a flood of birthday memories crashing over her as Vi's words sunk in. She shook her head. "Wait a minute. You didn't just want the cash more than a party?"

"Are you kidding? With all the presents *you* scored at your birthday parties? I would have much rather had the party."

"Huh," was all Lacey could say, history as she knew it being rewritten in the span of a second.

Suddenly, and for the first time in decades, Lacey didn't feel envious of Vi.

Lacey had two friends waiting home for her right now, fixing a special dinner to celebrate her closing. They had filets ready to be grilled and probably a bottle of champagne chilling, knowing Maeve. Lacey could even picture Bess hanging silly crepe paper or maybe a big congratulations sign above the kitchen table.

They were just that kind of friends.

Lacey had a beautiful, healthy baby at home who she got to hold whenever she wanted. She was even about to become a godparent along with Maeve.

Meanwhile, Vi had a ticket to London. Vi's life was exciting, but Lacey felt contented right here in Annapolis, in a little house on the water that was filled with more warmth than she had experienced in eighteen years growing up in the Owens' household.

Suddenly, Lacey wished Vi was right with her so that she could give her a hug. "You know, Vi, I'm really proud of you, too."

"I know. You tell me all the time," Vi answered dismissively.

"Good. I just wanted to make sure you knew that."

"'Course. I've got to hang up now. I'm almost at the Queens Tunnel and I'll lose my signal. Love you."

"Love you too. Have a good trip." Lacey snapped her phone shut and dropped it back into her purse.

To hell with her parents. She'd send them an email later.

The sun was low in the sky, just about to dip behind Maeve's house, as Lacey pulled into the driveway. The Bay called to her from the backyard, and Lacey fingers longed to wrap themselves around a glass of wine as she watched the last of the day's light melt into the blue horizon.

These past weeks, her memories of love and friendship on the back porch wrapped a comforting embrace around Lacey, as she'd watch the setting sun reflect in the waves and pray for Mick, wherever he was. Sitting in one of Maeve's wicker chairs, she could close her eyes and picture him there with her, sulking behind a bad set of Scrabble letters, eating a piece of pizza. Laughing. Listening to her. Holding her hand.

As though life were normal.

Putting the car in park, she squinted against the sunlight, certain the fiery beams were causing a mirage. A hallucination, maybe. One that looked like…

Mick.

Sitting on the front steps, the image's face lifted and eyes met hers. He stood, and her heart nearly stopped.

Mick?

Stepping out of the car tentatively, she wasn't sure if she said his name aloud. She blinked several times, terrified that all the sleepless nights had taken their toll and she was only imagining him.

But even as tears welled in her eyes and her vision blurred, he was still there.

Frozen at the side of her car, she stood paralyzed. For seconds or minutes—she'd never know. *Mick.*

He was alive. He was home.

She darted toward his open arms and melted into him, so grateful for the feel of his body against her that she was struck speechless.

They held each other in silence, and when Lacey finally began to pull herself back from him, Mick only squeezed her tighter.

She choked back a sob when he finally let her retreat from his embrace. "You're okay." Her voice was breathless as she cupped his face in her hands, still unconvinced he was real. "Thank God. Thank God, you're all right."

She leaned in to hold him again, but then stepped back awkwardly, remembering the way their last conversation had ended. Blinking back tears, she longed to erase that last evening from both their memories so that this moment was not clouded with confusion. But he was alive, she reminded herself, touching his cheek cautiously, letting his warmth seep into her chilled hands. Even if he never trusted her again—even if their relationship could never be saved—it should be enough that he was simply alive. "I've been so worried. We all have. Jack heard some of your team were admitted to Landstuhl."

"I know. I talked to Jack en route here from Andrews. He said I better come straight here, and make you promise you won't kick his ass for the false alarm."

She shook her head. "Never. He's been a good friend." She sent a questioning glance in the direction of the front door. "Maeve's not home?"

"No, she's home." Mick grinned, amusement stirring in his tired eyes. "She gave me a hug, then told me she won't let me inside till I apologized to you."

Lacey couldn't suppress the laugh. A more dedicated friend she would never find.

"I can't say I blame her, the way I left things with you." Mick paused. "I'm not sure where to start."

Lacey averted her eyes. "You don't have to apologize. I do. What you said to me that night hurt. But it hurt so much because it wasn't too far from the truth."

"Lacey, I—"

She drew herself away from him, battling futilely to keep her composure. Her lip trembled. "I did crash funerals to try to get business. And I did volunteer to help Edith because I hoped she might need my services one day. I guess it wouldn't be too much of a stretch for you to assume I slept with you for the same reason. But I didn't. I hope you already figured that out on your own."

"God, yes. I said that out of anger. I wasn't thinking."

Lacey nodded, feeling a grim sense of closure. "Good." She pressed her lips together thoughtfully, sadly. "I'm relieved that you're all right. And grateful. That's enough."

"Lacey, please let me finish. I overreacted. I was hurt and shocked. And—" his shoulders slumped, "—scared. I've been deployed nearly my entire career. I've never really experienced this kind of life. I've never gotten so used to watching someone sleep at night or spent time picturing a future together. I've never fantasized about having someone waiting home for me. So then when I learned that you had been holding something back from me," he shook his head, "God, I was so hurt by the thought that our entire relationship may have been nothing more than a way to build your career. It scared the crap out of me—the power you had over me. The power you still have over me. No amount of body armor can protect me from you."

"Why didn't you call me?"

"Captain Shey showed up the morning after our argument and recalled me. From that moment on, I could have no contact with you until the mission was complete. Till now." He took her hand. "It was killing me to not be able to tell you the truth."

"The truth?"

Mick stood silent a moment. Inhaling sharply, he pulled a tiny box from his pocket. "That even though you make me weak and vulnerable and it scares the hell out of me, I love you and I want to spend the rest of my days loving you."

Tears streamed from Lacey's eyes unchecked.

He opened the box, and the diamond shimmered in the evening sun. "I bought this two weeks before our argument. I carried it around in my pocket waiting to get the nerve to ask you. But instead, I found an excuse to push you away. I should have trusted you more. I should have seen the position you were in and offered to help you rather than turn away from you."

He pulled the ring from the box. "I don't expect you to answer now. I don't even want you to. I have to prove to you how much I love and respect you again. I need to earn your trust. You deserve that. Take all the time you want. Ten years could go by and I'll still be waiting for your answer."

"Mick, I don't need ten years to know I love you. I never stopped, and I never will."

He kissed her gently, almost reverently, as though he had been imagining this kiss for a lifetime. "Just wear this and think about it. It's yours Lacey, no matter what your answer is. There's no other woman who could wear it."

He slipped the ring on her finger.

It was a perfect fit.

A baby cried inside the house, and Lacey smiled, picturing Maeve, Bess, and Abigail crouched beneath the open window listening to every word. "It's time you came inside, Mick. There's someone you should meet."

Hand in hand, they walked through the door, greeted by their friends and the gentle coo of Abigail.

And the house sighed with contentment.

EPILOGUE

PALM BEACH, FLORIDA

LATER THAT YEAR

Lacey and Maeve eased themselves into the chaise lounges and took lingering sips of their raspberry margaritas. The resort's private beach was nearly empty. No hordes of tourists crowded these delicate sands, Lacey thought. Who could afford the prices?

Except for her wildly successful sister and her mogul fiancé. She grinned at the thought.

The mournful cry of seagulls and hypnotic crashing of the waves carried themselves over a breeze to Lacey as she dipped her toes again into the warm white sand.

"Perfect," Maeve purred, nearly emptying her first salt-dipped glass.

Pure bliss raced through her veins as Lacey finished her drink. "This has got to be the best margarita I've had in my life," she said, her eyes slightly crossing.

"It's not the margarita—it's the view. Will you look at that? I can see why Vi picked this place for a wedding. If I were ever stupid enough to go down that road again, this is where I'd go."

Bess came up behind them with her baby in her arms. Donning pink sunglasses and an over-sized polka dot hat trimmed in lace, little Abigail was covered from head to toe in thick sunscreen. Bess eyed the margaritas. "Tonight, when you guys are pulling baby shift, I'm having one of those."

"Or two or three. But you'll have to wait till we've recovered first."

"Works for me. Did Mick's plane arrive yet?"

"He called from the airport a few minutes ago. He's taking a cab over now," Lacey answered, giving up her chair under the umbrella for Bess and the baby, and pulling up another next to Maeve. She gazed at the water again. "I'm glad he could be here for the wedding tomorrow. But I have to admit, I'm kind of happy he couldn't take the whole week off from work. It's been nice just having some girl time, you know?"

"Palm Beach shopping is something no man could possibly appreciate the way we can," Bess sighed.

Maeve's grin was speckled with sea salt from her drink. She licked her lips. "You know, this is just what I needed. I hope I've told Vi that enough."

"Me, too," Bess added. "Tell her anytime she needs a short order bridesmaid in exchange for a ticket down here, sign me up."

Lacey shook her head, remembering the conversation with her sister. "I can't believe she went for it." When Vi had called her, upset because her fiancé was insisting on having two more people stand up for him than she had, the idea just came to Lacey.

"And I'll never be able to repay you guys for bailing me out." Vi, wearing movie-star sunglasses and a beach hat, had crept up behind them. "Imagine him insisting on two groomsmen as well as a best man. Groomsmen," she snickered. "What does that even mean, really? Are they supposed to groom him or something?"

Lacey swung her legs around so that she could share her chaise with her sister. "Why aren't you with your doting fiancé right now? Trouble in paradise?"

"No trouble. It's his last day as a bachelor, you know. He's with his friends."

"And you're with yours," Maeve offered. "Have a drink. We bought in bulk."

"Smart idea."

Lacey took another sip from her freshly-refilled glass, and her ring flashed in the sun, noticeably catching Bess's eye.

Turning to Vi, Bess peered out from behind her sunglasses. "You've set a pretty high standard for weddings. How is Lacey going to top this place?"

"If she ever sets a date." Maeve winked.

Lacey's eyes shone bright behind her sunglasses. "Hey, I haven't even said my official 'yes' yet. He said he wanted me to think about it."

"Yeah, but how much time do you need? You really shouldn't make him suffer."

Lacey smiled lazily, remembering the feel of Mick's hard body against her own the night before she flew to Palm Beach, and a blush crept over her. "Oh, he's not suffering," she said coyly.

Vi gave her a smug look. "I'll bet."

Lacey gave a little nod to herself. "I was actually thinking

I'd give him my answer after Vi's reception. You know, end our vacation with a bang."

Maeve grinned and held up her glass. "To tomorrow, then. May the only surprise on Vi's big day be the one Lacey has in store for Mick."

Vi laughed.

Bess held up the baby bottle in toast. "And to Vi, for giving us the time of our lives."

"I'll drink to that." Lacey raised her glass. "And to friendship."

Vi's glass met theirs, and her face relaxed into a contented grin Lacey had never seen before on her sister. "To friendship."

FROM THE AUTHOR

Thank you for reading *SEAL the Deal* and allowing me to take you to a place dear to my heart, Annapolis, Maryland. I hope you'll return to this beloved town with me in the next book in the series, *The SEAL's Best Man*.

In my mind, I often revisit the places and people in my books. So, from time to time, I love to share with my readers **free bonus scenes** I've written. Please check my website at www.KateAster.com/bonuses to see my latest.

As an avid reader myself, I know there are plenty of books available. So it means a great deal to me that you took a chance on an independent author like me and purchased my book. **If you enjoyed it, please consider recommending it to others, or even write a review.**

Your reviews truly mean so much, and I am grateful for your support!

Above all else, I want to thank you for valuing the service of our military. Mick, Jack, Tyler, and even Captain Shey were each inspired by the traits of real-life heroes I have had the honor of knowing over the years—including my husband.

I am so grateful that there are people like you who never forget that in times of war and peace, a small percentage of our population willingly stands in harm's way to protect our nation. Your support is greatly appreciated by our service-members and their families.

Thank you again for your wonderful support!

BOOKS BY KATE ASTER

~ SPECIAL OPS: HOMEFRONT SERIES~

Romance awaits and life-long friendships blossom on the shores of the Chesapeake Bay.

SEAL the Deal

Special Ops: Homefront (Book One)

The SEAL's Best Man

Special Ops: Homefront (Book Two)

Contract with a SEAL

Special Ops: Homefront (Book Three)

Make Mine a Ranger

Special Ops: Homefront (Book Four)

BOOKS BY KATE ASTER

~ SPECIAL OPS: TRIBUTE SERIES~

Love gets a second chance when a very special ice cream shop opens near the United States Naval Academy.

No Reservations

Special Ops: Tribute (Book One)

Strong Enough

Special Ops: Tribute (Book Two)

Until Forever: A Wedding Novella

Special Ops: Tribute (Book Three)

Twice Tempted

Special Ops: Tribute (Book Four)

BOOKS BY KATE ASTER

~ HOMEFRONT: THE SHERIDANS SERIES ~

When one fledgling dog rescue comes along, three brothers find romance as they emerge from the shadow of their billionaire name.

More, Please

Homefront: The Sheridans (Book One)

Full Disclosure

Homefront: The Sheridans (Book Two)

Faking It

Homefront: The Sheridans (Book Three)

BOOKS BY KATE ASTER

~ HOMEFRONT: ALOHA, SHERIDANS SERIES ~

Even on a remote island paradise, a handful of bachelor brothers can't hide from love when they leave the Army.

A is for Alpha

Homefront: Aloha, Sheridans (Book One)

Hindsight

Homefront: Aloha, Sheridans (Book Two)

Island Fever

Homefront: Aloha, Sheridans (Book Three)

BOOKS BY KATE ASTER

~ BROTHERS IN ARMS SERIES ~

With two U.S. Naval Academy graduates and two from their arch rival at West Point, there's ample discord among the Adler brothers ... until love tames them.

BFF'ed

Brothers in Arms (Book One) - available now!

Books Two, Three, and Four

are coming soon.

Sign up at my website at ***www.KateAster.com***

to be the first to hear the release dates.

BOOKS BY KATE ASTER

~ FIRECRACKERS: NO COMMITMENT NOVELETTES ~

For when you don't have much free time… but want a quick, fun race to a happily ever after.

SEAL My Grout

Firecrackers: No Commitment Novelettes (Book One)

Available now!

Novelettes Two, Three, and Four

are coming soon.

Sign up at my website at ***www.KateAster.com***

to be the first to hear the release dates.

LET'S KEEP IN TOUCH!

Twitter: @KateAsterAuthor

Facebook: @KateAsterAuthor

Instagram: KateAsterAuthor

www.KateAster.com